VIVA BRAZIL

DIRTY MONEY – BOOK THREE

NEIL ANDREWS

ISBN-13: 978-1515291961
ISBN-10: 1515291960

Dedication

To my loving wife who has to deal with the aftermath of my using too much energy writing, to James S for inspiring this part of the story and to DK and Pete the Pilot for invaluable input.

Contents

Foreword

The characters and events depicted in this book are fictional and the creation of the author's imagination or have been used fictitiously and are not to be construed as real. Any resemblance to persons living or dead, actual events, locales, business establishments, or organisations is entirely coincidental. We would all however do well to remember that sometimes elements of truth can be stranger than fiction.

Chapter 1
In Too Deep

MAX SAT ON THE UPPER LEVEL of the North Terminal at Gatwick airport in a daze. He called Rachel to arrange for her to meet him at Malaga when the flight landed which was expected to be just before eleven. He'd had a few hours to think since the meeting with Bashar and the more that he thought about things the more worried he became. Bashar's words rung in his ears; "*You're vouching for your brother.*" That wasn't the plan; Paolo could get in trouble in a locked room sat by himself; put him in Brazil with access to money women and drugs...well...an instant recipe for disaster and if anything went wrong his nuts were on the block. *Shit what was Rachel going to say, how could they get out of this alive?*

He looked up at the screen trying to find something to distract him from his melancholy mood, time had passed by without him being aware and a gate number was now flashing up for his easyjet flight. If he didn't get a move on he'd end up with his carry on bag getting checked into the hold which would really tick Rachel off. Max arrived at the gate and joined the back of the queue, if the staff had cattle prods the picture of farmyard animals would be complete, he shuffled forwards noting the mix of young Spaniards who had been enjoying the highlights of London and the older well tanned couples who presumably had popped back to the UK to see friends and family. The flight was always packed and today was no exception. He managed to squeeze his bag into the overhead and tucked himself into seat A row twenty three, near the back of the aircraft, at least he had the window and wouldn't be disturbed. He had a notepad in his hand with a pencil, he needed to clear his head and look at alternatives. *Stay alive...how do we stay alive?*

The flight taxied out as the crew carried out their safety briefing. Max was in his own world scribbling down notes and working out how much money he and Rachel had and whether they could just disappear. Halfway through the flight he snapped his pencil not realising that he was so worked up. *Fuck, fuck, fuck.* He closed his eyes and tried to relax but images of being dumped in the jungle or shot in the head kept flashing through his mind. He tried to focus on better times, to focus on Rachel; he couldn't wait to hold her against him, his rock, his everything, what a year they'd been through.

The flight landed on time but the gate was a long walk from Passport control. Max rounded the corner and hit the back of a queue that seemed not to be moving. He stood for five minutes before texting Rachel.

Hi Babe, Landed but passport control seems to be on a go slow. I'll see you on level two when it eventually gets moving. Love you. Xx

Various expats wandered to the front of the long line before heading back to take up their place. Max asked one of them what was going on only to be told that the automatic barriers weren't operating and that the National police officers hadn't turned up at the booths yet. *Welcome to Spain, service as usual* thought Max. Eventually things got underway and Max walked through aiming for the lift to take him up one floor to the arrivals concourse where Rachel sat patiently waiting in the car hoping not to get moved on by the Gaurdia or even worse to get a ticket. She spotted Max as soon as he came through the big slow circular doors; he'd reverted to type, blue jeans, white T-shirt, comfy loafer style shoes topped off with his trademark mop of wavy brown hair. She opened the door and stood waiting as he rushed up and just held her in his arms. Rachel was taken aback by the emotion coiled up in what should have been a simple hug.

"Hey...come on Max, it can't be that bad can it? I know the flights are crap and it's great to see you too but why the emotion? Come on whatever it is we can sort it, we're a team; we can deal with it." Rachel was upbeat, they'd come a long way recently and their money worries were a thing of the past. Life was looking good.

"Babe, I wish it were so simple. Come here, you know I love you don't you?!"

The drive back to Los Milnos was unusually quiet. Rachel could sense that Max was troubled and babbled on trying to keep the conversation light and easy going. News and gossip about people on the community, things in the local press, invitations from friends to nights out, nothing seemed to be working. Whatever was troubling him needed to be discussed in detail behind closed doors preferably with a very large Bacardi and coke in her hand. Once they were back at their two bed apartment cocooned from the world her wish was granted, she sat with her feet tucked under her and a glass in her hand as she listened to Max recall the details of his trip to London.

"I can't see how we get out of it Rach, he's mad, I'm not joking, he threw a bloody glass at my head and said that whatever Paolo does we're responsible. I don't want to be responsible for my feckless git of a brother, he's bound to do something wrong, what the fuck are we going to do Rach?"

"Calm down Max, it hasn't happened yet has it. Look on the bright side we've made money from the diamonds, we've got a bit of cash from the drugs and we're getting paid off from the club, we'll manage. What are you so uptight about?" It was unusual for Rachel to be the peacemaker; normally it was the other way round with Max trying to placate her. He should have stayed quiet but the mention of the club set him off again.

"Don't mention the club...I've a funny feeling that our problems aren't over yet. Tony's behind on his payments and I've got no idea why. Can't we just do a runner Rachel, get away from it all? I've got a really bad feeling about things, we're in too deep."

Rachel got up from her chair walked across the room and cradled Max's head in her ample bosom. "Max, Max, Max...come on we've been in worse places than this; let's just take one step at a time, let's go to bed, it'll all seem better in the morning.

Chapter 2
Witch

MAYBE RACHEL HAD A SIXTH SENSE, or maybe their luck was changing, just as she had predicted things seemed better the following morning and improved no end a few days later when Jack telephoned with an update.

"Hi Max, how yer doing me old mucker? Still dodging glasses?" He laughed at his own joke heartily.

"Yeah, yeah Jack; I'm good thanks, did you get the papers I sent over yesterday?"

"They'll probably arrive later today but it's all in hand so it is, Paolo is fixed up with a flight for next week and the lawyers out there are sorting things out. Anyway, I wasn't phoning about work; I was phoning with good news, put me on speaker Rachel will want to hear." There was a delay as Max fiddled with the phone before asking Rachel which button to press.

"Can you hear me Rachel?"

"Hi Jack, loud and clear what's the news? Are you getting married?"

"Don't be daft now...." He paused. "Well...not yet anyway. No the news is that Lynette has had a healthy bouncing baby girl this morning weighing in at eight pound two ounces."

Rachel's face lit up. "That's fantastic news but how come? Max told me that Bashar still hadn't found her and was in a foul mood."

"Ha...stranger things happen, when she went in to labour she phoned Martin because she needed a friend, anyway to cut a long story short Martin brokered the peace on the basis that if Bish stepped out of line or tried to take the baby he'd personally kill him. Oh by the way you should see the shiner that Martin gave him, it's a cracker, needed half a dozen stiches so it did, split his eye something rotten."

"Jack! I don't care about bloody boys and their egos, how's Lynette and how's the baby? Oh and where is she and what's the baby called?"

"Bloody women eh Max, all they want to hear is the news about the little one. She's called Millie because to quote Lynette it's a one in a million chance that she was ever conceived and they're both in The Edinburgh Royal Infirmary for another night before they go back to Lynette's place for a week or two to reacquaint themselves and play happy families, I'd wager that they've got a lot of talking to do and Bish is going to be in for a hard time...she's strong minded Lynette... yes she is."

Max cut in before Rachel got a chance to reply. "Why Edinburgh? I thought she was supposed to be somewhere over here in Spain."

"Ahh, she's a clever girl, weaved a false trail but anyway let's just say that Bish is a changed man, he was gooing and gaaing down the phone so he was. Things should be smoother now, maybe even back to normal, fingers crossed eh?"

"Anyway, that's the news, I've got to go, she who must be obeyed is calling for me. I'll catch you both soon."

Once the call was over Max had a huge grin on his face; "You're a witch girl! You said things would get better, amazing eh? Who'd have thought that Lynette would ring Martin and that he'd sort out the problems, anyway good news for us at least we know that Lynette is on our side after she made a shed load of money from us."

Rachel reminded him of the truth. "And don't forget that she made money for us too. I'm definitely happier having her back around curbing Bashar's excesses."

"You and me both, he needs a women by his side."

A light bulb flicked on in Rachel's brain. "Hey back up a minute." Rachel wagged a finger before grabbing Max's nipple and twisting it hard. "I object to being called a witch."

Chapter 3
Fatherhood

AFTER THE BIRTH and their reconciliation Bashar moved into Lynette's little nest in Edinburgh for the first two weeks. He was paranoid that if he said or did the wrong thing that she might bolt again and take his precious daughter with him. It was good to be away from the rat race of London and good for the two of them to have time to talk around the house and on their slow strolls through the park pushing Millie along in her convertible baby buggy. Trust was building between them again. He would never wish the turmoil of the last few months on anyone; it had been humbling, all his wealth, all his power but he still couldn't snap his fingers and fix it. Martin had been the one to finally make him see the light. What would he do without Martin?

For the first time in his life Bashar felt responsible, not just in the way someone could feel about business or a deal but completely responsible for the small bundle of joy cuddled in to the crook of his arm. As he crooned over her he played the game of seeing who she looked most like; it was hard to tell, she had deep brown eyes that you could swim in and an olive complexion that could have been inherited from either of them. How could he even have thought of treating her differently to a son? He would deal with the problems of going against his culture later, it would not go down well with his family or wider circle but for now Millie and Lynette were all that mattered. He had to change, if he didn't he'd lose them both, a fate worse than death.

As Millie once again started to cry he lifted the bottle out of the jug of hot water and checked the temperature on the back of his hand. He had insisted that Lynette started expressing milk so that he could look after a least one of the night feeds while she rested. He could see that she was tired; the emotional journey over the last few months must have been traumatic for her; all because of his stubborn pig headiness. "I'll make it up to mummy sweetie, you'll see."

He jigged Millie gently trying to get her to take the teat and suckle on the bottle. "None of that matters now little girl, you're safe with Daddy, c'mon now, be a good girl and drink up."

Realising that it was the bottle or nothing Millie reluctantly started to suckle and as the level of the bottle slowly went down she dropped back off to sleep, Basher flipped her onto her front on his hand and gently patted her back. "C'mon sweetie, let's have a big burp for Daddy." Millie obliged with an explosion in her nappy and a deep belch to accompany it.

Bashar really hadn't got to grips with nappies yet. He placed her on the changing mat, and took off her baby grow to find a long yellowy brown stain up the back of it. He grimaced and continued with the excavations trying to tear the sides of the nappy as Lynette had shown him but succeeding only in covering both of them in a film of liquid yellowy brown excrement.

"Jesus, how can someone so small produce so much crap? Daddy's failed again and it's shower time for both of us." He stripped off his boxer shorts turned the shower to luke warm and washed both of them off. He loved her even when she was messy, just like when she was born...Besotted.

Chapter 4
Rio

ON THE FLIGHT TO RIO DE JANEIRO, Paolo for the first time in his life was actually doing some homework reading travel guides to try to get familiar with the size and scope of Brazil's second largest city and the sixth largest city in the Americas. He was taken aback by the sheer scale of the place at almost one thousand three hundred square kilometres and the fact that six million people lived there. He probably should have been more aware but like many others his knowledge had been limited to seeing clips of the annual carnival or football tournaments on TV, he had no idea that it was so important to the Brazilian economy or the importance of its rich cultural landscape. The more he read the more he liked the idea of starting a new life there and leaving his problems in England far behind. He decided there and then that he may even stay long enough to get to see the 2016 Summer Olympics, certainly the finals of the World Cup in a few years' time; although he wasn't really much of a football fan, in his youth he preferred to chase the girls rather than a blown up leather sack.

For once he was excited without having drugs in his system and read on taking note of how the city was carved up, the Centre or Centro being the core of Rio on the plains of the western shore; the North zone which had the highest density of people and the South zone reaching the beaches fringing the open sea. He was surprised at how mountainous and hilly everything looked and how they sliced through the city separating the areas. To start out with he was staying near Cococabana beach, a prime tourist zone on Rio's famous Atlantic coastline. His language school was somewhere nearby in either Glória, or Catete, he'd forgotten the exact address but for some reason both of the areas rang a bell with him. He put his book down, he was sure that he'd work it out sooner or later. Hiring a car was a non-starter, the roads were complex and the traffic heavy and he had no desire to become tourist fodder.

The British Airways flight was pleasant enough although his request for a business class seat had fallen on deaf ears with Bashar his one concession was an upgrade to World Traveller plus which gave him a little more legroom and in theory access to a few more treats although as alcohol was his main crutch for the flight he was disappointed when the bar ran dry on the plane halfway to the destination. He thought that maybe the stewardess was trying to ration him but having sidled up to one of the other trolley dollies the bad news was confirmed. As the plane approached Rio the Captain's voice boomed out over the intercom asking the for the cabin to be prepared for landing and advising the passangers that they would be landing at Galeao airport in around twenty minutes time and that unfortunately low cloud would obscure some of the views today. There was a collective sigh indicating that everyone had been as keen to see the stark granite bluff of Sugar Loaf Mountain as he had, still at least he would have time to do the tourist thing and go up in the cable car at some point, some were flying on to other South American destinations the same day.

As he departed the aircraft the heat and humidity hit him and the wait to clear customs didn't help. The airport infrastructure was old and in the process of being renovated adding to the confusion of where to go and how to get through with his luggage. After being accosted more than once with offers of help which he brushed off, eventually he found the official cooperative taxi rank. His expectation of being able to hop straight into an air conditioned car were soon dispelled, but it didn't take him long to realise that a few reals or dollars in the dispatchers hand moved you up the queue quickly.

His driver was shabbily dressed, old and of dubious hygiene, much like his car which had seen better days. A rosary with a cross hung down from his mirror and a statue of the Virgin Mary adorned his dashboard; the air conditioning was limited to a small fan stuck to the windscreen and an open window. Paolo tried to strike up a conversation but couldn't understand the guttural response that he got. He contented himself with the toothless grin that was flashed his way and looked out at the scenery along the motorway.

As they drove along the beachfront the area was much more to Paolo's liking, beautiful people seemed to be everywhere, well more precisely beautiful girls and the tourist areas were definitely more salubrious than some of the slums they had passed on the way. The cab pulled up outside of a small boutique hotel that was to be Paolo's home for the next few weeks, set back off of the strip it looked a bit utilitarian for his tastes but as long as he had a decent bed and a shower things should work out. He paid the taxi driver and got another grunt in return. *What was the culture on tipping here? He should have read that section more carefully.*

Tomorrow was a rest day after the long flight but Bashar hadn't cut him any slack. Twenty four hours was all he was allowed to get over his jet lag and then it was down to it. He woke early on the first day as he failed to adjust to the six hour time difference but made the most of being up ealy and walked along the board walk and sampled a few of the local cafés. The afternoon was spent lazing by the small pool area on the hotel book reading his language notes before the real work started tomorrow. He felt a million miles away from the problems of his past live. Nothing could touch him now. Sunshine, a rum and coke in hand, anything had to be better than scrabbling to make a living dealing drugs in Essex.

Chapter 5
Language School

PAOLO WOKE EARLY AGAIN the next day, pulled back the curtains and looked out over the beach at the rising sun and pure blue sky. "What a day! Paolo... life is on the up." He jumped in the shower, shaved dressed and went down for breakfast to try out his pigeon travel book Portuguese on the waiting staff. He was due at the local intensive language college at nine and had high hopes, not about the learning experience but more about the beautiful women that he'd seen. Maybe he could find a red blooded Brazilian girl and teach her a few things about the language of love in exchange for learning Portuguese. "Yep, life is looking up."

The college was pretty dingy, four small classrooms above a small café in the backstreets but within walking distance of the beach. The flash website and pictures of students sat in small groups seemed a long way away from reality. From what he could make out, the focus seemed to be teaching students English rather than foreigners Portuguese according to the scraps of paper pinned to the scruffy noticeboard on the first floor landing. It was clear that this was a language school working on a budget. Despite the rough surroundings the teaching was good; Paolo had one on one tuition for two hours before his tutor called for a break. As they walked down the concrete stairwell students poured out of two of the other classes and the whole group headed for the café below. Paolo's energy level suddenly picked up, he could see more than one suitable candidate for his plans. He sidled up to two beautiful local girls wearing tight jeans and skimpy tops more than showing off their ample assets. Both had long black hair framing nicely made up faces, a little mascara to emphasise the lashes, a small amount of eye shadow and strong red lipstick. Paolo introduced himself with his new found language skills and waited for a response. The reply was in broken English, perfect!

Paolo made good progress during his coffee break quickly picking up phrases the girls taught him. As his tutor called time he said his goodbyes and made plans for them to meet up at the same time tomorrow. He hoped that Maria and Loretta would become good friends, very good friends. By the time Friday came around the girls were going to meet him at his hotel and take him to one of the local mambo dance clubs. He was told to dress down. Jeans and a T shirt, no watch, just some cash, no credit cards and no Jewellery; it felt odd, normally he liked to at least wear his fake Rolex and a thick gold chain around his neck, it was part of his sleazebag uniform. He really did feel naked.

As the taxi twisted and turned through the back streets Paolo began to realise why he was dressed down; away from Cococabana beach poverty was rife. A man could be killed for a gold chain and his wallet. Loretta and Maria were full of bounce as Paolo paid for the cab; they grabbed him by either arm and pulled him to the front of the queue where two huge doorman blocked their entrance before hugging Maria and waving the girls through. Paolo was stopped with a heavy hand on his chest but soon realised that as the man of the group he was expected to pay. With his newly found language skills Paolo asked for three tickets and thought that he understood that they formed part of your bar bill, with luck the girls would fill in the blanks, he was struggling with the doorman's heavy accent. Once inside Loretta explained that the first three drinks were free and whatever else you had was marked up to be paid at the end of the night. Only the doorman and owner handled cash, a very sensible security option in this run down area.

As he walked further into the club the high tempo beat of the music assaulted his ears and his eyes smarted from the haze of blue smoke, bodies writhed on the floor in unison, it was as near to group sex as he could imagine while being fully dressed. He stood drinking in the scene until the girls dragged him to the bar for rum shots before joining the throng on the floor. Paolo couldn't believe his luck. Loretta and Maria toyed with him and teased him as they pushed and pulled him getting him into the rhythm of the dancing throng. Sweat began to soak his T shirt in the steamy atmosphere. They stopped briefly every so often to refuel on rum and coke before switching to a local drug and water later in the evening. The girls took turns in kissing him and grinding against him, the sexual tension combined with the beat of the music and effects of the drug had Paolo thinking he was in heaven. The club closed up at three and a queue of people formed with cards in their hands to pay the owner. Paolo laughed at the simplicity. Once you'd paid for the drinks and special medicines marked on your card your hand was stamped with the image of a tiger cub. Provided the stamp was visible the doorman waved you good night, good luck getting past them without a stamp on your hand and don't even think of accidently losing your card which would result in a minimum of a hundred dollar payment.

The three of them poured into the back of a taxi and headed to Paolo's hotel to continue the party, scoring some cocaine from a local contact along the way. As they fell through the door of the room the girls were pulling at Paolo's clothes and shedding their T shirts and jeans until all three were stood naked apart from the girls still wearing their high heels. Loretta prepared three neat lines of coke on the glass top coffee table which they snorted before taking to the bed. Paolo stood mesmerised as the girls fondled each other's breasts and kissed passionately, this could be a long night, he reached in the drawer and grabbed a triple power penis ring slipping it over his cock and balls almost instantly feeling the steeling effect it caused by restricting outward blood flow. He smirked; it should keep him rock hard for hours making sure that he enjoyed the girls to the full. Maria moved herself down Loretta's body until she could tug gently at her pubic hair forming the perfect half inch wide Brazilian landing strip, she followed it down inhaling her heady scent in heavily before taking Loretta's soft folds in her mouth causing her to moan with pleasure; she wiggled her backside provocatively in the air before looking round and blowing a kiss at Paolo with glistening moist lips. He needed no further encouragement and entered her from behind pumping rhythmically while reaching over to grab her ample tits and tweak her rock hard nipples. Loretta screamed out as she hit the first of many of the night's orgasms with Maria quickly following.

Paolo woke in a tangle of arms and legs and grinned from ear to ear. He kissed Loretta gently while putting his hand down between Maria's legs sliding his fingers along her moist entrance; she groaned and rolled over to give him better access while searching out his cock. The three of them sleepily fondled each other laughing and giggling. Loretta turned to Maria with a grin on her face.

"Don't you think we should make sure Paolo has a happy ending after our fun last night?" She said nothing but moved round to take his cock in her mouth before moving to the side to allow Lorreta to share his morning glory. Between them they licked, sucked and slowly rubbed his cock and balls until he could take no more ejaculating strongly up over his chest as both girls giggled and rubbed his semen into his skin.

The three of them showered together in the huge bathroom before heading down to the street to get a café de monha and skillet toasted French bread rolls. Paolo's language skills had improved no end and the grin on his face said it all, Brazil was his kind of place.

Chapter 6
New Life

JACK AND BRIDGET SET ABOUT creating a new life in Spain with gusto viewing plots and Hacienda style properties with at least ten acres surrounding the house. Jack wanted somewhere that he could make secure; somewhere he could protect Bridget if it came down to it. He wanted clean lines of sight, more than one exit and commanding views and definitely not one of the millionaire's council houses as Joey called them on the big urbanisations above Marbella. He couldn't put his finger on it but would know it when he saw it. In the boom years before the Spanish property crash many small farmhouses or Fincas were illegally converted into brash over the top palaces with infinity pools where the owners could sit and admire the views out to Gibraltar, they were too northern European for him but maybe if the plot could be legalised they could provide a starting point. When looking at the old fincas they had one big advantage where many buyers would be put off due to the difficulties in arranging finance, for Jack and Bridget it didn't matter, they were true cash buyers and there were some real bargains to be had.

Wandering round the small lanes above the coast road after yet another failed viewing they came across the perfect plot when they least expected to. In truth Jack had got slightly lost but hey, real men don't need maps.

The property was set down one of the back lanes behind Estepona built on top of a hill and conveniently had a reasonably high wall along the roadside already built. There was a gaudy day glow orange "Se Vende" sign on the gate with a brief description of the property, six beds, five baths, sixty thousand metres, being sold by the owner direct, one million five hundred thousand euros. Jack picked up his mobile and dialled the number. He was greeted by a gruff English voice. "Hello, who's this?"

"Hi my name's Jack, I'm sat outside of a big property at the back of Estepona and your number's on the for sale sign so it is; any chance of having a look around?"

"Not if you're a property agent you can't, I'm not interested."

"Nope, just a genuine buyer looking for a good price on a property." Jack could hear the cogs turning.

"Are you alone? No, I see you've got a woman with you, that's you in the soft top right. Hang on I'll open the gates, come on up to the front of the house, the name's Harry."

Jack's head was on a swivel as they drove through the gates, he was calculating how safe he could make the place. The drive was block paved but not with real blocks, it looked like it was polished concrete, the driveway climbed up to the house at a steep angle and was around one hundred metres long, ideal to block unwelcome guests. The house itself was two stories, of typical Spanish construction with a concrete frame and probably filled in with the local poor quality clay air bricks before a daub of render was smeared over the outside to hide the lack of skill of the local bricklayers. It would need work but it had potential.

Harry stood outside on the terrace as Jack parked the car next to a round tiled fountain with water spouting from the mouths of three fish which formed the central feature. Virtually every Finca they had seen over the last few months had a similar statement outside the front door; he'd have to find out why the Spanish loved their fountains so much at some stage when he had more time. Harry fitted in with the property; he was a typical older style rough diamond ex-pat, he had long grey hair tied back in a ponytail with a scraggly beard, he looked like he could do with a good wash, and despite his tan his skin had the pallor of someone who hit the bottle hard. He was wearing shorts a polo shirt and flip flops and looked disheveled. He strolled over and held out his hand.

"You'll have to take the place as it is, I wasn't expecting visitors, it might be a bit messy but it's a fantastic spot to live, close enough to town but far enough away if you know what I mean and look at those views." He waved his hand expansively at the skyline and out to Gibraltar. "I've been doing the place up for the last few years but it's time for me to move on now; come on, I'll show you around."

Bridget couldn't work him out. He hadn't even looked at her let alone greeted her, his sole attention was Jack. Not that she was worried, she stared at the view, looked lovingly at the covered terrace running the length of the house and was already imagining having parties there and if they were lucky maybe kids running round or splashing in the pool. The gardens were a bit unloved with overgrown grass, dumped building materials and what looked like an old spa bath cut in half but beneath the clutter she could see that it was once loved with mature Canary palms, fruit trees and an abundance of rose bushes. She hadn't even walked inside and she was sold on the place. She looked back to the house and noted that Harry had moved Jack on leaving her to her own devices. *No matter* she thought. The open glass door led straight into a decent size kitchen, it wasn't to her taste with rough pine doors but they could rip it out and start again. More importantly there was a nice flow to the space and the terracotta flooring kept the building cool in the heat of the day.

Surprisingly for a man obviously living on his own and concerned that they might find it messy the place was tidy, the kitchen led onto a large lounge dining room area with a white tall mantelpiece framing an open iron fire grate at the far end. Three settees faced a huge flat screen TV and the bottle of scotch on the rustic wooden coffee table was a giveaway as to where Harry spent most of his time. Light wooden doors leading off from the lounge led to three very acceptable bedrooms, one with an en-suite and the others with a shared Jack and Gill set up. The more she saw the more she liked it. All it needed in her mind was a woman's touch, curtains at the windows, soft furnishings, a few accent walls and some statement paintings. She mentally slapped herself for 'moving in' without even talking to Jack. This was her dream but was it his?

She went through a small corridor coming across the stairs leading to the next level. Typically Spanish they were concrete, tiled over with a wrought iron bannister to one side. As she reached the top the space opened into an upper lounge where a large wood burner sat against one wall and glass patio doors opened on to the upper terrace; it felt much warmer and was probably where Harry spent his time in the winter, although it looked unused. A quick peek in one of the rooms showed why, all the rooms were bare, no bathroom fittings, no tiling, just bare pipes and bare sockets. She hadn't noticed it as she climbed the stairs. She turned back towards the wood burner in the main room to find Jack to see what his thoughts were. No point in getting excited if he hated the place.

He wandered back along the corridor without Harry in tow and sidled up to her with a huge grin on his face. "What do you think sweetheart? Like it? I know it needs work but it still feels Spanish rather than the over the top marble mansions we've been looking at." Bridget was non-committal supressing her natural wish to jump for joy.

"Well, it's okay but it needs a lot of work, do you know how to use tools Jack? I know you're handy when it comes to some things." She grabbed at his pants cupping him. "But I wouldn't want to be living in a half finished place and it might cost a fortune to finish." She cracked unable to keep the pretence up. "Okay, it's gorgeous, or at least it could be and the views are stunning but isn't he a bit ambitious on price?"

"It depends whether he wants to sell it or not. You can ask whatever you like but it's only worth whatever someone's prepared to pay so it is; and he wants a quick deal, says he's got to disappear so he does...Maybe you could do some of that there snoopy stuff on the web and find out a bit more, give us a bit of an edge when it comes to pricing."

"Why's he got to disappear?"

"Don't ask me? That's what you need to find out. Gerald Harry Bailey, maybe it's GBH eh? Okay don't laugh, it wasn't that funny. Anyway says he's 62 years old and was born in Whitechapel."

That evening Bridget set off a meta search trying to find out as much as she could about Harry and why he needed to sell. She found his court records, GBH was the least of it, armed bank robbery, extortion, he was a proper old time gangster but she couldn't see why he had to vanish. She followed a thread looking up associates and spotted a link that might just be part of the reason. The armed bank robbery ended up with one person being shot who subsequently died. The man who pulled the trigger was up for parole in a few months, could that be it, a good old fashioned double cross? She shared the information with Jack and by the size of his grin she'd hit gold.

"Argh, it'll be fun to tag him along a bit then...Tell him his buddy is on his tail. Can you find out how much was stolen and what's unaccounted for? The more information we have the easier it'll be to push his buttons so it will."

"You need to see what his problem is with women as well. Didn't you notice that he couldn't even look at me and he didn't say hello? I can run another search, he has been married but I don't know where she is now."

"Let's keep digging, there's more to it I'm sure."

Chapter 7
Up North

WITH HIS LANGUAGE SKILLS now more than acceptable Paolo arranged flights to Recife and car hire onwards to the beach project. He had one last night with the girls and had promised them both sales jobs once the project started to take off. He was confident that both of them would fit the bill perfectly, savvy, sexy, numerate and most importantly with luck potential investors would be blinded by their charms. He picked a little Suzuki four by four as his hire car and applied the magnetic boards to the side that he'd had made up in Rio. He stood back and admired them. 'Turtle Bay Eco Development'. "Yep, that about does the job, even the car fits the bill, small, efficient, locally built, I might even start to believe this myself."

Over the next few weeks Paolo settled in to the local community. The local bank manager welcomed him with open arms and opened a line of credit for the Company after Head Office had confirmed the receipt of a large deposit. The local Mayor saw the opportunity to earn a few more bribes and listened intently to the plans and the ecological philosophy that was going to be adopted; that and the provision of a new school would keep the electorate happy while he could make hay. The fact that the gringo spoke passable Portuguese also helped matters when he appeared at the local bar. He was affable, had an eye for the girls and always bought a few drinks. Even the surfers had time for him.

Paolo needed to find a local builder for the preliminary construction contracts to build some show villas, park like gardens a permanent office block and an imposing entrance way. He knew that he would probably end up paying the market rate but at this stage it didn't matter. Bashar had made it clear that things needed to get underway quickly so that clients could be brought to site to see the beach, the grounds and the show homes. Providing local jobs would increase his popularity and he couldn't wait to get out of the prefab offices that currently sat on site or at least to get the air conditioning hooked up. The heat was debilitating.

His follow up appointment with the bank manager was a tick the box sort of affair. Bashar had arranged for a line of credit to be set up in Sau Paulo and the local branch just had to arrange a cash facility and a few local accounts to provide slush funds to pay the inevitable bribes. The manager was probably about Paolo's age, neatly dressed with a crisp white shirt, grey slacks and polished shoes. He seemed a bit out of place, 'stiff' if you like; he did however know his clientele and explained who was who around the surrounding area over lunch at Paco's. Pretty early on Paolo decided that future meetings could be dealt with by the Surveyor, the man was tee total and didn't even seem to notice the girls serving them. Not quite his cup of tea, although he did say that he liked to party at night, maybe the bank had a no drinking rule at lunchtime or Paolo had mistranslated things; it was easy to get over confident with the language and entirely misconstrue things.

The local Mayor was much more to his taste, the man knew how to have fun and lunch involved more than a few bottles of wine before they moved on to the rum. He also made his position very clear early on...if Paolo 'happened' to use his brother's construction firm to carry out the preliminary work he was sure that he would be able to slide the initial works under the table. Of course a bit of slush money would help grease the wheels and he was upfront about asking for ten thousand dollars before the two of them went on to enjoy the company of the girls at the bar.

A few weeks later the Mayor gave Paolo the nod to start work even though planning had yet to formally go through. It was highly unlikely that the locals would complain given that they would have months if not years of employment. The gravy train was getting its station ready and they all intended to be on board. In the short term some his prefab offices were hooked up to the grid providing a cool place to work and somewhere to put up schematics of the development and glossy pictures of the proposed villa's. A hastily laid gravel drive and some rapidly planted garden beds made the whole thing look presentable. He now had an office to work from and a base set up for the British Surveyor who'd been hired to deal with the construction phase. He had relied heavily on his expertise when arranging his first local deal and was looking forward to someone else arriving to do all of the hard work. Paperwork was not Paolo's forte, talking, smooching, and entertaining now those were things that he could do. And party, well it was his middle name.

Chapter 8
Local Mafia

IT DIDN'T TAKE LONG for Paolo to reacquaint himself with the white stuff. The local bar seemed to be swimming in cocaine and the local girls, well...let's just say they were more than willing to play games with the stuff, although he had to admit he'd never had it rubbed in to the tip of his cock before, it brought a numbness to the extremities but also excitement, he really struggled to describe it but it was still playing on his brain sat at his desk a day later. He shook his head slugged some more coffee and tried to concentrate on the plans in front of him. He was due to see the local Mayor and Regional Councillor to negotiate fast track permission on the second block of land; he had to be on his 'A' game or they would demand astronomic bribes. Maybe he could take them to the bar to party afterwards, buy a few girls and get some compromising photo's...*concentrate Paolo.*

The crunch of wheels on the gravel outside the sales office had him rushing to clear his desk and straighten himself up in the mirror. He wanted to look the part... the Uber smooth gringo holding all the cards, his ego meant that playing the part would not be difficult; he really did believe his own PR. He rubbed his Italian shoes down the back of his trousers and wiped his hands with a tissue to make sure they were dry; satisfied he slowly walked to the door to hold it open. As he pulled on the handle the heat hit him head on in contrast to the icy air-conditioned environment he'd been sat in. His eyes struggled to adjust to the sunlight and as he took in the scene he realised that something was off. The car in front of him was a huge Lincoln Navigator, an American seven seater beast with fully tinted windows making it impossible to see inside; it was a stark contrast to the Mayor's beaten up Toyota which was always covered in red dust from the local tracks.

The two front doors opened. The driver and his accomplice both stood and pulled out hand guns while scanning the area. *What the fuck do they need guns for?* Satisfied that the area was clear they walked to the back doors and opened them to release their precious cargo. The Mayor and Regional Councillor exited as expected but it was noticeable that they were deferential to the third man, someone that Paolo hadn't seen before. He looked to be in his mid-forties or early fifties, five foot nine, long black hair pulled back in a ponytail and a typical Mexican moustache running down either side of his mouth. His face was pock marked and he had a grizzly scar running down his left cheek. In contrast to his features he liked his gold and bling, wearing a heavy thick chain around his neck, a matching bracelet around one wrist and a bling watch on the other which was either real or an exceptionally good fake. The trio took in Paolo holding the door open and sauntered across. The Mayor held out his hand to shake, whilst the other two ignored Paolo's proffered hand. This wasn't going as expected. *I'm supposed to be holding all the cards, what the fuck?*

He ushered them into the conference come board room with a large round table and comfy executive chairs. The Mayor headed straight to the drinks bar and poured three large Tequilas before asking Paolo to name his poison. For a change he decided to stick to coffee he had a feeling that he was going to need a clear head.

"So Paolo, things are progressing with phase one no?" The Mayor waved his hand at the window indicating the infrastructure work that was underway.

He turned towards the new man. "This is Senor Garcia, he is a very important local businessman and he is going to be your security advisor for the projects. He knows all of the important people in the area and has many many business interests. He will make sure that you get approval for the second stage and will keep you protected."

Paolo failed to read between the lines; he'd missed the words 'going to be'. "That's a very generous offer Juan but we don't really need security or protection, I thought we were here to negotiate our contribution to ensure planning for the second phase."

"You don't seem to understand Paolo; the protection offered by Senor Garcia is non-negotiable, he will be your advisor and you need to agree terms with him."

Paolo couldn't quite work out the dynamic. He could see that the Mayor was not his usual effable self, nervous even, something was off. He laughed trying to lighten the mood. "Everything's always negotiable."

"The Mayor looked slightly panicked and pulled Paolo to one side talking in a whispered voice. "Paolo, we have talked about this...you must have security and Mr Garcia provides it...not just to you but to all of the Town...there is no choice, you remember?"

The Mayor turned back to his two compatriots with his arm round Paolo's shoulder. "Sorry my friends, I was just reminding Paolo of our conversations about security and protection. Now then Paolo what do you have to say?"

"Well it seems that I'm between a rock and a hard place; I don't have authority to agree a security deal. My investors don't think they need it, they say they can provide their own." He finished his remarks with one of his best slimy grins while holding his hands palm outwards in a placating gesture.

"There's not much more I can say."

The three locals went into a huddle and Paolo respectively gave them space. It seemed that Senor Garcia had thought that the security issue was a done deal and from the shouting and cursing he was not a happy bunny. The trio broke apart and the Mayor continued as the spokesman.

"Paolo, I beg you to reconsider, we have discussed this, Senor Garcia will not take no for an answer."

"Well, sorry the answer is no, can we get on to planning now? I thought that today's meeting was about how to get permission."

His flippant attitude seemed to make Garcia snap, his face went black with fury before he waved at his two henchmen and shouted some orders at them. They wandered slowly to the back of the Lincoln and pulled out two old machine guns from the back, they stood waiting for their boss to join them and then proceeded to unload the magazines from the guns into the windows and walls of Paolo's office. He hit the floor covering his head and ears. Juan shrugged his shoulders and held out his hands in a conciliatory gesture before also hitting the deck...Paolo couldn't believe how calm he was. As the firing stopped he got to his knees and continued talking as if nothing had happened.

"There are many problems in Brazil Senor Paolo, it is always wise to have how do you say...'a sponsor?' It would stop you having problems with your machinery, your workers and it would smooth the way with many things in the corridors of power."

Paolo picked himself up from the floor and brushed himself down; he was inwardly quivering but knew in macho Brazil he had to try to stay calm, he steeled himself; he wasn't going to roll over easily. "You realise who you are threatening? It's not just my family anymore we have serious external investors who won't take kindly to your attitude, they make people disappear; they trade arms worldwide. You're picking a fight with some of the biggest drug dealers in Europe and they don't play nicely with people that threaten them."

The Mayor's face lit up. "Ah, drug money, so let's be more open shall we, maybe there is more that we can do together eh Senor Garcia?" Garcia shrugged and looked disinterested. "Senor Garcia here runs the operations for the Escobar cartel in our area, he is a very important man, and maybe he can arrange some supplies for your investors. You understand though, you are now on his territory, you have to contribute to the cause or you will be shut down no matter what I say or our esteemed Regional Councillor says. The Escobar cartel owns the police and politicians here in this area of Brazil."

Garcia stood and walked to the bar to pour himself another drink. He knocked it back before trying to intimidate Paolo with a stare straight off of a spaghetti western film. "You Gringos are all the same; you think you're important, superior. You need to understand... Here I call the shots; you can't even piss unless I say so. He threw his head back and comically tried to stand tall to make his point. "You understand?!"

Despite quaking inside Paolo stood his ground and stared back at Garcia, Max had warned him that things could get rough and spelt out that he did not want to upset Jack or Bashar under any circumstances whatsoever.

He took a deep breath and gambled. "I think you'll find things a bit different when you meet my friends Senor Garcia but let's not jump the gun, what do you propose as your fee?"

"I want a quarter of a million dollars up front to sort out your planning and a protection fee of twenty five thousand US dollars a month." He didn't smile, he was serious.

Paolo choked on his coffee and let out a guffaw which instantly offended Garcia yet again. He wiped down his shirt and around his mouth with a tissue before trying to recover the situation in his usual smarmy way. "I'm sorry Senor Garcia, I must have swallowed my drink the wrong way or perhaps I misheard you. Let me just check my understanding." Paolo stood and walked round the table to the bar buying himself time to think while pouring himself a soft drink. He needed to stay alert and to tread softly. "Twenty five thousand a month is a lot of money Senor Garcia, the local barman only earns four thousand dollars a year, your idea sounds more like big city money but I will talk to the investors and make your offer and..." He waved his hand round expansively at his damaged office across the corridor..."And explain your, ermm, shall we call it your terms? I'm not sure it will go down well but all I can do is talk to them. You understand that I'm not the decision maker?"

He turned to the local Mayor and Regional councillor. "In the meantime gentlemen I can assure you that you will be amply rewarded if you are able to ensure our plans go through unhindered." He smiled his best serpentine grin hoping to diffuse the situation. "I will of course try to deal with Senor Garcia's requests as quickly as possible." He nodded in his direction acknowledging him.

Garcia snorted and turned on his heel heading straight out of the door to his Lincoln Navigator, the Mayor and Councillor hurried out behind him. "You have seven days Senor Paolo, no more! We cannot keep you safe from the cartel."

Chapter 9
Snow White

BACK IN ESSEX Tony was also starting to have problems with his drinking and drug habits. Working every night at the club where the girls and clients were routinely off of their heads coupled with a steady flow of white powder from Joey in Spain was proving difficult to manage. He worked hard at trying to limit his alcohol intake only really starting to have what he called a 'proper drink' after closing usually with the staff and maybe a few select patrons. He tried to make it seem like it was leisure time but in reality he missed the late night wind down somewhere other than where he was working. He loved the people, loved the place but he just didn't like himself that much, he was struggling with his internal demons and using alcohol as a crutch earlier and earlier in the evening. Just a whiff of pizza on the way to work would bring back images of trying to hold his army buddies together after the IRA bombed their regular take away haunt, as the memories deepened and his dreams became more vivid inevitably it led to a Jack Daniels or two before anyone else arrived just to get himself back on track and functioning.

It didn't take that long before the lure of Snow, Blow, Crack, Charlie; whatever you want to call it, started to take hold. He'd had a fresh delivery which Giselle noticed and she badgered him after the club had closed to let her have some.

"You tried it before Tony? It's fucking great, instant high, you feel like you can scale Everest. Come on Tony, I'll fuck you for some, blow job, anal, whatever you want, you won't be sorry."

Thankfully Tony was strong enough to say no, at least this time. He gave Giselle a small twist, sent her on her way and then spent the next two hours staring at the bag. *Was it really that good? Didn't it really ruin people's lives? What was all the fuss about? Everyone in London took it didn't they?* He knew that it was the after dinner drug of choice in London, wheeled out as the 'digestive' to finish the meal as if it was nothing more than a Brandy or Whiskey. Fear of the unkown and the stories of celebrities burning out their septum had so far scared him off. *Come on Tony, pull yourself together, for fuck's sake it's not the first time you've had flashbacks. Be strong!* He placed the stash securely in the safe and tried to push all thoughts of it from his mind.

He closed up the bar, took a deep breath of the cold morning air and put his head down as he set off in the direction of home. Not having Freddie around for a month was a real pain in the arse. He worked one month on one month off and to be fair to him he tried hard to be at the club between his long haul shifts. Tony pictured him in Shanghai on his current layover shopping until he dropped picking up fake bargains to bring home for friends. *Hey, the fakes make up half my wardrobe. Fuck I still miss his smiling face, especially when I'm having a bad time.* Sleep did not come easily, his black op sorties playing through his mind, holding in Denny's guts after the bomb, getting stuck in a trench for two days hiding out while on an off limits reconnaissance mission. He was beating himself up badly, tossing turning, sweating...

Why are so many dead, why did I deserve to live? He woke gasping for breath, sweating profusely. His mind turned to Charlie...would it help? *For fuck's sake Tony pull yourself together.*

The smell of fresh pizza on the way to work the following afternoon was the straw that broke the camel's back, rather than reaching for Jack Daniels, Tony pulled out a wrap from the safe and cut himself a two lines using his credit card as he'd watched the girls do every night. He rolled up a twenty pound note and paused. *Would it be better than using alcohol as a crutch? Would the clients know he'd used it? Fuck it.* Tony snorted the Charlie up his nose. *No time to turn back*...The rush was instant as the blood vessels in his brain opened and a feeling of euphoria washed over him. He felt like he could take on the world but to quote Jackson Browne: "When you do a line of coke, you feel like a new man. The only problem is the new man wants one, too." *Fuck I feel good; I can do anything!*

The quote was all to true. Sure the high on day one took him right through until morning, he was buzzing doing the work of two men, the life and soul of the party but by the end of the first week he'd get to around two in the morning and feel like he needed a pick up. As much as he tried to resist by week three it was six lines a night and by week four, well, who was counting? He started sharing his drug fuelled mornings with Giselle who was happy to share his bed for a wrap or two and to have a companion to get off her head with.

It wasn't long before the staff nick named him Snow White so he took down the UV lights. He didn't know who he thought he was kidding but there was no point in advertising his habit. What started out as a dabble to help exorcise his demons soon began to run his life. He was dipping his hand in the sweetie bag too often and sooner or later Joey would probably start to ask what was happening to the missing cash. Tony started to duck and dive, losing a bit from each stash, skimming the till on other occasions, so much so that he started to "forget" to make the repayments agreed on the club. Money for the Charlie came first.

On his first monthly stint back at the club Freddie tried to get Tony to talk about his problems. He could see that he was bottling up something and he suspected that he was hitting the sauce hard again, there was something different about him, it could be his hook up with Giselle but Freddie was sure there was something else. Tony just laughed it off telling him that he needed to retune his gaydar to filter out some of the emotions. Only Tony would get away with such a comment but the smokescreen didn't put him off the scent. The following month Freddie decided it was time to confront his business partner. The staff were openly singing "Hi ho, Hi ho, it's off to snort we go." The row that followed was immense; Tony still swore that everything was under control even getting aggressive trying to prove his point. Freddie backed off...for now.

The façade crumbled completely with a phone call from Max. "Hey, Freddie its Max, how's things?" Some small talk later and Max got to the real reason for his call. "I was just a bit worried Freddie, you know with the last two payments not being made and all, I thought maybe the club was failing or something." Max left a long pregnant pause but Freddie stalled, he didn't want to admit that he had no clue that they were behind. "Yeah, umm yeah Max, probably my fault because I've been working away so much, you know what Tony's like when it comes to the admin, I'll chase him up later and get back to you. Give my love to Rachel; make sure you give her a big hug from me." Freddie placed the phone carefully back into its cradle before thumping the bar top with his fist. "Fuck it, fuck it, fuck it!!! You're not wiggling out of it this time Tony Brown."

Freddie opened up early and sat in the corner of the club with the lights out. He watched as Tony came in, went straight for his stash and cut himself a line on the bar. He waited until Tony had snorted the powder up his nose using a rolled up banknote before turning on the lights. "Feeling good now Grumpy? Had your fill of snow? You're a fucking lying bastard Tony Brown, I've talked to Max and you've missed the last two fucking payments on the club, what's your problem Tony and no more fucking lying! You're fucking up my life as well as your own after all the work I've put in to this place." The emotional dam that Freddie was holding back broke, he sobbed, broke down into tears and somewhat over dramatically threw himself onto one of the brown leather settees. He wiped his eyes with a big white handkerchief before drawing breath, letting the words flow between intermittent sobs. "I've put my life and soul into this place and you go and stick it up your nose; why Tony, why?"

Tony put his head in his hands. He could never have taken the club over without Freddie, his investment and all of his help, he deserved better. "Oh fuck...I'm sorry Freddie, look just don't cry, I don't cope well with tears and hugging you well that would just be wrong wouldn't it...you've caught me bang to rights, yeah I've been chuffing the white stuff, I lied last time you challenged me but you've gotta understand Freddie it's the only way that I can cope."

"Cope! Cope with what? A hugely successful club? Living the dream of owning your own place? What's there to cope with Tony? You've got a house, you could have a long term girlfriend if you wanted, you're getting your oats with Giselle, you've got friends Tony...Where's the problem I don't understand? If you want to know about problems, try growing up with a homophobic family and a father that tries to beat femininity out of you. Like to see some of the marks from the sticks or the cigarette burns Tony? Get over yourself and man up!"

Tears started to roll down Tony's cheeks. "That's the problem Freddie, I can't.." He stammered..."I...I see the faces...the...the faces every night, I can't sleep, why me, why did I survive when my friends were all killed?" He wiped his sleeve across his face and poured himself a large JD that he threw down his throat as if he would never taste another.

Freddie stiffened; he'd never thought of Tony having problems, he was a big rough tough guy. *Tough guys didn't cry did they?* Well here's the evidence, a big strong guy with tears running down his cheeks. He took charge. "We're not opening tonight Tony, open a bottle of JD put it on the table and get ready to talk. I'll phone the girls, Tuesday's are slow anyway; we only took four hundred quid last week. We're going to sort this Tony Brown, with or preferably without Snow White and the seven dwarfs."

Chapter 10
Off To Rehab

FREDDIE STEWED for a day or two after his heart to heart with Tony, the guy was suffering badly, the drugs were just a way of him trying to deal with his demons from his time in the army. He'd listened, he hoped it had helped but he knew deep down that it would take a lot more than a few words to get Tony back sober and functioning properly, he couldn't understand why it had taken so long to manifest itself but a discussion with a pilot who was ex-forces pointed him towards some combat stress charities and the web where he found that it takes years, even decades, after the events for the problems to come to the surface. The more people pushed it to the back of their subconscious and the more they bottled things up the worse the swing back could be. Tony had kept it all deep within not wanting to seem less of a man. He found it incredible that it took so long to break out but the more he read and learnt the more he realised that he was in over his head especially as a number of the charities insisted that people were "free from alcohol" before they would help. Get real...alcohol helps them deal with the problem. Not able to turn to the charities for help or able to persuade Tony to talk to his GP Freddie was left with few choices. *It's a long shot but maybe, just maybe...*

He scrolled through Tony's phone whilst he was upstairs until he found the log for yesterday. There was only one foreign number listed. It had to be right. He quickly scribbled it down, put the phone back onto its home screen and set it back underneath the optics. It was a good job that Tony was still old school and that he didn't have one of the new fingerprint recognition phones, he'd guessed Tony's security pattern by watching carefully each time he used the phone. A simple Z swipe was not very original or difficult to guess.

The following morning Freddie had made up his mind, grabbed his mobile and dialled the number. He hoped that Tony would forgive him. *Too late now he thought.* As the phone was answered Freddie garbled his words trying to get them out before he changed his mind. "Joey? It's Freddie, I've got big problems at the club, Tony's hooked on the white stuff and he's suffering from combat stress, trauma, shellshock, whatever you want to call it, I don't know how to fix it and I need Jack's number, he'll listen to Jack...he won't go to rehab or treatment for me. So have you got the number please Joey?"

"Whoa, for feck's sake Freddie calm down will yer. Yer talking at a thousand miles an hour and I can hardly understand ye. Now deep breath let's start again, slowly."

Freddie gave himself a mental slap; of course Joey was prepared to listen. He sat on his kitchen stall took a sip from his mug of coffee and went over the events of the last few weeks and months leaving nothing out. "Feck, feck, feck! It always fecking happens to the good guys, it's an operational hazard to be sure Freddie. We've all been there at some stage tempted by the white lady but the stress thing I don't know much about. Now to be sure if I give you Jack's number he'll fecking kill me given that he's retiring and all. I'll relay the information and he'll call you back so he will, he likes Tony, he's sure to help. Now one last thing Freddie; how the fuck did you get my number, I've only had this SIM for four days so I have."

Five minutes later and Freddie's phone jingled to tell him that he'd received an SMS although there was no number or name showing, he opened it anyway.

Freddie, I'm on the case, I'll talk to Tony later and I'll arrange his rehab. I'll call when it's organised. Unfortunately you can't ring me I only accept incoming traffic via a secure website and ring back via a hidden network if it's someone I know....Hang in there. Jack.

He shrugged, it all seemed a bit secret squirrel but he was sure that Jack would have his reasons. At least he wasn't battling this on his own now, he had allies.

By opening time the following day Freddie still hadn't heard back from Jack and he was starting to get worried. He set about cleaning up and polishing glasses to keep himself occupied when he was interrupted by a knock at the door. Animal Frank and Tommy Two Tones walked through wearing their usual black Crombie coats, ten hole Doc Martin boots, smart button down collar checked shirts, braces and skinny leg jeans...Just their everyday intimidation uniform. "Alright Freddie, how's it 'anging mate? Hear you've got a bit of a problem so we've been sent to help 'ent we Tommy." Tommy nodded his head as he made his way round to the fridges to grab a beer.

"Don't mind do you Freddie?" Not that he was going to take no for an answer.

"It's nice to see you lads but who sent you and what are you here for?"

"Bloody hell Freddie, not like you to be slow is it? Jack sent us to pick up Tony and get him to rehab." He looked at his watch. "Should be talking to him around now...hope the news goes down well, don't fancy having to strong arm Tony but we can always use the Rohypnol."

"The what?"

Frank reached into his pocket and pulled out a packet with half a dozen small tablets inside. "Ere this stuff... you'll have to pour us all a drink when he gets here and drop one of these tablets in his JD and coke...'ang on let's fink about this...he's a big bloke, he won't 'ave been drinking earlier... so we better chuck some more in....make it two tablets Freddie."

"Isn't that stuff illegal? It's the date rape drug isn't it?"

Tommy laughed at Freddie's innocence. "Bang on Freddie but don't worry we won't let anyone near 'is arse, you can be first to convert 'im."

Freddie was not impressed. "Pig! I don't know why they call you Tommy Two Tones...you'd need more than one brain cell and I doubt there's more than one in there." Freddie rapped the front of his head causing Tommy to kick away his bar stall and lunge across the bar at him."

"Alright, alright, come on Tommy, you were out of order and he's got a point. Put your fucking brain in gear before you open your gob." As Frank calmed the situation down the door swung open and Tony stormed through looking as if he was chewing a wasp. He was not a happy man.

"You fucking grass Freddie! I've had that fucking piece of Irish scum on the phone telling me that I've gotta go to rehab to get off the white stuff and to talk about combat stress. I wouldn't be suffering from stress if it wasn't for those Irish wankers. What right has he got to lecture me?! What fucking right! You told him didn't you!" He stopped mid stride as he realised that Frank and Tommy were sat at the bar. "Sorry boys, I don't wanna involve you in this it's personal between me and Freddie. What you doing here anyway, Vince not been paying his bills?"

"Somefing like that Tony, fought we'd drop in for a drink and say hello...Bad time is it? We'll just have a quick one wiv yer and get out yer hair. Come on Freddie three large JD and cokes, let's not be rude." He stared at the Rohypnol and raised his eyebrows at Freddie making his request clear. "What's this about stress then Tony? Fucking nightmare when you get stressed out init Tommy?"

"I don't want to talk about it Frank."

"Alright mate, we can see we're not welcome, no hard feelings, here drink up."

Tony not wanting to offend the boys more than he already had chugged the JD straight back and offered them one for the road before apologising for his foul mood. Tommy nodded at Freddie for him to put more in. His eyes went wide and he mouthed back," you've got to be kidding." Tommy just made a fist and stared, luckily the others were distracted; Frank had his arm round Tony's shoulder and was steering him over to one of the tables with the comfy leather chairs.

"Yeh, look Frank, you and Tommy are welcome here anytime, sorry I was a bit of an arse when I came in, I've not been sleeping too good and I've been a bit wound up lately, you know how it is."

Freddie came over with two more drinks, sliding the one with the meds in over to Tony. He took it and drank it more slowly but still finished it off in under ten minutes...he needed a good drink after talking to Jack.

"Fucking hell Tony; got a 'first on yer boy? Here have mine, I've gotta drive later and the old bill are getting right hot with the old roadside checks, can't be driving without a licence now can I."

Tony reached for the other glass before looking quizzically at Frank, he was getting suspicious. "I thought you dropped in for a drink? What really brought you this way Frank, nothing to do with Jack or Joey is it?"

"Well you know how it is Tony, Joey's been a bit concerned about the returns on his shipments, seems to be a bit down on his margins. Asked if we could drop in when we were in the area; wouldn't know why he's down on his margins would yer?" Tony shifted uncomfortably in his chair sipping from his glass. "There's nothing wrong with his margins, he'd have phoned me if there was, everything's fine." He got up and walked over to the bar shaking his head on the way before pouring himself a coke. As he headed back he was having difficulty with his co-ordination and stumbled on the table. "What the fuck? Have you slipped me a fucking mickey?"

"Yeah, sorry Tony, but it's for your own good, Jack says you've gotta go to rehab so we're the taxi service. Told you I had to drive didn't I?"

"Well fuck you I'm not going and you and Tommy have got a fight on your hands if you think you can make me. I've already told Jack he can stick it."

Tommy came over with the bottle of Jack and poured some into Tony's coke. "Ahh, Tony, Tony, Tony...enjoy your last drink, you won't be having one for a while so take it while you can. You see we're all mates and that's why we've drugged yer. You'll be asleep soon and there's nuffing you can do 'bout it. It's for your own good Tony; just try it for a couple o' weeks." Tony took the glass, swigged it down and swung a right cross at Tommy who tried to catch him as he collapsed to the floor taken off of his feet by his own body force.

The boys picked him up under the arms and walked him out of the back door before placing him in the back of a black Land Rover Discovery laying him out flat on a mattress placed lengthways along the boot and folded down rear seats.

"No offense meant Tony, you're a proper geezer, a good bloke, and geezers don't take drugs, they 'ave a good drink, 'ave a bit of fun, maybe a bit of a dust up but that's it. So you gotta try Tony. We're taking you to rehab to exercise your demons, make the most of it mate." Tony reacted with his last strength trying to catch either of the brothers in the head with his foot but in reality he was just flailing around. "Ah, ah Tony, be a good lad, I don't wanna 'ave to hit you wiv a dolly or let Tommy chin yer. Snuggle down and go to sleep there's a good lad."

Tony was in a surreal world. His mind was spinning, he could hear what Frank was saying but he couldn't respond, his thoughts became fixated on his discussion with Jack. He was going off to rehab whether he liked it or not.

Chapter 11
Unwelcome Message

WITH THE LOCAL DRUGS LORD GONE Paolo set about clearing the place up or at least trying to find his handyman to clear the place up, manual work wasn't his thing. He did at least check the security cameras to upload the machine gun scene. He was lucky that the system hadn't been damaged and he was also able to get some footage of Senor Garcia making his demands. A few short video clips would explain things far better than he could in an email or over the phone, who would believe him anyway? He attached the file to an email and sent it to Max and Bashar before loading it onto the secure website he'd been given for Jack. He had the upload password here somewhere; it was just frustrating that the thing changed every bloody week. With the job finally done he decided that he needed some rest and relaxation and he knew just who to go and see at the local bar - big breasted Belinda and maybe a line or two of coke. *Yes, he needed to unwind.*

Martin and Bashar sat in front of the large on wall screen playing the video clips backwards and forwards with Martin picking out details that Bashar would never have seen. "See how this guy holds his machine gun? He's not been trained, definitely not ex-military, probably just a local hoodlum, same with the other guy, sloppy with the firearm and look at his shoes, they haven't seen polish since they were new. The car is also a bit of a giveaway, it's clean but it's an older model, probably six or seven years, it's a hand me down from his boss who has the real power. He's a small fish." He sat back letting Bashar digest his views.

"Well, what do you recommend Martin? I don't want to alienate the locals entirely but there's no way I'm paying some jumped up little prick protection money. You might say small fish but he clearly thinks he's a big fish. We need to make him realise that his pond is a puddle even in his own country...just don't start a war Martin, it's a headache I could do without, and DON'T tell Lynette."

A grin spread across Martin's face. "Still wearing the trousers then?" He laughed as Bish grimaced. "Let me talk to my local contacts; we need to play this carefully rather than going in all guns blazing. I might send in Enrique Fernandez." Martin sat back in his chair deep in thought before reaching a decision. "Yes... yes he would probably fit the bill very well along with a few ex-military guys in tow. Here, let me pull up a picture on the laptop so you can see him on screen." A few key strokes on the keyboard later and there was a small collage of photos of a suave looking tall bearded Brazilian with key facts about him listed down the side of the page; Martial arts expert, small arms expert, covert ops, skilled linguist, member of upper echelons, links to Brazilian presidency staff, enjoys knife play. "Well what do you think, looks a bit like you in some ways Bish but he's not such an arrogant git."

"Aw come on Martin, give me a break that was months back and I've learnt my lesson, I'm much more relaxed and open now." Bish perused the information on screen carefully. "Hmm, I'd believe he was from the government or a drugs cartel if I met him; but how does he find the pressure point?"

Martin tapped the side of his nose. "That's need to know Bish, that and don't bark yourself if you own a dog. I'll set it up."

Max and Rachel didn't take things quite so calmly. Rachel threw a wobbly and hit the Bacardi while Max tried to calm her down. "Look Rach, the local Mayor's changed, it's not the guy I was dealing with and anyway we're not in the front line anymore, Bish and Jack will deal with it. I'm not even going to bother replying." *That's a lie but what you don't know won't hurt you.*

"I'm going out Max; I can't sit here and listen to crap. It's our names on the deeds and we own part of the company, our necks are on the line if this goes wrong! We're supposed to be enjoying our money and getting back to a normal life. Since when is getting threatened by drug lords normal?" Rachel dramatically put her hand to her brow and oozed sarcasm. "Oh, I'm sorry... I forgot you're used to be threatened by drug gangs and dealing in contraband... silly me, I forgot that you were a part time hoodlum..." Her face turned dark with anger and her eyes narrowed. "Sort it Max, you promised me that we would get out of this and lead a clean life, let's not go back there." She turned on her heel and stomped out of the apartment, someone would be in for a coffee...Sylvia?

Max flopped onto the cream leather settee in the apartment and pushed his hand through his hair as stress got the better of him. He'd already tried phoning Bish four times without a response, he'd seem like a stalker if he phoned again. He had hoped to have answers before Rachel got to the email but although he'd hidden it on the main PC he'd forgotten that the emails pinged automatically to Rachel's phone until she came storming out of the bedroom wailing like a banshee. She had a point, they had spent hours talking about getting as far away from Bashar, Jack and Joey as they could and here they were getting dragged straight back into things. "Fuck, why is life so difficult!!" He slammed his fist down on his leg. He was so angry. He'd managed to win Rachel back but things were starting to fall apart again all due to things out of his control. In reality they both knew that they wouldn't be allowed to just walk away, and as yet the promised up front proceeds from the property sales had yet to arrive in their bank account. Bish had told him that it was something to do with a BVI structure being needed and that Lynette had it in hand. He trusted Lynette; she'd had his back more than once and had never let him down. *But now she has a child with Bashar, can I still trust her?*

He picked up his mobile and dialled Paolo's number. *Where was the little shit?* It was typical of him to send an email with a burning fuse and then disappear until the dust settled. "Fuck it, Paolo its Max, I don't want to talk to a fucking voice mail, ring me, we need to talk about your unwelcome news!"

Chapter 12
Paco's Bar

PAOLO LEFT THE HANDYMAN clearing up at the offices and jumped in to his small Suzuki four by four emblazoned with the Turtle Bay eco development logo on each door. He gunned the engine and headed down the track towards Vistamar the local Hamlet with around five hundred permanent residences boosted by the beach bum tourists who come to smoke the dope and catch a break on the steady stream of waves formed by the reef. When he first drove out to the site from Recife he thought that he was being sent to the back of beyond but as he drove along the palm lined coastline framed by the azure blue seas and white sand beaches he began to change his mind. Vistamar sealed the deal; wonderful afro -Caribbean culture, beautiful girls and plentiful bars for such a small place. His American dollar was king, everything was so cheap; he could have a good meal, get drunk and get laid with change in his pocket from a fifty dollar bill. Paco's bar became his local haunt with a mix of locals drinking beer or rum and beach bums smoking spliffs. He liked the vibe and more importantly he liked the local girls on offer.

He pulled up outside the bar put his keys in his pocket without bothering to lock the car and walked past the white wooden bench style beds and hammocks. A few surfers were draped effortlessly across the beds shooting the breeze and talking about today's big rolling surf. It sounded as if they'd had a great day with "Awesome" being heard every other word. Give them a few more hours and they would either pass out where they were in sight of the beach or they'd crawl back to their camper vans or lodgings. Nobody worried...be happy.

Paolo sprawled out on one of the outside beds and caught Belinda's eye as she served drinks to the surfers.

"Ah Belinda, Belinda, you bewitch me. Are you busy?" She made a non-committal face. "Will you join me with a bottle of rum? We can have a few drinks perhaps find a few joints to smoke and then..." Paolo jiggled his eyebrows. "Then maybe you'll let me unbutton your shirt and we can have some real fun." He placed his hands firmly on her breasts and ran his thumbs over her nipples, receiving a firm slap in return. A few minutes later Belinda returned with a jug of Mojitos, a bottle of rum and a couple of glasses. She also had a small bag of coke.

"Senor Garcia left this for you. He apologises if his men got a little carried away." Belinda's eyes were fixed on the bag. "I hear that they shot your place up...you don't seem concerned."

"Nah, my friends will deal with Senor Garcia, it's not going to be a problem." Paolo leaned forward and poured two mojito's topping them off with a bit of rum for an extra kick as Belinda slid in beside him on the seat cupping his balls. They raised their glasses and chinked. They both knew the game they were playing and both knew where it would end up...in one of the upstairs rooms with both of them naked enjoying each other's bodies in a drug and alcohol fuelled orgy.

Paolo eyed up the cocaine in the bag. It wasn't what you would call a small present even though the drug was cheap in Brazil; it was generous, thoughts rolled around his mind. *Should he give it back? Would it complicate matters if he accepted it and used it?* He placed it in his pocket and poured another drink as two of the regular surfers looking to bum a shot or two wandered over to the table.

"Hey, Paolo dude, any chance of a hit of rum? We're running low on funds until the end of the month dude, just a loan you know."

He waved at one of the waitresses and ordered another bottle and a couple of glasses. He had no interest in the guy but the pretty girl with dreadlocks dyed white at the tips by the sun...well she could be another matter entirely. He mentally slapped himself. Not today while he was focussed on Belinda but there was no harm in keeping the shelf stacked. With the rum on its way the surfers rolled a spliff using their home grown weed, sharing it round between the four of them. Paolo kicked off his shoes and removed his shirt, there was no way he was going back to work today and tomorrow also looked decidedly dodgy.

Chapter 13
Financing Structure

LYNETTE FLICKED THROUGH her contacts pages until she found the number for Senor Rodriguez, she was shut away in her office while the nanny had taken Millie for a walk around Hyde park and as much as she loved her daughter she also craved alone time in the real world. She hadn't wanted to employ a nanny but Bashar had convinced her that having someone in for a few days a week would make all the difference and how right he had proved to be. She picked up the house phone and dialled the number and now that her name was on the approved list she was put through immediately.

"Ah, Ms. Smythe, or should I say Lynette, it is a pleasure to hear your sweet voice, what can I do for you today?"

Lynette could picture him in her head sat with his feet up on the desk cigar in hand, perfectly turned out and ogling every secretary that came within ten yards, he would be the same until they took him to his grave. "Hello Juan you old smoothie, still buttering up all the girls I see. I have a few BVI companies that I need set up with more precise articles than the usual Table A format and I was wondering if you could arrange the administration and set up until I have time to come over to finalise details."

"It would be a pleasure to see you again and of course we can fulfil your requirements just email whatever you need to John Linton, do you remember John? Copy me in and I'll make sure that it happens. Ah, and maybe this time I'll get to take you to dinner."

"Full marks for trying Juan but I've already told you that I'm spoken for and this time you'll get to meet him and maybe my baby daughter as well."

Juan put on his best dramatic voice. "Ahhh, my heart has been pierced, you have found another and have borne his child, what am I to do? Seriously Lynette my congratulations, may your daughter turn out just like you. I shall have to meet this man that has stolen you away. What was his name again?"

"As sharp as ever Juan; I never told you his name but as I'll be emailing it to John it makes no difference if I tell you now. Do you have your pen and paper at the ready?" Juan smiled to himself, he was indeed sat poised ready to write it down, he liked to know who he was dealing with. "Prince Mohammed Bashar Aahdil Kaddouri, for simplicity he goes by the name Bashar Kaddouri which is what we'll use on the documentation, that's Kilo, Alpha, Delta, Delta, Oscar, Uniform, Romeo, India...got that Juan?" Lynette could visualise Senor Rodriguez paper in hand perusing the name and racking his brain trying to recall if they had any dealings in the past.

"He may be a Prince but he is still a lucky man to have found you. I look forward to meeting you both soon."

Lynette wrapped up the call and set about typing out the e-mail to John Lynton detailing what she needed:

Dear John,

I hope this finds you well.

Senor Rodriguez has nominated you to set up a number of companies for me, I hope you don't mind. I'm going to need five in total as follows:

1. *Turtle Bay Eco Development Community Master Company Ltd: Standard property holding Company to be run by the developer until the conclusion of the whole development process. We need an option to place the company with the communities but it's important that they have no right to buy. I'd also like the standard Articles tweaked though so that the Developer retains a golden share so that they can take back the company at any time; Hide it away somewhere, I'd prefer if this wasn't too obvious.*
2. *Turtle Bay Eco Development Community zone one Ltd: Standard property holding Company to be run initially by the developer and then taken over by the residents to manage the maintenance of the development.*
3. *Turtle Bay Eco Development Community zone two Ltd: Standard property holding Company to be run initially by the developer and then taken over by the residents to manage the maintenance of the development.*
4. *Sterling Eco Finance Limited: This company will be the main channel for funds and will need to have full banking powers, if you can't get a licence for the word 'Sterling' in the title let me have suggestions of other official sounding names that you can get.*

5. *All the above companies need to pay a licence fee for image rights and exclusive introductions to MKS Limited (also to be set up).*

Any problems drop me a line. I'll try to send over details of the proposed non Island based directors and shareholders later.

Best wishes

Lynette Smythe

As she pressed send she had second thoughts and looked again at the white board on her office wall which had her plan for the structure of the deal and money flows between different countries mapped out in multiple colours. She'd forgotten to include the Fractional Ownership Company in the email, (fractional ownership being the new name for time share), never mind she could send that one later. There were more pressing things to hand. Millie would be back from her walk soon and would need her afternoon feed, Lynette didn't need a clock she could feel the ache in her breasts, they were full and demanding to be emptied. She didn't mind substituting bottles for some feeds but she wanted to make sure that Millie had both types of milk especially as she was lucky enough to produce it in abundance much to Bashar's disgust when he inadvertently got soaked in bed with oozing milk.

Once Millie was fed and happily sleeping Lynette got back to work. She needed a bank guarantee in place for the financing company from a recognised European bank and also one for the fractional ownership company. Seeing the name of a long term respected bank on the documents safeguarding deposits and documentation inevitably helped the sale process. People were gullible, in reality what did a big name guarantee mean? At best ten years fighting through the courts in an attempt to get your deposit monies back from some foreign territory and at worst, 'nada or nothing'. Fighting in a foreign jurisdiction was throwing good money after bad and merely keeping the lawyers happy. To get the bits of paper in place she needed Bashar.

"Baz honey, can you tie up the final bits of paperwork on this deal for me with a couple of phone calls?"

Bashar was in a playful mood. "What? The revered business woman Lynette Smythe, LLB, MA and more other letters after her name than I can remember needs my help? Moi? A lowly Prince?"

"Get over here Mr Kaddouri before I give you a good spanking."

"Oh, is that a promise?"

Lynette smiled, they had been full on with Millie lately and they could do with some time on their own. "After I've finished up if you're a good boy, you can take me to the steak place near Covent Garden to wine me and dine me and then we'll see...I'll express some milk and Emma can deal with the night feeds."

Bashar draped his arms round her shoulders, moved her hair to one side and gently kissed the back of her neck. It sent a shiver down her spine and stirred her loins. "Your wish is my command my lady, how can I be of service?"

"Mmm, well...I can think of lots of things for later but for now you can phone that dog turd Hartmut Muller and tell him to expect an email from me. His bank is going to provide some guarantees at market rate and when we've sold half of the properties he's going to pay us the value of the mortgage book. Oh, and he can take the first fifty properties off our hands to sell on to his clients, immediate payment into the MKS account held by Monsieur Monnier.. I'm not expecting any of it for free, he'll make good money but I'm not spending eight months jumping through hoops with committees. Just tell him to get the thing approved ready to sign up with the Companies next week."

"I take it from the dog turd reference that he's still not forgiven..."

Lynette scowled. "He invaded my personal space and threatened me and the baby I was carrying. If he didn't have kids I'd be paying for Martin to top him."

Bashar winced. "Ouch, you hold a grudge my love; remind me not to cross you! He's had his initial punishment and now he is indebted to us, I'll call him for you and tell him to tread very carefully around my Tigress and her cub." He swiped a mock claw through the air with a "Ggggrrrr" and headed back into his study."

He pulled up his contacts on his ipad and dialled the bank's number in Luxembourg having first checked the name of Hartmut's PA in the record. *Heidi, yes that was her name Heidi.* It always paid to know the names of the gatekeepers and those that did most of the work. Bashar prided himself on being able to build a rapport. The phone rang and he asked for the assistant rather than Hartmut himself.

"Good day Heidi, we haven't spoken before. My name is Prince Mohammed Bashar Aahdil Kaddouri."

"A pleasure to talk to you your Highness, what may I do for you?" Heidi rapidly typed in his name to the client database to bring up his records. There were no deposits or investments but the file was double red flagged. '<u>Calls to be passed to Herr Hartmut Muller immediately</u>.'

Bish continued with the soft soap. "I realise that Herr Muller has a busy diary but would you be so kind as to have him call me at my London residence urgently?"

"Would you mind holding for just a few minutes your Highness and I'll see if he can leave the meeting that he's currently in, I'll try to be as quick as I can."

"No problem Heidi, I have time to wait but it would be easier, if he could make himself available."

Bish listened to typical lift or on hold music whilst Heidi went about her business. She buzzed through to Hartmut's office interrupting an internal meeting with one of the banking officers. "My apologies Hartmut but I thought you might want to take this call. It's a.." She looked down at her notes to remind herself of the correct name. "...a Prince Mohammed Bashar Aahdil Kaddouri on the phone...for some reason you've double red flagged him so I assume it's particularly important."

Shit! He'd thought that the kidnap and extortion episode had been consigned to history. "Yes, um yes, thank you Heidi, can you hold him for one minute and I'll finish up with Kurt as soon as I can." His brow started to break out in a line of sweat. "Sorry Kurt, I really have to take this call, I'll catch up with you tomorrow at some stage."

Once the door was shut Herr Muller buzzed the internal connection giving the all clear. Heidi was disappointed to pass the call over; she was quite enjoying chatting to Mr Kaddouri or Bish as he insisted on being called. "Just transferring you now Mr Kaddouri, enjoy the rest of your day."

"Ah, Herr Muller, I assume you know why I'm calling?"

Hartmut almost spat down the phone. "I've no idea and I will not be bribed or manipulated!" It was easier to be strong and confident when the other person was a thousand miles away.

"Hmm, you seem to forget that you've signed a document in return for a very very large favour. Now if you would like to annul that agreement then it can be arranged, I'll just pass the paper to Ms. Smythe to do with as she will but I assure you Hartmut she is much less lenient than I am and whether you like it or not you threatened the Tigress and her unborn cub."

Hartmut was getting flustered. *He had promised to do anything in return for his life.* "What do you mean cub?"

"Well you see Lynette was pregnant when you sent the heavies after her and which means you not only threatened her but her unborn child and you know what a Tigress does if her cubs are threatened don't you Hartmut. Anyway, we're wasting time, apparently you can be of service to me and she has allowed you to make a normal market profit on the transactions which I think is being over generous but such is life."

Hartmut's resolve broke. "What do you want?"

"Lynette will email the details over to you and our lawyers will draw up the contracts. Your bank is going to act as guarantor to some finance companies involved in the Turtle Beach Eco Development. You are also going to have the opportunity to buy the first fifty units from us off plan to sell on to your clients via your investment officers; it should be mutually very beneficial. Don't disappoint her Hartmut. She wants things turned around in under ten days and as you know 'what Ms. Smythe wants Ms. Smythe gets.' I'm sure you know the old saying...Happy wife, happy life...You'll be receiving details by email at some stage today." Bashar hung up. There was no point in talking to the mealy mouthed slime ball more than necessary. He was confident that he would toe the line without any reminders.

Chapter 14
You Can Run...

PAOLO WAS BEGINNING TO FEEL more and more settled with his new life in Brazil. He had money, status, girls and drugs on tap and more importantly he'd left his outstanding debt problems in the UK a long long way behind, at least he thought he had until he got a reminder. The incoming call wasn't one that he recognised but then with a new phone in a new country and with his new found status probably fifty percent of the calls were from new numbers. He picked up expecting another sales or contract enquiry.

"Turtle Bay Eco developments, Paolo speaking."

A gruff voice with a Russian accent responded from the other end. "Ah, Paolo, how good to hear your voice. We were beginning to think that you didn't want to talk to us anymore, no phone calls, no emails,... you wouldn't be thinking of skipping out on your old buddies would you Paolo?"

Paolo instantly broke out in a cold sweat. *Keep cool Paolo, keep cool, they're thousands of miles away.* "Olaf, what a surprise, how did you get my number?"

"I'm sure it's a surprise Paolo...thought you could skip the country without paying your debts did you? Just remember Paolo you can run but you can't hide. It doesn't matter where you go we will always reach you or your family."

Paolo tried his usual tactic of bluffing his way out of things. "What you on about Olaf? I'm all square with you guys; I've paid all of my bills, the slates clean, I thought that last ten grand left us cool...Cristal might still owe you a bit of money but that's not my problem anymore, you should talk to Vince I hear that he's taken her on as his bitch. He'll pay her debt I'm sure."

"Paolo, Paolo, Paolo. Always the slimy little shit bag who blames anyone that he can and misdirects whenever he can. This time Paolo the shit sticks, you've got no chance of wriggling. Viktor wants his hundred grand and he doesn't care how we get it from you."

The figure caused Paolo to lose his cool and he inadvertently ended up confirming the debt. "One hundred! I thought the figure was seventy five."

"Haven't you heard of interest Paolo? You've been gone a long time, how long is it? Two maybe three months, you're lucky it's not more. By the way it's going up to a hundred and twenty grand if it's not paid by the end of the month.".

Paolo pulled at his shirt collar as if he was struggling with the heat or struggling to breathe. "Listen Olaf, be reasonable, I've started a new life, I'm earning now, as soon as I get the money I'll wire it across to you, and I'll pay interest Olaf, tell Viktor that his money is safe with me, I'll be good for it."

He could hear Olaf laughing at the other end of the phone. "What do you think we are? A bank? You'll pay up by the end of the month or we'll either sell our debt to the local Brazilian boys or even better we'll extract it from your precious brother or his girl Rachel seeing as they're nearer to home. No more dodging and no more running Paolo just fucking pay up or else."

The line went dead. Paolo placed his phone on the table and had a minor rant around the room pulling at his hair as he walked up and down. “Shit, shit, shit!! Oh Jesus, now what Paolo, think, think, you’ve gotta get the money from somewhere, who knows what the bastards would do to Max or Rachel....Oh fuck how did I get into this mess?”

When Max and Bashar had agreed to him coming over to Brazil he really had thought his troubles were over, a new continent, a new life and surely the loan sharks wouldn’t bother tracking him to Brazil. How wrong he’d been. Thoughts ran through his head. *Maybe Bashar could get them called off, they weren’t the sort of people you stitched up, he’d seen first hand what they were capable of and it wasn’t pretty. Should I warn Max and Rach to be on their Guard? Kidnap and chopping bits off to send by mail was one of their favourite modes of operation. What the fuck am I going to do?*

Paolo spent a few hours drinking and considering his options. He toyed with his phone considering whether to phone Max but couldn’t face it, or more precisely he couldn’t face Rachel’s scorn. Not coming up with any answers he did what he always did when the pressure came on. He went on a booze and drugs bender that lasted almost three days, the net effect being that he could hardly remember what month it was let alone the phone call from Olaf. *Job done.*

Chapter 15
Dr Jones

THE BLACK DISCOVERY stayed within the speed limit and headed out towards the A127. Frank didn't want to attract attention, there were always a few too many police cars around with the traffic cars section based just up a few miles up the road at Laindon and if you gunned the motor it was all too easy to be picked up. Tony groaned quietly in the back for the first few miles before beginning to snore softly. The Rohypnol had done its job. Frank turned East towards Southend before taking the slip road marked Wickford and Malden. Tommy looked perplexed. "Where we going Frank? I fought we were taking 'im to Marbella?"

Frank didn't take his eyes off the road. "Change of plan little bruvver. D'ya remember that place out on an island near Heybridge that Jenny went to?"

"Yeah, yeah I fink I do... Osea Island I fink, couple of the big shot entertainers went there before it got closed down and didn't Amy Winehouse go there? Fantastic voice...such a shame she got in with the wrong crowd..."Yeah, well we're going near there that one's closed."

"Well it ain't much fucking use if it's closed is it!"

"Get yer brain in gear Tommy boy. It might be closed but there's another place nearby out on the Dengie marshes, and more importantly some geezer who specialises in combat related stress problems lives nearby and works there. Jack's arranged for him to and see Tony once he's has a few days in the place drying out."

Tommy shrugged; unconcerned with the change in plan. They rode in silence as they left the built up urban area passing fields on either side heading out towards the Heybridge basin and on out in to the Marshes. As the late evening temperature began to drop mist swirled eerily across the road caught by the beams of their xenon headlights. Tommy remarked that it looked like a horror movie filmed in the swamps; given that they were actually below sea level he wasn't far wrong. As they went round yet another bend in the road Frank slowed the car and pulled onto a gravel driveway, the tyres crunched as they pulled to a halt in front of a pair of huge steel gates held up by neatly pointed brick piers with gargoyle like structures staring down daring people to come in.

"Go press the buzzer; they're supposed to be expecting us."

Tommy was not happy; he had an overactive imagination from watching too many late night horror movies and was convinced that a mad axe man would jump out of the bushes. Frank knew his little brother all too well and rolled his eyes.

"Go on then, press the buzzer... don't be a fucking tart."

A crackly voice came over the intercom. "Good evening, may I help you?"

"Umm, yeah, Tommy Helsdon, I've got Tony Brown wiv me, I fink you're expecting 'im."

"Come to the front of the house and someone will meet you."

The gates swung open automatically, Tommy walked through while Frank edged the car forward hoping that the gravel didn't chip the paintwork. As they headed down the driveway to the house loomed out of the mist. It wasn't pretty; whoever built it wanted to make a statement but clearly didn't have the money so successive generations had tagged bits on without much thought to aesthetics. The large spotlight illuminating the building was wasted, it would have looked better remaining in the pitch black. As they arrived in front of a huge set of black doors with stained glass detailing a man dressed in a light blue set of nurses overalls opened the door and came out to meet them.

"Ah, you must be Mr Brown, welcome, welcome."

"Nah, mate...Tony Brown is in the back...sleeping like...Where's his room? Me and Tommy'll take him up for yer."

The male nurse looked confused. "Can't you just wake him up? He's got to fill in a few forms and sign in before he's allowed in to the secure section of the facility."

Frank loomed over the nurse in a threatening manner. "You ain't gonna be trouble are yer? Like I said me and Tommy will take 'im up to his room...now lead on Tonto."

The nurse was used to the odd diva wanting to get their own way and responded accordingly. "Well, I'm not arguing but you won't get past Dr Jones so easily, he's thrown people more famous than you out of here. Follow me, second floor."

Frank put Tony over his shoulder using a fireman's lift and told Tommy to pick up the two sports bags from the floor in the back. One had his overnight gear in and the other was full of clothes, shaving and wash gear selected for Tony, it was mainly tracksuits, T-shirts and sweatshirts with one pair of slippers and a set of trainers that they had thoughtfully taken the laces out of not realising that he wasn't actually going to prison. The nurse led them to a room with a large bed after going past a number of camera controlled doors.

"Put him on the bed please." He crossed his arms in front of himself trying to look stern. "You do know that he can only stay here if he signs in of his own free will don't you." He stared at Frank who stared back firing off a quick retort.

"Fuck off, I'm his free will, now jog on and find Dr Jones. Tommy. Pick me up here early evening tomorrow and drive carefully through those back lanes, oh and see if Tonto can rustle up a cup of tea, milk and two sugars."

Frank set about getting Tony into bed pulling off his shoes, socks and trousers before struggling to get his Jacket over his arms. Satisfied that he would be comfortable enough he pulled the duvet over the top of him and propped his head on the pillow. Tony had hardly moved. The room was basic even a bit sparten but it did the job. The bed was a good size double placed centrally in the room with a small desk and chest of drawers at its end. A large leather wing backed chair sat in the corner next to the huge wooden sash window; it looked like that would be his bed for the night, not that he was tired yet. Looking round Frank noted the lighting and tried to find a switch to brighten things up a bit but without luck. He shrugged; maybe the lighting was part of the treatment

Tonto arrived with a cup of tea in a melamine cup, frank tapped the side with his finger nail clearly unimpressed. "That's all you're getting, plastic knives, plastic forks and plastic cups...we don't want any of our guests to have an easy route for self harming. And don't get the idea that I'm your servant or that this place is a hotel. I see you've found the wardrobe and put his clothes away. His wash gear can go in the bathroom." He pointed towards a door near the room entrance. "Dr Jones is seeing another patient and will be with you soon. You're lucky he's here, he normally goes home around eight o'clock." He looked at Tony sprawled on the bed. "Believe me he won't be impressed with what you've done." He turned on his heel departing rapidly making it clear that small talk was not part of his job description.

A stocky man walked in the room, around five feet eight tall, a barrel chest, glasses stuck on top of his salt and pepper hair, jeans, sneakers and a checked shirt. Frank looked him up and down and assumed that he was just another inmate.

"Sorry fella, Tony's sleeping; I'm visiting like...what's this gaff like then?"

The man pulled out a chair from beside the desk and sat on it with his legs either side of the back. "Oh, it's alright I suppose, it depends whether you want to get clean or not. If you know you need help then this place is pretty good but if your mate has been brought here kicking and screaming then...well...it probably won't do that much good...all we can do is try."

"Fuck me you're cheerful ain't yer, how long you been here then?"

"About a year now, I get to see the place and our guests every day." The man stood and held out his hand. "I'm Doc Jones but we're really informal here so people call me John or JJ. The nurse tells me that you've drugged your friend and brought him here against his will. Is that right?"

Frank sneered. "Depends what you mean by against his will Doc, dunit. He needs to get sorted; having terrible nightmares about action in Northern Ireland and using coke to help him get through the day; don't sound to me that he knows his own mind so it's 'ard to say that he's 'ere against his own will ain't it. You know what they say...don't shoot the messenger; I'm just here to help. I'll make sure that Tony sees the light when he wakes up if you know what I mean."

Doctor Jones considered the man in front of him. A typical East end rough diamond, the sort of guy you would want next to you if you were in the trenches. Always positive, bright, intelligent although only educated via the University of Life, a man's man and a true gentleman with the fairer sex, he grinned as he reached a decision. "I tell you what; let's see what happens when your mate wakes up. You can have an hour to convince him to stay but if he wants to leave that's it."

Frank nodded his head in agreement. "Fair enough Doc."

"Please, John or JJ. Now what have you given him to knock him out?"

Frank spent the next hour with JJ filling in forms and giving as much history as he could and owned up to the amount of Rohypnol. The Doc was unimpressed at the dosage and insisted that Frank spend the night in the chair awake in case Tony was sick and choked on his own vomit. He showed him where the coffee machine was and where he could find the charge nurse if he needed any help. Frank decided that he liked the Doc, he seemed genuinely interested in Tony's problems.

The night hours passed slowly with Frank re-reading The Bourne identity that he found on one of the bookshelves to keep himself awake. The facility seemed to start early with Tonto coming round with a cup of tea just after six. Breakfast was a communal affair in the dining room but patients only usually joined in after a few days trying to straighten themselves out so he gave it a miss; anyway, Tony was still crashed. He pulled back the duvet and checked that he was still sleeping, once he was satisfied that Tony was settled he hopped in the shower to freshen up but soon returned to his chair keeping watch over him. At around ten in the morning the Doc put his head around the corner.

"Still sleeping then?" Frank nodded. "Well I've got to see a few patients over the next few hours so I'll pop back in around lunchtime to see if sleeping beauty has woken. He's probably going to have a whopper of a headache so make sure you've got plenty of water or tea for him to drink and give him a couple of these to help his head." The Doc handed over four tablets, Frank didn't even think to ask what they were.

Tony began to rouse around eleven and was not a happy camper. "You fucking bastard Frank, what the fuck did you give me and where the fuck am I?"

"Chill Tony...'ere take these the Doc says that it will help wiv yer raging headache, he also says I've gotta get you to drink plenty of fluids."

Tony eyed the pills suspiciously but his head was pounding. *Oh well...here goes.*

Listen mate, I really didn't want to slip you a mickey but let's be honest snorting coke ain't going to sort your problems is it? I've met the Doc, seems like a decent geezer but he says it's up to you...we can't make you stay here, you have to decide. He's gonna drop back when he's finished wiv his other guests...fancy some tea?"

After a cup of char Frank persuaded Tony to have a shower; he was still very antsy and he wasn't too sure whether the Doc would be able to persuade him to stay. He felt like he was treading on glass, making small talk, trying not to set Tony off on one. He just needed to keep him talking until the Doc arrived to explain things, it was proving difficult. He made the mistake of mentioning Jack and Tony went off on a rant about the Irish, mention of Freddie didn't fare much better. He was angry, very angry. Frank couldn't work out why but was happy to be the focus of his venom rather than have him beating himself up. *When the fuck would the Doc arrive?*

"Who d'ya think you are Frank, giving me a fucking mickey, I've fought for my country to keep dickheads like you safe and you fucking drug me...wanker! People don't appreciate what the Army does for them. I've given my fucking life for this country!"

As the diatribe subsided JJ walked through the door. "Keep going Tony; tell the tosser what you think...He's got no idea. I've been on the frontline in Kosovo, done two tours of Afghanistan and still can't explain it to the man on the street. Whatever you say they just don't get it, unless you've been there and seen it you can't understand." Tony stopped dead in his tracks and stared at the Doc.

"Who the fuck are you? And how come you've been on the frontline?"

The Doc looked at Frank and cast his eyes to the door. He took the hint and wandered out leaving the two of them to talk. "Well Tony, it looks like you've got some pretty good mates. Not many people would pay in advance for six weeks treatment and risk drugging you to get you here; they obviously care about you but do you care about yourself? Frank might have already told you that we only accept people here that want to get better, that are prepared to give themselves to the program. Believe me Tony I understand what you're going through. I've been there, got the badge, got the T shirt....I joined the TA when I was at University for a bit of excitement and extra bunce, never thinking that I would be on the front line but I've seen more than I ever want to, I've had dark days...I've questioned why I should survive when friends have been killed...there's no logic...it messed me up big time but I've got myself on the straight and narrow and I've sworn to try to help others who've gone through the same....Life's a bastard Tony, you have to do what you can to claw your way through." He paused and sat back in the chair. "Sorry mate, I'm downloading my problems onto you. Let's start again...I'm the Doc and I'd like to help. I've got loads of experience of dealing with combat stress, I can't cure it but I can help you learn how to manage it. I'm happy to share my own experiences with you. I don't have a panacea Tony, but I'll try my best." The Doc stopped talking and put his head in his hands before taking a deep breath and standing up. "It's up to you Tony, you've got great mates, a real support network, you just need to learn to like yourself...it's up to you whether you stay or go." He turned to walk out of the door. Tony had tears falling down his cheeks. "Wait Doc, please wait...I want to get well...will you help me?" The two embraced, step one had been completed.

Chapter 16
Negotiations

By the time Bridget had finished on the web Jack had a dossier of information about Harry and about the history of the property going back over the last twenty years. The Spanish data had been difficult to find and Bridgette had ended up subcontracting the work to a whizz kid advertising his services on the web. They had paid handsomely for his 'express' services but now it was all starting to look worthwhile. According to the local council records it was a single story two bedroom country Finca, if only they could see it now, its footprint must be at least three times the original. He mulled on how best to go about things overnight before ringing Harry the following morning to go back for a second viewing with a builder whose sole purpose in life was going to be shaking his head and sucking his breath in over his teeth whenever Jack asked about build quality or what it would cost to fix anything. Jack intended on softening up Harry before the serious dancing began.

Two hours of checking the property over with the builder and anyone would think that the house was in danger of immediate collapse, even Jack was worried. Most of the problems seemed to stem from the fact that it was built on multiple slabs rather than one complete concrete raft. As Southern Spain was well known for soil heave and movement inevitably the building would crack.

The builde pointed out where Harry had tried dry lining, papering, and using flexible filler, all of which had failed to varying degrees. The locals never worried, it was standard Spanish practice, each summer they would get out the filler, plaster the cracks over and cover it with a coat of emulsion claiming it was "Rustic", job done until the next set of rain caused ground heave and the process started all over again.

A private chat down the drive with the builder before he left put most of Jack's fears at rest; the building could do with a damp proof course being injected, gutters and soakaways, new windows , an electrical check although it seemed quite passable and of course a complete new kitchen and bathrooms; essentially a very full refurbishment which would cost the best part of two hundred to three hundred thousand euros depending how over board Bridget went on the finishes. Jack wandered back to his car theatrically shaking his head before reaching on to the back seat to pick up a bag with a bottle of high quality Irish Whiskey and a bottle of still mineral water inside, he'd even brought his own crystal glasses as he wasn't too sure whether Harry just drank straight from the bottle given the evidence around the house. The pair of them sat on the terrace and Jack poured two generous measures before clinking glasses. *Let the dance begin.*

"So Harry what are you thinking having heard from the professional builder? He's a knowledgeable guy so he is." He sat back admiring the amber liquid in his glass before commenting on the view. "Tis a shame no one would be able to get a mortgage on the place, it limits your market so it does and it's such a lovely vista." He waited before topping up Harry's glass while examining his face closely. He could see the turmoil running through his mind. *Was Jack his only chance of selling?*

Harry coughed as he swallowed his drink in one. "I've had other people interested you know, not offering the full price like but keen to proceed but if you're a cash buyer and can complete quickly then I'm willing to do a deal."

Jack suppressed a grin before topping him up again. "Well you heard the man Harry, your price is out there on a wing and a prayer when you take it all in to account. Has anyone else had a surveyor or builder here yet?" Harry shook his head. "Well what's your bottom line Harry?"

"One and a quarter million and you need to complete within two months."

"Harry, Harry...you should have talked more with my girl, she's proper clever so she is and she tells me that your old mucker gets out of prison in two months' time and that he's going to be looking for his share of the proceeds of your robberies. It sounds to me like I'm your only option if you really want to disappear quickly. You do want to disappear don't you Harry?"

Harry grabbed the bottle and poured himself a full tumbler of whiskey before gulping half of it down in one. "Did she tell you that my ex-wife ran off with my best mate when I was inside? Stung me for some of the proceeds before she told me as well, bitch! I don't have a lot of time for women, prefer my own company, I'll probably go live on an island by myself somewhere. Bloody women are nout but trouble." He paused before fixing Jack with a stare. A million... five hundred in cash and five hundred on the table through the proper channels, oh and you pay all the costs."

Jack contemplated the offer, he knew if he wanted he could push it further but it was a fair price. He raised his glass. "A million it is then but we each pay our own costs."

Chapter 17
The Road To Recovery

FOR THE FIRST FIVE DAYS of treatment Tony wished he was still on the Rohypnol. Instead the Doc had put him on a cocktail of drugs including diazepam and baclofen. He felt completely out of it but to be fair he didn't crave a drink or cocaine so the medication must be of some use. Apart from three times a day rounds to make sure he'd taken his medication he was pretty much left to his own devices, a nurse would check on him every hour and once a day JJ would drop in to see how he was getting along. At the end of day five he was informed that he would be starting group classes the following morning and spending an hour and a half with the Doc in the afternoon. He was pleased to be getting underway at last, he'd spent too long cooped up in his room thinking which was the last thing he wanted to do when nightmares filled every sleeping minute.

In the morning group session Tony learnt the basics: You don't recover from an addiction by stopping using. You recover by creating a new life where it is easier to not use and if you don't create a new lifestyle and escape your shackles, then all the factors that brought you to your addiction will eventually catch up with you again. After a few hours in group therapy Tony's head was spinning. How could he change his life? How could he avoid the things and behaviour that had been getting him into trouble? He ran a nightclub for god's sake and he wasn't going to let that dream go. There wasn't much point in following the HALT acronym about high risk situations when his whole life was high risk. He had to get his head straight; he had to be honest with himself and those around him, he had to find a way. Wanting to get clean and admitting that he had a problem was only stage one.

The session with JJ in the afternoon left him feeling even more bemused, they sat, they talked, but he didn't see it as treatment. In reality the Doc was trying to get a handle on how deep rooted Tony's problems were and how best to treat them. Unless he could put some bounds on the scope of his issues treatment would be difficult. By week two Tony was beginning to get bored. He had heard much of the discussion in the group sessions before and JJ seemed still to be skirting round some of the issues. He took to working out in the gym and running across the fields and was starting to feel much stronger. JJ noted the change and decided that the time had come; most of Tony's tablets were now just placebos anyway.

The following morning Tony was stopped by the nurse from going to the group session and led along the corridor to a small room with a large whiteboard and a projector. The Doc looked nervous. If it's okay with you Tony Nurse Jason will stay with us during this session, it's hard to say how you'll react but one thing's for sure you've got to stop blaming yourself for things that were out of your control. Today is going to be tough, we're going to relive your nightmares and use a combination of Eye Movement Desensitization and Cognitive Behavioural Therapy to help you cope with combat stress, it's just like addiction Tony, it won't cure you completely but it will give you mechanisms to help cope.

When Tony finished the first session he took to his bed, he was emotionally rung out and physically exhausted. He'd even had to excuse himself at one point to go and throw up. His next session was booked for two days' time and in all honesty it would probably take him that long to process what he had learnt and to try to push some of the trauma back down below the surface. If he wasn't so exhausted he'd be howling at the moon or trying to decapitate people whilst running round the grounds naked. He breathed in deeply. *What was he supposed to do, relax, breathe in, breathe out, breathe in, and breathe out.*

By week five Tony had lost over a stone and a half in weight, was running five miles every other morning and was feeling better than at any time since being in the forces. With JJ's help he'd faced his demons, he'd stopped blaming himself and he was coping without alcohol and without drugs. One more week and he'd have to face the real world and then the true test would begin. Frank had visited once a week updating him on the figures for the club, filling him in on any tittle tattle and offering whatever support he could. Tony had forgiven him and couldn't thank Jack enough. He was lucky to have met such a good crowd. Today was visiting day and Frank had brought along a few sweets and chocolates as a treat which he spread out on the bed before making himself comfortable in the chair opposite. He popped a Tutti Frutti into his mouth and was instantly transported back to his childhood.

"Blimey, the taste of that makes me fink I'm ten years old...come on Tony try one."

Tony reluctantly picked up a sweet and slowly unwrapped it. It was clear that something was bothering him so Frank sat quietly waiting for it to come out.

"Frank, I'm feeling good but I've only got one week left here and I'm starting to get nervy. I'm supposed to keep myself out of high risk situations, avoid places with temptation, try not to let myself get hungry or angry but the thing is Frank...well you know...I reckon I can cope with handling alcohol but there's no way I can deal in the white stuff anymore, the club is going to have to go back to being clean...I was wondering whether you could talk to Joey like...put in a good word for me...I just can't handle having the stuff around me."

"It's in hand Tony. You've gotta pay back ten grand over the next year but we've arranged to move distribution to Vince's place...you do realise that you might lose a lot of custom?"

"It's not the sort of custom I want Frank. The club was better when it was clean, the people were nicer and we made just as much profit with a lot less hassle. Vince is welcome to it. He'll be insufferable but that's life, I want to stay clean and temptation needs to be kept well away. Is he still with that Floosie Crystal? She'll probably stick most of it up her nose if he is, one of my...hang on... no sorry, one of Joey's best customers that girl."

Chapter 18
Enrique Fernandez

ENRIQUE HAD BEEN BUSY planning since he'd received the call from Martin. He'd called up his regular black ops crew who regularly carried out anti-drugs work for the DEA and called in a few favours to find out precisely where Senor Garcia sat in the drug lord hierarchy and who he was going to upset if he accidently topped him. The Escobar cartel reached a long way into government and the police and it wouldn't do to upset people too close to home. He sat behind his desk wearing his aviator sun glasses and stroking his neatly trimmed beard as he listened to an update from his second in command. Martin had been right; Garcia was a big fish but only in a very very small pond; taking him out wouldn't cause too many waves but it had to be done the right way hence the beard stroking, he was deep in thought, how did he get Garcia in line without risking the cartel having an impact on the planning process? He'd thought enough and made a decision.

"Julio, we need a show of force, something that demonstrates our fire power without starting a major war...I think we'll visit the site as if we are intending to take part control of it. Get Paolo to tip the wink to the Mayor and the Regional councillor that there are some important investors with links to the drugs trade visiting the site. We need to have the two hummers, eight guys suited and booted and the Mercedes Limousine with the two of us in. Anyone who comes near us needs to be frisked and intimidated, think of it as a Royal visit. Make sure we have a grenade launcher with us in case we have an opportunity to blow up something for fun. We'll fly up in three days' time, get the guys to drive up tomorrow...this should be interesting. Oh and make sure Paolo doesn't tell Garcia, I want him to find out from the local grapevine."

Enrique and Julio flew up to Recife Guararapes airport in a small Cessna Citation jet with seats for five passengers and a two man crew. They could both fly the aircraft if needed but as they couldn't be sure how long today's demonstration would take an extra pilot gave them options if things got difficult. He could refuel the plane and file return flight plans while they went to site. It had been many years since Enrique had been to Northern Brazil; Rio was his home now and he considered himself to be more of a multinational being with the amount of travelling involved in his work and his linguistics skills. The plane came in over the green hills which he noted had considerably more buildings on since he was last here. The scar from the quarry and sandpit where machinery gouged at one of the hills to satisfy a clearly booming local building industry was still visible; it was much smaller when he was here last. The hilltop towns and villages gave way to greenery before they overflew the edge of the city passing the motorway, a smart business campus and some old warehouses; typical of many places in the developing world the final run in to the airport had the inevitable shanty style areas with buildings and people packed together trying to scrape a living. He shrugged, it was always the same, the poor don't complain about the noise or the fumes.

The plane touched down smoothly on Runway 18 and taxied to an area with half a dozen small business jets parked up. Off to one side Enrique could see the stretch limo and a two man team waiting to greet them. As the flight was domestic formalities would be minimal and they would be on their way in under ten minutes, he settled into the back seat of the Mercedes, unfortunately the drive to the Turtle Beach eco resort would not be quick, depending on traffic probably two hours. Still it could be worse, the aircon was efficient, his seat reclined comfortably and there was ample legroom to stretch out. He flicked his mobile open and sent a text to Martin.

Landed at Recife, en route to development, will let you know the outcome

As the headed along the coastline away from the City the gaps between the towns and villages steadily increased leaving unmarked pristine beaches to the locals and wildlife. The only problem was that as the population decreased the roads became more rustic with some stretches more suited to horse and carts. As they approached Vistamar the roads turned back to concrete and people stopped to stare at the two black Hummers with a Mercedes Limo sandwiched in between as they passed by scattering leaves and dusts in their wake, older workers in the fields bowed slightly and tugged at their forelock; just the reaction that Enrique wanted.

They pulled up outside Paco's bar in the hope of making an impression and instantly succeeded, a crowd of small boys fawned over the jet black cars and enjoyed scrabbling after coins tossed down the streets by one of the drivers. The crew moved the surfers out of their favoured seats with a flick of their thumb, a nod of their head in the direction of the beach and a scowl over the top of their aviator glasses. Paco scampered out to wipe down the tables and shouted over his shoulder for his wife to bring out more cushions.

"Welcome, Senor, welcome to my humble restaurant." He bowed and scraped while handing out menus and bringing across the blackboard where today's specials had been hastily scribbled. Julio threw a hundred dollar bill at him and barked orders in Portuguese.

"Fresh fish, grilled shrimp, salad and cassava or fries for everyone, oh and bring out half a dozen bottles of still water, some coffee and a couple of cokes." He deliberately turned his back to him. "And make it snappy."

Paco knew when new money was in town and made sure the prettiest girls served up his simple barbecued food while he slaved away in the kitchen baking bananas in rum and brown sugar to finish the meal. They hadn't asked for a desert but he hoped his initiative might be rewarded at some stage in the future. While he cooked and the girls served his wife took care of the phone calls informing Senor Garcia that he definitely needed to be at the Turtle Bay Development to make the acquaintance of the chefe (the boss), he was a rich important man. Everything was going pretty much as Enrique had planned, the town was buzzing with rumours. After dessert Julio tossed another one hundred dollar bill at Paco and grunted. "Chefe says that his fish was good."

Paco stared at the money in his hand as the team loaded back up into their cars -Two hundred dollars in one lunchtime; he sometimes didn't take that in a week!

The cars tyres crunched the gravel as the convoy pulled up in front of the hastily patched up portable office at the Turtle Bay Eco Development. Paolo was standing on the front decking with the Local Mayor and Regional Councillor doing what he normally did which was making sure everyone had a drink in hand. The ten man heavily armed team took up positions around a thirty meter perimeter while Julio walked slowly towards the trio with a Beretta pointing at them at waist height.

"Put your arms up in clear sight." All three nervously complied; Paolo had not been expecting this. One of the guards frisked all three of them. "Clear" he barked making them jump. The door to the Mercedes opened and Enrique slowly appeared looking every bit a member of minor royalty or a debonair drug lord. He turned his back to them and looked out to sea breathing in the salty tang in the air. He nodded his head and turned slowly.

"A nice spot, the air is fresh, the sands are white and the seas are turquoise...I like it...When will the first phase be complete?"

Paolo looked at the Mayor and Councillor unsure how to proceed, the lack of introductions and the frisking had unnerved him, he felt like the ground would swallow him up. He coughed clearing his throat and talked while staring pointedly at his two compatriots. "Umm, well eh, it depends how long it takes to get our permissions in place."

Enrique waved his hand in the air in a flourish. "That is not a problem ...Is it gentleman! I am sure that Gia Alonso will wave it through for me which means locally we have no issues...correct?"

Gia Alsonso headed the Regional council and was god as far as the two local politicians were concerned, what she said happened and if Senor Fernandez knew her personally then the plans would fly through....that only left the problem of the drugs gangs."

The Mayor piped up. "No problem, no problem at all Senor Fernandez." He was almost grovelling while smoothing gravel backwards and forwards with his shoe as if it was the most fascinating thing in the world. "But there is one other minor issue...we erm... we cannot control the local drugs gangs, in particular the Escobar cartel and they always want their protection money and their slice of the action." As if on cue a commotion was underway at the site entrance punctuated with two gunshots. Enrique winced. He had told Julio not to kill anyone...yet!

Juan Garcia was unceremoniously dragged backwards by his arms with his heels scuffing in the gravel before being dropped in front of Enrique and kept there by a heavy boot. "Sir, this man claims to be a friend of the owner and the Mayor but he had two armed men in his car and threatened our security team."

Enrique looked down his nose at the crumpled man in front of him before adjusting his sunglasses to look over the top of them. "And did you kill them?"

"No Sir, you gave strict orders not to kill anybody ... yet. The shorts fired were from his men as they were incapacitated."

Enrique looked at the Mayor whose face was ashen. "You know this man?"

"Yes Chefe, this is Senor Juan Garcia...the local representative of the Escobar Cartel we were talking about earlier."

Enrique flicked his head at his operative who immediately lifted Garcia to his feet. His face was like thunder but Enrique ignored the vile tirade coming out of his mouth and immediately started to smooch him. "Ahh, Senor Garcia, forgive me we did not expect you here today." He brushed some of the dust off of Garcia's suit and straightened his lapels before putting his arm around him and leading him into the office. "Come let's get you a drink." Paolo and the politicians went to follow but Enrique stopped them. "Gentleman...A private conversation if you don't mind."

The three of them could only watch through the large glass window as Enrique poured two drinks and toasted Garcia. They watched as Enrique dominated the conversation in a very relaxed manner and could see Garcia getting agitated and throwing his arms in the air before Enrique leaned in presumably talking quietly in to his ear. They could tell that the words had been important. Garcia had stiffened and walked carefully to the door guided by his elbow which Enrique had in his vice like grip. They stood on the terrace while Enrique ostensibly admired the view but in truth he was making a statement, Garcia was cowed and he wanted the politicians to see it.

"Gentlemen, Senor Garcia and I have reached an accord. He will no longer be demanding protection money and will be happy to help further the project however he can." He turned to Paolo. "The shack further down the beach...Are you getting rid of it?"

"Yes, the bulldozer hasn't got round to it yet."

"Do you mind if I let my boys have some fun? They've had a long journey and need to let off some steam." He didn't wait for a reply and two of the operatives pulled out a grenade launcher from the boot of the hummer and took turns in bracketing the shack. Enrique laughed. "Okay enough playing boys, Julio, this one in the centre please." Julio barked his orders and the next grenade with some added juice inside blew the shack skywards leaving a trail of burning thatch raining down on the beach from above.

"Don't you just love fireworks? Thank you for your time gentlemen." He circled his finger in the air and the team loaded up in less than thirty seconds roaring out of the gates leaving gravel spinning in the air. Paolo stood open mouthed for once he had nothing to say.

Chapter 19
Fortification

JACK WAS AS GOOD AS HIS WORD and arranged for the property deal to go through quickly. He'd picked up Harry from the Villa, taken him to the Solicitor and Notary to sign the various deeds and documents and had now returned to the house with him and a briefcase full of one hundred and two hundred euro notes. Harry sat and stared at the money and seemed reluctant to pick it up and leave.

"I'm going to miss this place Jack. It's all I've known for the last ten years, it's got bits of my soul here. I'll miss the view and listening to the sound of the cicadas rubbing their legs together while enjoying a glass or two."

Jack could see the emotion was real and hoped to comfort him with a few words. "But you need to move on Harry, you know that as well as I do. Is there anything else that you want from the house?"

"Nah, I've moved my computer and clothes. I did say that I'd be leaving all of the tools books and everything else didn't I? It's up to you what you do with them."

"And what'll you be going to do then Harry?"

He fondled the money in the briefcase. "Well, I'll go to Gibraltar and pay some of this in to my bank then I'm going to Canada to look at a small Island where I can happily live by myself."

Jack stood making it clear that the discussion was over. He shut the case and handed it to Harry ushering him out of his seat and towards his car. "Nice doing business with you Harry but I need to get started on the place, Bridget's coming round with a couple of cleaners in an hour or two to sort stuff out."

"Yeah, yeah, umm thanks Jack. I'll be seeing you then." Jack watched him walk down to his car and drive out of the gate looking back over his shoulder. He cut a lonely figure. Jack pondered; it could have so easily have been him if it hadn't been for Bridget. *God that woman's important to me.*

The house clean turned into more of a house clearance. The bedding and towels were bagged up, a drawer full of Harry's underwear and socks was emptied into a black sack and taken to the bins down the road and everything was washed down even though the builders would be arriving tomorrow and creating dust that would cover everything. Once the cleaners had finished and loaded up their spoils Jack walked on to the terrace and put his arms round Bridget from behind as she waved them off. "Well, my sweet little angel, are yer happy?" She turned and kissed him passionately. "I'll be happy once it's finished Jack...once it's got our stamp on it and once I can cuddle up on a sofa out here with you... then I'll be happy...unbelievably happy ..."

The following morning the builders turned up in force with a couple of diggers and various bits of heavy machinery. Jack was on site to direct operations and to make sure that they all understood that their pay and bonus depended on them finishing on time as promised. Kieran, who had done a grand job sucking air over his teeth to convince Harry that the property had major problems, gave the orders to the guys on the JCB's to get digging at the back of the house to create the space where they planned to put in a panic room that was being fabricated off site and that could be craned in to position before nine tonnes of concrete was pumped over and around it. It was more of a nuclear bunker with water and air recirculation, hidden GSM telephone links and even a satellite link through a dish that was tucked away at the bottom of the garden. Jack had tried to think of everything. If they came under attack he wanted Bridget to be safe and to be able to access the internet to wreak her special brand of havoc.

A week later after a visit to Bashar in London Jack was amazed at what had been achieved. New heavy weight doors and windows had been fitted throughout changing and modernising the look of the whole building. The weight was not just the frame but a double layer of laminate, which while not bullet proof, should slow down the first or second bullet from small arms fire. Inside was less pretty with holes drilled in all the walls at ankle level and plaster hacked off where needed to waist height. A damp proof course was being injected into the walls using a compressor to force the fluid deep into the brickwork. Kieran was not happy with the results.

"Listen Jack, I can't guarantee the damp proof course; we can only do our best." He picked up a lightweight brick in his hand to demonstrate his problem. "These crappy bricks don't really have enough guts to them to take all of the chemicals, will you look at the bloody holes in them...piece of bloody crap to be sure... It'll be a lot better but I can't say it'll cure everything, you understand now don't you? Don't be looking for me if it's not perfect."

"Argh, it'll be fine Kieran, what about the rest of the works?"

"Upstairs is all skimmed out, your bathrooms are in, the tiling's underway but I haven't got your fireman's pole in yet, the middle floor has enough concrete and reinforcing in it to make a good runway, you could land a bloody jumbo on it. Darren's going to bring the oxy cutters tomorrow."

"What about the kitchen?"

"Jesus Christ Jack, give me a bloody chance. I told yer eight weeks and as long as you don't go changing your mind or getting all fancy it'll be eight weeks give or take. I've got ten guys on site today, I couldn't organise anymore even if I could get them."

Jack ignored the plea in his voice. "And the car stopper bollards in the driveway?"

"They're on order Jack but I can't promise them in the timescale, because you want stainless and the extra deep variety it could go over by a week or two."

"Change them back to ordinary steel if the lazy fucker can't have 'em ready, the Costa del Sol isn't exactly swimming in work at the moment now is it?"

Kieran put his hands on his head and walked up the other end of the terrace before he blew a fuse. "Jack. Do me a favour and fuck off for another week, go on holiday, go visit some friends but keep out of my hair for a week or two and let me do me job..."

Jack took the hint and nodded. "I'll think about it." He turned and walked to his car at the bottom of the drive. He so wanted everything to be right. It would have been easier if Bridget had agreed to move somewhere else like Australia but she insisted that she wasn't going to hide. The Costa del Sol was her home now and she wasn't going to be driven out by anybody. Hopefully the veritable fortress that Jack had specified would keep her safe, his life didn't matter, Bridget had already saved it but he couldn't let anything happen to her."

Chapter 20
Toby Trelawney

DESPITE HIS RECENT PROMOTION Toby still looked like the model computer geek. His skin was still greasy and spotted in places, his clothes although more expensive still looked like they'd been thrown on his thin angular frame, his thick rimmed heavy glasses accentuated the look and his feet seemed too big for his body; in fact he looked like Tom Hanks in Big when he shrank back to being a schoolboy. He'd now spent the last five months with a small team under his control trying to find where and how Bridget had hidden Jack's information on the dark web. Although he was considered one of the best in his unit and had received accelerated promotion he still had an inferiority complex when up against the famous Miss Donovan. The woman was after all a legend and her old professor would have nothing bad said about her and even less said about her techniques. He was a dead end. They'd tracked his mail for months, even had him tailed but any communication with Bridget was above board and seemingly impossible to trace at her end.

It was that evening that he had a huge breakthrough as to how she had managed to 'lose' all but one pound of the ministers pay in the Payroll system. He'd caught the end of a conversation when some of his parent's old friends were round for dinner laughing about how they'd met over a comp machine when he was a young auditor and she was the operator hired for a week to add up the reports. Toby in his innocence asked what a comptometer was and received the answer that it was a ten kilo calculator that was devilishly difficult to operate but a good operator could add up thousands of figures a day with a very low error rate.

As a child of the modern age he was bemused. "And what would you want to do that for?"

"Well in those days computers didn't always get things right, sometimes the total on a page didn't equal the figures shown."

He shook his head. "Surely that's impossible."

Seamus swirled his red wine round his class before leaning on the table and shaking his head. "Toby, Toby, Toby, you'll be telling me next that you believe the answer that a spreadsheet gives you without double checking."

Toby went slightly red around the cheeks. "Umm, why shouldn't I? I know sometimes they're wrong if the wrong formula's been used, like someone's left the top row out of a calculation or something similar, but it doesn't happen often."

"Well that's a matter for debate, it you're assuming that the error is an accident, something missed. Anyway in the old days people like Mollie here would check that the computer had added up all the lines correctly and counted the minus numbers as deductions. They weren't often wrong but it did happen. I remember one audit where we just couldn't work out the stock figures until we realised that it was double counting a sub-total. That put a bloody hole in their so called record profits I can tell you. You should have seen their faces."

Toby's jaw hit the floor and he muttered "Oh shit." Before putting his head in his hands. "How could I have been so dumb?! It's so obvious it's brilliant. He turned to his parents dinner guests. "Seamus, Mollie, I think I owe you a huge thank you you might just have solved a problem that I've been trying to solve for weeks....Idiot, idiot idiot...." He slapped himself on his forehead with his open palm before leaving the room and heading upstairs to his electronic world.

Back in the office the next day Toby put a team onto the payroll program. "Re-write it to exclude all subtotals. Just take the total of all the prime figures direct, don't rely on anything that's been added by a sub routine."

Two days later after a few trial and error runs to get the code right they hit gold. "It doesn't add up, it doesn't bloody add up...It's out by exactly the figure we were looking for, how can that be?" Toby lifted his head from his screen. "Because she's used a subtotal as a suspense account; run the next three weeks reports and I bet they're all out by the same amount...it's so fecking obvious, how did we miss it...Hidden in plain sight."

Finally he had a breakthrough or at least he thought he did. They'd made too many assumptions, over complicated things because of her skill with morphing codes, did they need to look nearer to home. It was a hunch but what if it was hidden right under their noses on their own servers? He booked into the Security Ministers diary with the usual argument with the battle axe of a secretary. "Yes, it is important, no I can't just send an email...Look, I don't have time for this, just tell the minister that I've found how Miss Donovan had fiddled the payroll and it has implications for our search. Ring me when he stops shouting at you for refusing an appointment." He slammed the phone down. He could visualise her as Helga from the Hagar the horrible strip cartoon..."Bitch!"

He gripped his desk until his knuckles went white. "What am I doing in this shithole dealing with a bunch of dickheads?" He looked around. Brown dingy carpet with more coffee stains than pattern, vertical blinds that were yellowed with age and had seen much better days, old school type massive radiators that failed to heat the place in winter but boiled you on a spring day. "I shouldn't be here; I should be working in a high tech office."

One of his minions lifted his head from his screen. "What's that boss?"

"Nothing; just pissed off at trying to get past Helga Iron pants to the minister and pissed off with this dreary bloody office." He walked as far as the water cooler and filled the clear plastic cup with cold fluid before turning back to his desk as the phone rang. "If that's bloody accounts again about our internet costs they can feck off!"

"Hello!"

"Argh Miss Helga Iron pants, Mr Power would like to see me now would he? What a surprise... and do you know what Miss Iron pants, it looks like my diary is now full. He'll have to come to my crappy office if he wants to see me today, otherwise I can make tomorrow at ten in the morning." Toby slammed down the phone again before going in to panic mode. *Did I really say that? Oh well, job today gone tomorrow...Feck it.*

Toby dismissed the fact that he was probably about to get fired and sat back down playing through scenarios in his mind and scribbling them on a pad. He mapped out the main servers that he was aware of and drew others with dotted lines where he assumed they existed but couldn't be sure. *Would she really hide it on their servers? You're a clever one Miss Donovan but I'm on your tail.*

The door at the end of the corridor opened and in walked Michael Power the Security minister heading straight for Toby's desk. "Toby, Helena tells me you've found something, what's the news?"

Toby's head span. He'd expected to get fired...maybe; just maybe Helga Iron pants hadn't dropped him in it. "Umm, yeah, umm hello Minister...take a seat and I'll show you. It's not much but it leads me onto another theory that's going to need your backing if we go down that route. The minister was of a similar school to Toby and assumed that computers were always right, to get him to understand that they were actually fallible and just as vulnerable to human error Toby had to map out a small spreadsheet with one column showing a subtotal and another with just the primary data. The penny dropped. "Well feck me!"

"Exactly what I said when I realised what she'd done, it was hidden in plain sight which brings me onto another theory. What if she's hidden the treasure trove of information on our own servers and it's not on the dark web? Look at this." He pulled the A3 bit of paper to the centre of the desk. "These are just the government servers that I'm aware of, there's probably two or three times that many all interlinked, all exchanging data, nobody thinks about the storage capacity and nobody checks if another hundred or so megabytes of space are being used up. It's perfect but we're never going to find it without access and a lot better equipment than what we've got here."

True to a politician's colours the Minister wouldn't make a decision on anything. He needed a report and he needed diagrams to discuss with a committee. Toby inwardly died a little bit more, yet another day or two would be wasted producing needless bits of paper when real work could be getting done. He turned to his team "Fecking bunch of tossers, nobody has the balls to make a decision. Wind it up lads; let's have an early night like the rest of them."

Chapter 21
The Dreaded 'S' Word

WITH HIS PROMISE to Kieran to try to keep out of the way Jack was finding it difficult to fill his time. Bridget still had things to do like organising bondage parties, swingers parties and introducing new dominatrices for long term clients and if she wasn't doing that then she was partaking in the drug for modern women, the dreaded 'S' word...Shopping! He could understand the nesting instinct and her wanting to make the best of their home together but he really struggled with the notion of browsing twenty stores before going back to buy the item you saw in the first one. Jack was a man's man. You decided what you wanted and you bought it or killed it first shot, no fuss, no messing around.

Joey had laughed like a drain at his plight but at least he had an explanation although god knows where he got it from. Joey's theory passed down by his uncle was that the desire to shop and touch every bloody item in every store before changing your mind fifteen times went all the way back to our Neanderthal roots and was programmed in to a woman's DNA. The theory went like this. Men liked to group together in pubs and in tribes at football matches. These groups or tribes were the hunters in stone age times, then they would set out on a hunt kill the first animal that they came across that was suitable to feed the village, eat a few choice bits and then head back to goon around for the next day or so. Their job was done so they'd just hang out with their mates. Woman on the other hand split up into much smaller groups and went out to gather produce. They would go from tree to tree or bush to bush testing the softness or ripeness of the fruit to see if it was suitable to eat. Often the best fruit would be back at the first bush and they would return to pick it. QED. Women were programmed to have small groups of close knit friends and to shop until they dropped. The instinct was programmed in to them.

Jack sighed; Bridget had insisted that he help choose some of the colour schemes for the main rooms but his heart wasn't in it, choosing some of the anti-personnel systems well hey that was a time consuming exciting business. It was a good job he loved her so much, if he saw another throw or had to choose another set of curtains he'd go mad. Finally, after several hours he was released from the prison known as La Canada shopping centre in Banus as Bridget wanted to check a colour back at the house.

Kieran had been as good as his word and so had Jack, he'd stayed off site for three weeks and things were getting much closer to completion. As they pulled into the drive in Bridget's soft top Mercedes the automatic security barrier shot out of the driveway some fifteen metres in front of them. Jack immediately craned his neck round and found a mirror image pillar poking up behind them.

Will you look at that, Kieran's got the first part of the security pack working so he has." He looked over at Bridget in the driver's seat who was staring at him quizzically. "It's simple sweetie. Anyone who comes through the gates without clearance gets trapped between the two pillars and it would take a bloody huge truck to shift 'em, it'll help keep you safe so it will."

Bridget looked over the top of her sunglasses as if she was addressing an overly enthusiastic school boy. "Jack... we've discussed this... there is absolutely nothing that they can do to find the vault or break the code, we're safe, home free...when are you going to believe me?"

He leant over and kissed her. "I always believe you darling but there's no harm in a bit of insurance now is there?" He hopped out of the car and bounded up the drive before getting dragged into yet another techie conversation.

A quick tour around the house revealed that Jack's other safety features were progressing well. A large oval column in the main bedroom cleverly hid a sliding door that gave access to a fireman's pole. Press a button and the door opened. Jump on the pole and slide down to the basement level and the door closed. When you 'landed' or arrived at basement level you opened the column from the inside and stepped out opposite the door for the safe room or bunker as Jack liked to call it. The three of them tried the pole although Bridget took a lot of persuading. Arriving outside the room she was suitably impressed.

"Is that a retina scanner to gain access Jack."

"That it is but you'll have to program it, tis beyond the competence of a t'ick Irish Mick like me."

"And the keypad, is that secondary or do you need both?"

"Both."

"Well Jack, I am impressed, you're learning. Can we go in?"

Inside the secure room there were four bunk beds similar to those you'd find on the cross channel ferries that converted from settees to beds and to the side was a small desk and chair with a bank of screens above it. Kieran flicked a switch and images of the garden, the terrace and the lounge came up as split screen. He tapped another button and you could hear the workman chatting as they painted the walls and Talk Radio Europe playing in the background. A shift of the joystick and the camera panned round to show them working on the feature wall which was rapidly getting a coating of a deep coffee cream.

"Nice colour choice Bridget. The boys will finish it today."

Heading deeper in to the bunker there was a small but functional bathroom, a small kitchen and at the far end a storeroom lined with shelves already stacked with dried foods, cans and bottled water. On the far wall Kieran opened a steel cabinet to reveal a gun rack with a selection of Kalashnikoffs, M10's, two pump action shotguns, some grenades and some nine millimetre Beretta pistols. The ammunition stacked at the bottom was enough to start a small war.

"I haven't got the water recirculation unit plumbed in properly yet Jack. I need the guy from the supplier to come down. Paddy can't make head not tail of the instructions and its best we get it done properly. If you have to use this we want to be sure that you're safe. There's one other room Bridget that's all yours, the comms room. You've access to the internet by four different routes - Satellite, radio signal via the transmitter on the Bermejo mountain; GSM and good old fashioned cable. We thought it best that you have back up systems in case things get awkward."

Bridget wasn't really listening; she was still staring at the array of guns in the metal cupboard. "Jack, you're starting to scare me...Do you really think that we need all these fortifications and our own armoury? Who would come after us with so much venom that we need all this? I can't get my head round it Jack." She turned on her heel and started to walk trying to keep her emotions in control. She called to Kieran who had wandered further into the facility. "Kieran, can you let my car out, I need to get away and think."

No matter what Jack said he couldn't get Bridget to see it his way. She sat in the car with tears in her eyes and reversed up out of the gate. Kieran put an arm round Jack. "Let her work it out big guy. It is pretty fecking scary, even the boys thought that you were intending to announce war against Gibraltar.

Bridget drove along the coast road unable to stop the tears dripping down her face. *I love him, I really do, but what have I got myself into?*

Chapter 22
Gambling

WITH STEVE CARTER handling the building contracts and the local end of the operations Paolo flew back to Rio ostensibly to set up a telesales operation to start selling properties off plan. In reality he didn't need to get things underway for a few weeks but it gave him a chance to reacquaint himself with Maria and Loretta and anoint them as his first sales employees. He also hoped that maybe they could introduce him to a little local action if there was a poker scene. He thought of himself as a reasonable player and he used to win more than his fair share in Essex and London. How good would the locals be? Surely it would be easy money; money that maybe would keep Olaf at bay.

With a new employee to do all of the work Paolo was starting to forget what his job was and whose money belonged to whom, company money washed around as if it was his own. He set himself up in a luxury three bed apartment overlooking the beach, bought himself a new wardrobe and flashed the cash in the local clubs and bars. The girls had hit the Jackpot and made sure that they made the most of the gravy train getting him to buy them clothes and jewellery and generally taking a kick back in every bar where they persuaded him to buy bottles of hideously over-priced champagne. They were even on a kick back from the local drugs supplier.

Introducing him to the local high stakes players was just another transaction as far as they were concerned, if he won, it was money for him to spend on them and if he lost, well, hopefully they could arrange for some back dated commission.

Four weeks in to his spree Steve Carter called him concerned about spending and the lack of invoices or receipts. "Hi Paolo, it's Steve. Listen, I've just been pulling the monthly accounts together along with an update for Bashar and we seem to have around twenty thousand dollars unaccounted for. Could you fax up an expense sheet for me?"

Paolo had no idea how much he'd been spending and didn't see why Steve should be questioning him. "It's not a problem Steve, it's promotional stuff and bribes, just stick it down as slush fund payments and I'll get back to you with the details."

"Whatever you say Paolo but just so you know Bashar's team are keeping a tight rein on me at the moment checking and double checking contracts and spend figures. Anyway when are you up here next? You'll be impressed with the progress."

"Yeah, soon Steve, soon, I'll let you know."

Paolo put the phone down and childishly gave it a reverse victory salute. "Fuck off Carter, who are you to question me? I can spend the money if I want to, who set it all up? They don't pay me enough for what I do." He cut himself a line of coke and snorted it to lift his mood. *Maybe I have dipped my fingers in a bit much; no matter I'll soon win it back at poker, better go to the bank and get a decent roll out for the first game tonight.*

That evening with Maria and Loretta on each arm Paolo strode into the Bilton club as if he owned it. He wasn't a member but with his high spending and an introduction from the girls the staff had been told to turn a blind eye. They walked through the air conditioned foyer through the dance club which was just starting to get a few early punters and out the back into a private room. Six faces looked up from the table where a discussion was going on about an American shmuck who'd been playing with them the week before. Maria stepped forward to make the introductions.

"Marco, Juan, Pedro this is my friend Paolo that I told you about." Pedro stood and closed the gap between them extending his hand in welcome.

"Pleased to meet you Paolo, I believe you've met my cousin Juan Garcia at Vistamar; you've got a pretty big development up there I understand." He turned to his compatriots sat around the table. "Juan says that the gringo has plenty of cash, he's building five hundred or so units in the first phase of a beach side development. Maybe we'll get him to share some money with us like the Americano eh boys?" Laughter broke out around the table and Paolo was waved into one of the empty seats with a hearty slap on the back.

A huge black Brazilian guy walked in through a door opposite the entrance that Paolo had come through. He was carrying an ornate wooden box, decorated with brass and inlaid shell, around the size of a briefcase that he placed on the table before slowly opening it. Paolo's heart jumped slightly as the rows of chips of various denominations glinted back at him in the light.

"Good evening gentleman, tonight's buy in is Ten thousand US dollars, you'll be playing standard Texas hold 'em, house rules are that limits can't exceed the chips purchased, if you run low there's an optional re-buy at midnight. The house charges a hundred dollar a seat cover charge and takes a five percent table fee. Chips can be cashed back in at the end of the night or if you prefer not to carry large amounts of cash we can wire transfer your winnings to you. Any questions gentleman?“ He slowly looked around the table making sure that everyone had understood the instructions. “No questions? Okay show me your money.”

Paolo was feeling lucky tonight. Texas hold 'em was his favourite variation of the standard card game of poker. Two cards (hole cards) are dealt face down to each player and then five community cards are placed face-up by the dealer. The first card is called "the flop", the next "the turn" with the final card being known as "the river" or "fifth street." Players have the option to check, bet, raise or fold after each deal and with five of the cards showing face up, Paolo considered it a game of skill. Working out your opponents strategy and tells or tic’s was essential to win big. Tonight was just a warm up as far as he was concerned.

The game started quietly but he immediately noticed that his fellow players enjoyed using the free alcohol liberally, he stuck to soft drinks at first trying to keep his head clear, he could always have a drink or two when he worked out what was going on. After the first ten hands he was about a thousand up. Pedro and the Mexican were also winning with the other players losing in equal measure. He was starting to feel comfortable. As the evening wore on the blinds or minimum bets were starting to get bigger fuelled by the alcohol and losing streaks of a few players. Paolo rarely chased the money when he was playing, either the pack was good for you or it was cold. There was never any point in trying to win back what you’d already lost, just play what was in front of you, amazing really considering his other weaknesses for excess in life. He folded on a couple of hands and sat back watching the Mexican and Pedro, they were both still winning regularly but he was starting to see a pattern.

He was sure that when Pedro was bluffing and trying to get the other players to fold he had a habit of stroking his right eyebrow. He could use that to his advantage. Similarly the Mexican stroked his chin when trying to bluff. He filed both thoughts away. At two in the morning time was called. Paolo was eight thousand up and elected to leave his stake pot and winnings with the house for a game in two night's time. As he rose from the table he couldn't help a small grin as self-congratulation run through his mind. *Well done Paolo. This could turn in to a nice little earner.*

He walked back out to the dance area and found the girls dancing to the music. Maria pulled him on to the floor rubbing up against him. "I'm horny Paolo; you've left us on our own all night, let's go score and party uh? Hey and can we bring Jonny home with us to have fun? He's been looking after us while you've been away." Paolo looked over to see Loretta gyrating to the heavy bass beat with a young stud.

"Does that mean that I have to share you?"

"Don't be a grouch Paolo; we look after you don't we?"

The girls made sure that Paolo had more than his fair share of shots using the excuse that he had to catch up and for a bit of fun they slipped him a mickey as well. Back at the apartment Paolo remembered all four of them being naked on his huge bed and frolicking but everything else was a blur and at some point he must have passed out which was just what the girls wanted. Loretta grabbed the camera and they had fun positioning Paolo in such a way as it looked like Jonny was having sex with him. To finish the theme off they grabbed a used condom, thankfully not containing any emissions and used a pencil to insert it up Paolo's backside. He was in for a huge surprise when he woke up and the girls couldn't stop laughing.

Chapter 23
New Resources

A WEEK AFTER THE PAYROLL REVELATION and three days after his report had been submitted Helga Iron Pants phoned Toby just before lunchtime. "Mr Trelawney? Your new office will be ready on Monday. It's on the fifth floor of the Atrium building, all of your data will be transferred on to a new server over the weekend but your team will need to move all personal effects and box up any paperwork that you need. You might want to view the space before moving so that you can allocate desks to your existing team. Oh, and you'll now be reporting direct to Mr Schneider the Chief Information Officer." There was silence on the line. "Mr Trelawney?"

"Umm, yeah, umm sorry...I'm stunned, I was so rude to you last time we spoke that I thought you'd consign me to the basement somewhere or arrange for me to be fired...wow...is this really happening?"

"It certainly is Toby. I found our last conversation enlightening, you're the first person in twenty years who's been brave enough to call me Helga Iron Pants rather than just whispering it behind my back. This government needs more people like you young Mr Trelawney. People with the courage of their convictions who snap the red tape when it gets in your way, I've pulled a few strings to get the best office and best facilities that I could, now get on with things and find where that Donovan hussy has hidden the data. Oh, and a box of chocolates wouldn't go amiss. Goodbye Toby."

He slumped back in his chair before putting the phone gently back in to his cradle. A moment later he was up on his feet and doing a robot dance around his desk then sliding across the grubby floor in a footballer style goal scoring celebration punching the air as he came to a stop.

"Good news boss?"

"Good news? Fecking fantastic news." He stood before yelling at the top of his voice. "Team meeting Murphy's bar, ten minutes time, no excuses, wrap up what you're doing."

Crammed in to the largest booth at the back of the pub Toby went through the details of the phone call with his team of equally spotty geeks, the excitement of being on the fifth floor of the atrium building was palpable, there was a lot of high fives and excited chatter mixed with concern at being so close to the reach of Schneider.

"Schneider's like god and he's going to be looking over our shoulder, what if he finds out we're just a bunch of geeks?"

Toby put his hand up to stop the chatter. "Listen guys, we're not just any geeks...we're the geeks that found out how the famous Bridget Donovan fiddled the government payroll...Nobody else has done that...just remember that we're the A team."

After lunch he left his team packing up their possessions and walked the half a mile through the shoddy old nineteen sixties office buildings and warehouses to the newly built business park with its open spaces, park benches and water features. He strolled up to reception where he collected a new pass from security before being directed to floor five. He exited the lift walked across the beautiful wooden floor then on to the thick luxurious carpet before waving his pass at the security tab next to the door. There was a satisfying 'click' as the lock disengaged. He pushed the door open with trepidation concerned whether his dream of a modern efficient domain was about to be dashed. He needn't have worried. Helga Iron pants had excelled. Modern work stations were arranged in pods of four, each desk having two screens, one PC based and one linked in to the Unix based servers, all of the phones had headsets to allow staff to talk on the phone whilst operating their keyboards which although a minor point would save a lot of sore necks. The main wall visible from all of the pods had a bank of white boards and screens across it and Toby could already see where he was going to be spending the weekend getting things ready for his plan of attack. He walked towards two glass partitioned offices at the far end of the room imagining that it would be for Schneider. He was wrong. One was set up with a round table and leather backed chairs as a meeting room and the other had his name neatly engraved on a plate attached to the door. He couldn't resist, he pulled out his phone, took a picture and sent it to his Mum and Dad. He'd arrived, now all he had to do was deliver.

On the way out he checked that he could get access over the weekend before heading straight into Town to buy the biggest box of chocolates, the best champagne and a huge bunch of flowers for Helena, PA to Mr Michael Power, arranging for all of them to be delivered before four pm, he owed her big time.

On Saturday morning Toby gave his mum a fright...he was up and dressed in jeans and his favourite grey Superdry T-shirt and it wasn't even nine o'clock. He grabbed a slice of toast, smeared it with butter and marmalade and set about tying the laces on his favourite retro converse sneakers while trying to eat at the same time.

"Slow down Toby, have ye wet the bed or something? Has the power of this new job gone to yer head?"

"No Mum and No Mum, I've just got things to do at the office, I've got to get my thoughts down on paper before my head explodes. It'll be nice and quiet, nobody to interrupt my train of thought and it'll be ready for the team on Monday morning. Thanks for the toast Mum, gotta dash." As he walked down the drive to the bus stop he couldn't help but chuckle. He was twenty seven years old and his mum still treated him like a teenager. Granted the gaming late at night gave her good reason but with his new job, new office and more responsibilities she needed to start thinking of him as an adult. He'd have to cut the apron strings sooner or later but good home cooking and a washing and ironing service was hard to find.

The security guard on reception took down details of his security card and nodded him through with a gruff "Good morning te ye Mr Trelawney." His converse shoes squeaked on the polished marble floor as he headed to the lift and punched the button for floor five. As he exited the lift he swiped his card on the door tab and surveyed his new home bursting with pride. "Look out, look out wherever you are Miss Donovan; I'm on your case." He opened a new set of marker pens and started to draw the results from his ponderings on the big white boards so that everyone could see the servers, data storage dumps, databases and links between systems. He split the boards into areas that he could identify by department.

Admin including payroll, HR, property and facilities;

Accounts, including purchasing, supplier data, cash transactions, and creditors.

Customer service, which was his catch all; An anomaly of data dealing with the local councils and external communications.

He was left with Treasury including customs and excise and defence. Both were above his pay grade and he'd not managed to get any details on them yet despite putting in a request a few days ago.

He stood back examining the boards. What was he looking for? "Definition, we haven't got a definition of what we're looking for, if we're looking for a needle it's no use looking unless you can show people a picture of a needle or at least describe what it looks like." Talking out loud helped him think.

He headed up his next two boards THE HAYSTACK, and moved on to a fresh board which he labelled THE LIKELY NEEDLE. He set about trying to describe what characteristics he thought it might have:

- An executable file
- A data cache including word documents and jpeg or pdf files
- Likely not to exceed 100mb
- A non-conforming batch name or header (see govt approved list)
- Needs access to external connection / The web
- Did not exist on our servers six months ago

He stood and looked at the board for inspiration. *Damn this was hard, how can it be executable and a cache?*

He heard the security lock on the main door click open and footsteps echoing off of the wooden floor before muffling on the carpet. A middle aged man with short salt and pepper receding hair and silver metal framed glasses was walking towards him carrying two Styrofoam cups of coffee from Starbucks.

"Good morning Toby, in early aren't you? My names Doug Schneider, we haven't had the pleasure of meeting yet. Here, I've brought you a Latte; I've got the sugar in my pocket somewhere. A coffee machine for the troops is being delivered tomorrow."

Toby froze to the spot before taking the cup and offering his hand to shake. "How did you know I was here? I thought I would be the only one in on a Saturday."

"Easy, the central system pings my computer with a list of anyone in the office out of hours or overnight. I had a hunch that you'd be here today so I checked the list. Good work on the payroll by the way, it takes me back to the old days in retail when companies used to fiddle their closing stock."

Toby almost choked on his coffee. "That's exactly what Mollie and Seamus said." He explained the story of the comptometer and adding up computer lists and how it gave him the break to find what had been done to the payroll program. "We'd been focussing purely on web based code violations up until then, I never thought about it being hidden in plain sight so I thought we better look closer to home before we put more resources into the dark web."

"Good thinking...do you know what's in the file Toby?"

Toby blushed. "I was privy to a conversation between the minister, a man named Jack Fitzgerald and a Miss Bridget Donovan, so I've got an idea but I'm sorry Sir, I'm not allowed to divulge the contents or my thoughts to anyone."

"Good lad, I see you've learnt the party line. Let's make this easier for you. The file contains information in written and picture form relating to several murders during the sectarian wars. Some of those pictures implicate members of our parliament which would not go down well. We believe the file also contains details of the promises made by the UK government 'not to prosecute'. Some of the ministers that signed off deals with known terrorists are still in the cabinet and in very senior positions. It's more than just skeletons in the cupboard Toby; it's a nuclear bomb waiting to go off. I've had two other teams looking at this and nobody else has even got close, we can't fail. I'll sanction whatever overtime your team needs, cancel all leave, and if you need more personnel let me know. Now then shall we look at what you've managed to piece together so far?"

Chapter 24
The Score

AFTER HALF A DOZEN GAMES of twice weekly poker Paolo was fifty thousand dollars up and feeling very pleased with himself, his only problem was the constant hassle from Olaf to pay up, in full. He'd offered to make stage payments but the Russian wasn't interested. He had less than a week to find the cash or Olaf would start taking it out on Rachel or Max, he even threatened to kidnap Rachel and make her into a sex slave to work off the debt. He still didn't have the guts to admit the extent of his problems to Max and did what he usually did when he had a problem...ignore it until it went away or go out and party so he could forget about it. Thinking of last night his head was pounding badly, too much cocaine, too much rum and a night of sex with the girls had him feeling pretty low. The fact that he woke with a condom sticking out his backside really hadn't been the way to start the day. He must have had sex with that guy last night. *What was his name again, Jonny*? He'd never slept with a man before and the thought repulsed him. It was pretty wild and he couldn't remember what had happened but being shagged up the arse by a man when you model yourself on Casanova was less than ideal. He hopped into a cold shower and soaped himself over and over again before pulling on a tracksuit and going down to his local café come coffee shop.

The owner greeted him effusively as normal before commenting that he looked a bit under the weather. "You want a pick me up? My Argentinian parents swear by Fernet Branca when the stomach feels dodgy and the head is spinning from too much partying...It's a quick fix...I'll bring you one with your coffee."

His morning latte was accompanied by a foul smelling black drink. He was sure it was Venos cough mixture but the café owner insisted that he knocked it back. The burning sensation started off a coughing fit and went all the way down to his stomach. "What the fuck?? How's that supposed to help?" He grabbed the bottle and tapped the name into the search engine on his phone. Apart from the regular story of Bill Crosby mistakenly ordering a whole cooked sparrow and using the dark stuff to chase it from his stomach a quote from Robert Misch, long the head of the Wine and Food Society of New York, caught his eye. "Fernet-Branca is the liqueur of Hades." Drinking it", he wrote, "is like hitting yourself on the head with a hammer; when you stop it feels great, when you down your Fernet, you're so happy it's gone you're bound to feel better."

His Phone pinged and a message came through with a picture from Maria showing him in a compromising position with Jonny. He read the text. *Wild night let's do it again some time, never knew you were so adventurous. Maria. Xx*

The photo brought back hazy memories making Paolo feel even worse, his stomach was rolling and he was sure that the Fernet Branca would finish him. He was due to view some offices for the planned sales centre today but bed was beckoning, bed a good meal and then the high stakes game that he'd been invited to by Pedro and the Mexican. *Fifty thousand buy in, no table limit - I'll make a killing and solve all my problems in one hit.*

After spending the day in bed and having checked his backside out thoroughly over the bath Paolo was starting to feel good. He dressed sharp for the evening and looked himself over in the mirror before heading out. He hailed a cab outside of the apartment and was surprised when it drove into one of the zones that he had been told was a no go seedy area. The cab driver seemed unconcerned so he assumed that the risks had been exaggerated. The venue was new to him and for a high stakes game he was surprised that it was held in a private house that looked out of place in an otherwise fairly ramshackle street. His fears were quelled slightly when the door was opened by the regular huge black guy who acted as stakeholder at the Bilton club, that and the ornate chandeliers in the cool beautifully decorated hallway. The opulence continued when he was shown through a set of heavily gilded doors into a library that wouldn't look out of place in an English stately home. Wood panelling and the spines of dusty old leather bound books stared back from two of the walls the third housing three large windows which would bathe the room in light during the day. The Mexican and Pedro were sat on some lounge chairs on the other side of the room which had a huge round table at its centre, presumably the venue for tonight's game. They called him over and pulled a leather chair closer for him to join in on the conversation.

"Welcome Paolo, the venue is different eh? Senor Gomez insists on living in his old neighbourhood although he could live in a palace if he wanted to, he has made big money and loves to play high stakes poker. You are sure you are up for this? You can win more but also lose much more than in our regular games, although you've been lucky so far eh Paolo?"

"I don't intend on losing Pedro. I'm here to take your money." Paolo slipped in to Bravado with ease. *Let the mind games begin.*

Gomez made an entrance expecting everyone to look round at him. He was not what Paolo expected, small build, keen dark eyes, hair slicked, a dapper deeply embroidered gold waistcoat with a pair of mirrored glasses peeking out of a pocket. No doubt he would be wearing them during the game. There was one other player with him, older, bearded scruffy by contrast; he looked slightly out of place. Pedro pulled Paolo close. "That's David Silva, don't be fooled by his looks, he's a sharp player with the money to back up his bets."

Introductions were made all round with Pedro emphasising that Paolo had a multimillion development underway up at Vistamar. He did nothing to correct the notion that it was his and his alone. Who would want to admit to just being a sales lacky? The game referee called the table to order confirming that each player had deposited funds for the fifty thousand buy in required and issuing chips from his ornate wooden case. The sight of the piles of chips made Paolo twitchy. *What if the cards were marked? What if this was out of his league?* His normal arrogance kicked back in as the stakeholder randomly picked out four brand new cellophane wrapped packs of cards and selected one at random after sliding them randomly around the table.

The first half a dozen hands went to plan. Pedro giving himself away over ninety percent of the time when he was bluffing with his eyebrow stroking, similarly the Mexican continued to stroke his chin when he was unsure of his hand. Both Paolo and Gomez were up when they stopped for refreshments and a comfort break. The only issue was trying to work out the strategy that Gomez was using, it was hard to get behind the dark glasses and he was careful what he did with his hands aware that any tic or nervous habit could give him away. Silva was also a good player but Paolo hoped he now had his measure. *Hell, I'm winning aren't I?*

As the night wore on the game heated up and the stakes were raised. The pre flop betting started routinely with a raise to two thousand dollars. Gomez then raised to six thousand with what Paolo hoped was a bluff for a weak hand; maybe he was trying to steal the pot. It was not a good time to try because Paolo sat with pocket kings. He played his hand strongly and re-raised to fourteen thousand sweating slightly as he did so. The action moved around the table to Silva. While contemplating his decision he asked Gomez how many chips he had. He was likely trying to get a read and deciding whether the hand was worth pursuing. On hearing that Gomez had eighty thousand Silva made the call, he stood to win a lot of money with the right kind of card turning on the flop (in other words, he figured he had pretty good odds).

The flop showed an ace of diamonds, a three of hearts and a six of spades. Paolo's key risk was whether someone was holding an ace but he assumed his Kings would be the best hand and bet twenty five thousand inwardly confident and wanting to win the hand right there. He'd checked the faces and body language. *He had to be holding the strongest hand.* Gomez folded. The flop was not good for him and his exit buoyed Paolo's hopes of a big win. Inwardly he'd convinced himself that the money was already his.

He was shaken out of his stupor when Pedro full of Bravado announced that he was raising to fifty thousand; with the chips he'd won and with those from the rebuy at the break he had a stack of around ninety thousand and he wasn't calling yet. The Mexican and Silva folded leaving Paolo contemplating the odds. He was caught off-guard by the bet. Pedro had been stroking his eyebrow. *He had to be bluffing didn't he?* Paolo understandably took some time to try to figure out whether to call. He mulled over what Pedro might have. *Maybe three of-a-kind, he could have threes, sixes or if he was unbelievably lucky, aces. No he was still stroking his eyebrow and looking nervous.*

Pedro's body language was stronger than the nervous tic; he went in for the kill. "You want to make it interesting Paolo, a quarter of a million each and we turn our cards together?"

Cool sweat started to run down his back. He sat thinking about all of the games they'd played over the last few weeks. He'd called Pedro's body language correctly over ninety percent of the time and one hundred percent of the time in the last week or so. He had to be bluffing, a pair of aces, three of a kind, but a quarter of a million. It would solve all of his problems.

He placed his palms flat on the table watched intently by the other players before taking his decision. "I'll take those odds Pedro, although you understand that I don't have two hundred and fifty grand to hand."

Pedro nodded slowly. "Senor Gomez is our witness and enforces all bets made in his house, isn't that right?" Gomez took off his glasses to speak. "All bets made in my house must be honoured." He stared intently at Paolo. "Only gamble what you can afford to lose."

Both men nodded and Paolo flamboyantly turned over his kings. A grin spread across Pedro's face. "Slowly, slowly catchy monkey my friend, I think a pair of aces leaves me the winner of the chips on the table and a cool quarter of a million on top." Paolo stared at the cards as they landed on the table. Bile rose in his throat and it was all he could do to stop himself being sick, he'd been played. Pedro deliberately used the tell to lure him in and he was now down well over three hundred grand on top of his troubles with the Russians.

Chapter 25
Eureka!

FOUR WEEKS ON and Toby and most of his team had dark circles around their eyes from burning the midnight oil. They had been given unprecedented access to government databases and the once pristine office now looked like a bombsite, coke cans, coffee cups, papers strewn everywhere, it was so bad it might even qualify as a teenagers bedroom. They had installed huge old school dot matrix printers dug out from a government store into a hastily screened off area and had run miles of reports off on the ticker tape wide spool green and white computer paper. Toby had only ever seen these types of reports when he was a schoolboy on a computing tour at a local factory but he was now an expert on "Was/Is" reports which show changes to masterfiles or program files between two dates. In the past when computing was a centralised affair such reports were a key weapon in the armoury against fraud, any change to a supplier Masterfile or a program file would have to be signed off by a senior person. Now nobody even bothered running the reports even though the underlying system was still based on the old Unix protocols. All that was different was that it now had a pretty user friendly interface sitting over the top. It was no wonder that government IT systems creaked throughout the UK.

Schneider had called in every Saturday to help Toby get his mind around some of the older technologies he could see a lot of his younger self in Toby, the boy had a spark and his mind thought differently, he looked for patterns not just straight lines, critical if they were to solve the issues facing them. Using his old Filofax and digging out numbers from the past he'd even managed to pull in a few contractors in their late fifties and early sixties who could run the report routines and write query reports for him. The influx left many of Toby's younger team reduced to reviewing paper reports with coloured pens to mark anything suspicious, it was a dull job but someone had to do it and follow up on every lead.

Toby walked from desk to desk checking ideas, conversing with the team and giving his usual encouragement, as ten o'clock rolled round there was a familiar boot kicking at the door. Doug Schneider and a security guard were standing behind it with their arms laden with coffees and Doughnuts from a local shop. The team welcomed the break, they got to talk to the main man directly and were encouraged to throw ideas or finds out into the open no matter how wacky they seemed.

Peter Jones was still terribly shy about speaking up but he thought he might have found something and was desperate for a pat on the head, as usual though the more confident members of the team were hogging the limelight. Sat next to Doug, Toby could see that something was bothering Peter, he kept bobbing up and down and fiddling with a sheet of green lined computer paper in his hand, he just didn't have the confidence to butt in. He caught his eye and mouthed "what's that?" Peter went straight back into his shell but was clutching the piece of paper as if it was a gold bar. Toby put his fingers to his lips and let out a blast of a whistle that stopped all conversation in its tracks. Schneider broke into a laugh. "Well team I think your boss has something to say."

All eyes turned to Toby. "No, not me; Peter, come on up show us what you've found, if this lot would shut up for five minutes you'd be able to get a word in sideways. Come on; scribble it up on the board."

Peter went beetroot red especially as there were a few cheers and jeers claiming that he'd found the fabled Honey Monster or Pirates gold. He steeled himself and was encouraged by the fact that neither Doug nor Toby were laughing. Toby always treated him equally and with respect, he had time for him even if he did stutter and was a real nerd. Toby listened. He went up to the white board with his piece of paper in his hand and started to draw; unfortunately it was so small that it wasn't really visible to those in the room. Toby appeared by his side to help him express himself.

He whispered quietly to him. "Don't let the jerks get the better of you Peter. What have you found?"

"I found this file on a 'was/is' report from the personnel data file. It always has loads of changes going through every week as people join and leave but this one stuck out, the file's much bigger than it should be for twenty personnel changes and when I try to query the file for Ted Shaafh it just bounces me out saying protocol not known, that and the fact that Ted Shaafh is an anagram of 'Fat Heads' but no one would do anything like that in real life would they? This lot a probably right...it'll turn out to be fool's gold."

Toby whistled again to bring the room back to silence. "Show some bloody respect. Peter's found an anomaly that might just be what we're looking for!"

Schneider stood and took the few steps over to the white board grabbing the piece of paper from Peter's hand. He scanned it together with Peter's scribbled anagram, read it again and the let out an exclamation of delight. "You bloody beauty!! Eureka!!" He grabbed Peter in a bear hug. "I think he's found it, I think he's bloody well gone and found it!"

After ten minutes or so of excitement and much patting on the back for Peter an end was called to the coffee break and people were tasked with more research before they set about the serious work of isolating the Personnel database from the rest of the network. What seemed like an easy thing to do was actually a huge nightmare. The Personnel database by its very nature of recording the active workforce, timesheets, joiners and leavers was linked in one way or another to just about every other department in government.

The first idea was to use a simple PC trick of placing the offending file into a virus vault. Great idea but in practice an epic fail, the file didn't respond to normal commands and steadfastly refused to be removed. Finally there appeared to be just one option open to them which involved a shed load of work but hopefully would be the safest way forward. By digging into the backups they had found a copy of the database that was six months old where the file wasn't present. By using the database back before its insertion and reloading all of the changes since that date, which were mammoth they should in theory get back to a clean state provided they didn't inadvertently reload the rogue file. It was going to take at least a week of work but it would be worth it. The ministers would now be able to sleep at night.

Chapter 26
Kidnap

BRIDGET HAD TRAVELLED AHEAD of Jack to spend some time on the beach in Rio and was booked in to a small boutique hotel just up the road from Paolo's apartment, it gave her a chance to get to know Rachel a bit better while Max and Paolo hung out in the bars ogling the perfect Brazilian girls showing off their booty as they walked or skated along the front.

To get over the long flight the girls chilled out on Copacabana beach which is one of the most famous and iconic beaches on the planet. The wavey boardwalk design,ultra tiny bikinis and striking backdrop fitted Bridget's idea of the classic Rio beach experience perfectly. They had elected to get sunbeds near one of the kiosks in the middle section, between lifeguard towers three to six, where the concierge had advised them that the sand was at its widest and the waves at their wildest. As they had no intention of going in the water it was the perfect spot to people watch whether it was trying to spot the rich and famous or whether it was just letting their eyes follow the tireless beach hawkers doing their bit to keep everyone refreshed. Of course in between people watching there was also a lot of girl talk with Rachel trying to get a bit more information about Jack and Bashar in the hope it might prove helpful. Bridget was no fool and just politely batted questions away or feigned ignorance. She was far more interested in talking about tomorrow's excursion to Sugar Loaf Mountain.

Dinner that evening was a strange affair. Max and Rachel had insisted that Bridget tag along and it appeared that Paolo thought her acceptance was carte blanche to make a move, it was water off of a ducks back to her but it did make her wish that Jack was here with her now, they, or more precisely she, had had a bit of a wobbly a few weeks back when everything just got on top of her. Jack had done a great job on their new house but underneath the happy façade he'd created a veritable fortress and it had really made her question what she was letting herself in for? She had faith in her IT skills to keep the two of them safe, surely there was no need to have grenades in the house, the next thing would be a tank parked in the front garden. A nudge from Paolo brought her out of her melancholy.

"Hey, Bridget, are you with us? C'mon, shots all round, let's party..."

"No thanks, Paolo, the Malbac has gone to my head already, it was great with the steak but I'm feeling pretty bushed now, probably jet lag..."

Rachel was also starting to wane. "I'm suffering as well, maybe a bit much sun today, is it safe for the two of us to walk back along the front.?"

Max looked to Paolo for reassurance. "Rio's a lot safer than it was and it's still reasonably early, you should be fine it's only a few hundred yards to the hotel and the apartment." He looked both girls over, not overly dressed up...casual even, he took no notice of the jewellery despite that probably being the key attraction to would be muggers. "Yep you'll be fine, stay in screaming distance of the bars and café's, we'll be along later. Max is still waiting on dessert; we'll get it at the bar. We won't be far behind you...My place for a nightcap?"

"Thanks Paolo but I'll take a rain check."

It was just before ten and there were still plenty of tourists and locals wandering along the boardwalk. As they walked they were approached by a couple of street urchins offering to polish their shoes with a toothbrush and magic water, the fact that they were wearing strappy heels was lost on the kids, they just saw a tourist and dollar signs. Rachel and Bridget chatted easily as they walked, their guard was down; they were enjoying the heat and the break, neither of them noticed the black van pull out from the side road and drive slowly up behind them keeping pace as a man craned his head out of the window trying to identify the girls. Everything seemed to happen in slow motion. Two men jumped out of the back, a white cloth was clamped over Bridget's mouth and nose; a hand stopped Rachel from screaming as she was dragged backwards losing her footing. Bridget thrashed furiously before the chemical smell started to dull her body senses. *What was it? Formaldehyde?* As she ran out of air and was forced to inhale deeply her resistance finally stopped. She was unceremoniously lifted off of her feet and dumped in the back of the van. Rachel despite being at a height and considerable weight disadvantage was still kicking and biting her assailant, drawing blood as she raked her nails down his face. He put a hand up to check and hit her furiously with a closed fist which knocked her to the ground, even though she was dazed as she landed painfully on her backside she had the presence of mind to wail like a banshee causing tourist and locals alike to come to her aid. Max picked up her distinctive scream and bolted from his seat at the bar sprinting along the street where he could see her sprawled across the pavement and a black van screeching off into the distance.

"Rach, Rach, are you okay, what's happened, where's Bridget?" His eyes were scanning the street and surroundings expecting her to emerge from a behind a bush or from behind the rapidly gathering crowd. "What's happened, who hit you?" He brushed the rapidly growing lump on her face causing her to wince.

"They've taken her...they took her, Max get help, hurry...HELP!"

The local police arrived within minutes but didn't have a lot to go on. Black vans were common and nobody seemed to remember the number plate, the officer was sure that they would have been false anyway. The three of them were taken to the local station and interviewed by detectives trying to get a lead as to why Bridget was singled out. Paolo was sweating. *Could Olaf have carried out his threat and taken the wrong girl?* He had no intention of coughing up information about his private life. He hadn't even found the strength to admit his problems to his brother. When in doubt act like an Ostrich and put your head in the sand.

Three hours later and they were released to make their way back to the apartment. Nobody talked. The police had told them that the kidnappers normally made contact within twelve hours and that a ransom would be demanded. Kidnap used to be rife in Rio but was less common now and rare when it came to a tourist, it was much more likely to happen with rich families or oil executives. The demand would hopefully be small; they police advised them to contact Bridget's insurers for help, without a firm reason they seemed to be brushing it away.

Max drew the short straw and made the call to Jack. He was business like, almost as if he expected it. "I'm sorry Jack, we shouldn't have let them walk the short distance to the hotel on their own, the police just can't think why Bridget was targeted; they reckon that it just doesn't happen to tourists anymore." There was a long drawn out ominous silence.

"Jack, you still there? Hello, hello."

"I'm here Max, I'm thinking. Keep your phone next to your bed, call me anytime night or day. I'll talk with Bashar and get a team out there." The call terminated. Jack had put the phone down.

There was nothing the three of them could do but wait. They sat in semi darkness sipping strong coffee, there was no hope of sleep; they were traumatised.

Max was clutching at straws. "Jack said that he'll get a team out here but I feel bloody useless. Is there anyone else we can call Paolo, have you got any local contacts?"

Paolo shock his head. "No, no one of any use anyway." *Do I confess? Jack'll bloody kill me; best stay stum Paolo, stay stum.*

Chapter 27
Rage

THE NEWS THAT BRIDGET had been taken from the streets of Rio threw Jack into a blinding rage. His language was vile and his head and heart were thumping. *This can't be happening, it's not possible! Calm down Jack think!*

All roads seemed to lead to one source. It had to be Dermot and his pet minister, Jack couldn't think of anyone else who would dare to touch her. "You're going to pay for this, you're going to wish you'd never heard of Irish Jack by the time I've finished with you all." He grabbed his mobile phone and rang the land line at The Office, Joey changed his number so regularly that he had no idea how else to get hold of him in a hurry.

"Hola Carlos, it's Jack, how ye keeping me old mucker?"

You could hear the smile in his voice as he responded in his good but grammatically incorrect English. "Jack, why we no see you anymore? I need to serve more Spanish coffee, I have to feed children and give mama dinero to spend."

"Argh, I miss the place as well Carlos but I'm building a new life. Would Joey be in The Office by any chance?"

"Sure Jack, sure. I get him for you. It take a minute, he talk with Seamus."

Joey stopped what he was doing edged his way round the booth, walked to the bar and picked up the phone, it had been weeks since he'd heard from Jack and he'd been a really important part of his life for years. He understood the reasons for him putting space between them but it didn't make losing your best friend any easier. "Jack! How are you! Long time no speak, would you be in Spain? If yer are I'll buy you a beer or two."

"I'm not Joey, but I could do with a friend right now, I've got serious problems so I have. Bridget's been kidnapped and I think it might be something to do with that fecker Dermot and the fecking scum in the assembly. This is a heads up Joey, I'm going to war and I'd be grateful if you could let that fecker Dermot know all bets are off. He can get me anytime by leaving a message at the ITS messaging service based in London. I call them twice a day and respond to any message left. If he's got nothing to say expect him to be dead within the month. They've no idea how important she is to me Joey, no idea at all...I'll kill the fecking lot of them if so much as a hair on her head is harmed. Feck the idea of passive defence and being on the untouchable list, it's time for the old school approach. I'll be seeing you Joey, I don't want to drag you into this, no I don't. I'll be calling in favours from Bashar as well...Don't get caught in the crossfire my friend. Hasta luego amigo."

"Jack, Jack! For fuck's sake." Joey shook his head and put the phone back down into the cradle. Jack had hung up...He wanted to offer to help him...He was a friend and if Dermot had crossed the line he'd be with him.

Joey followed the usual routine and picked up a disposable mobile and sent a text with five numbers and three letters. A few minutes later the mobile rang. It was Dermot with his hacking smokers cough identifying him before he even spoke.

"Joey, you need something urgently?"

"I wouldn't say that I need something urgently Dermot, more that you might need something."

"Stop fecking around Joey, what is it?"

"Have ye or your pals arranged the kidnap of Bridget Donovan?"

Dermot snorted. "Huh, I wish I could, she's causing bloody havoc so she is with her hidden data. We can't touch her, it must be a hoax. Where'd yer get the notion she's been kidnapped anyway?"

"It's not a notion Dermot. Jack has just put the phone down on me. He said to tell ye that all bets are off and that he's going to kill everybody within a month, old school was the phrase he used."

"Sweet Jesus, was he ranting and raging?"

"No, that's what was worrying. Yer know Jack...he usually blows hot when something pisses him off, let's off a bit of steam like with a swearing every second word, but he was calm and collected, just delivering the message. Talking of a message he says you can leave a number at the ITS messaging service in London and he'll call you back. You'll have to look it up on the web, he didn't leave the number."

"Feck, feck, feck! It's time to prey Joey. When Jack is calm and collected he's in a real rage so he is, there's no knowing what he'll do. I better get hold of the ministry and put them on alert, do the same with all your team Joey. This could get bloody very quickly."

Yeah right thought Joey, as if I'm going to set them against the one man I trust.

"Do you have any other details Joey, where did it happen, what time, anything at all? Shite this is bad..."

It was then that Joey realised that he had no clue where Bridget had been kidnapped, not even which country she was in, he didn't even know which country Jack was in. He didn't want to look bad. "It's best you get Jack to call you Dermot." He put the phone down realising that he had nothing else to say. He'd leave a message for Jack later offering whatever help he needed in Spain. *Fuck Dermot.*

Joey called the ITS service and left a message for Mr Jack Fitzgerald. "Any help you need you've got it. Joey McCann." He twiddled the phone in his hand; he needed information, maybe Bashar would know or perhaps Tony. He tried them both but just got voicemail. He left messages for them hoping that they might return his call.

Chapter 28
Viral Messages

WORK ON THE ROGUE FILE had been going on for three days and everyone was feeling pretty smug. They were still no nearer getting past the encryption but they could see that it contained a number of jpeg or picture files in its subroutines, it had to be what they were looking for, two more days and the employee Masterfile would be rebuilt and operations returned to normal. Toby still had a nagging itch, something wasn't right and after the initial euphoria he was still doodling trying to get to an answer. He picked up the phone and called Doug.

"Doug, it's Toby, listen we need to tread carefully, something isn't right, I can't see where the HR server has a link to the outside world so how would Donovan manage to broadcast it from there?"

"There's bound to be a link Toby virtually all of our systems can be accessed via the web."

"Exactly and the web has an encrypted firewall to stop unauthorised access so how did she plant the file?"

"There must be a back door...an old modem link for maintenance or similar. We've isolated the file onto its own server now. It can't communicate with anything else on our network so if it is a virus bomb we should be okay."

"Are you sure it can't communicate? How are the technicians accessing the server? If they're using PC's as slave terminals and they've got WIFI then it could technically get out."

"Shit!!! I'll call you back Toby." Schneider immediately shut down operations on the rogue file and ordered the purchasing departments to find some old green screen dumb terminals immediately. He didn't care how difficult they'd be to source, he wanted them now!

Having secured the server and banned WIFI in the same room Schneider thought that everything was now safe. The weekend came and went but Monday morning heralded a bombshell on screens across the various government departments. The IT department was swamped with phone calls. As staff opened their machines they were greeted with the word "FATHEADS" scrolling across their screen followed by an animated dominatrix telling a man dressed in a suit and a bowler hat to bend over and take his punishment. With pants around his ankles the dominatrix swished a cane through the air.

"Who's been a naughty boy?"

"Ouch, I have mistress?"

"And why are you naughty?" Swish!

"Ouch, because I underestimated you mistress and I searched for your file" Swish!

"And what do you say?"

"I'm sorry mistress, I'm truly sorry."

"Good, you may lick my boots."

The cartoon character was seen bending over sticking his red raw backside in the air and licking the dominatix's boots whilst she continued to talk to him.

"Would you like to see some pictures? Would it make you feel better?"

"Oh, yes please mistress!"

The screen cartoon faded out to be replaced by a collage of bondage and fetish pictures with faces carefully pixilated out, more than one senior advisor, parliamentarian and civil servant recognised themselves adding to the furore directed at the IT department to get it off the screens.

Schneider was tearing what was left of his hair out. *Toby had been right, they'd missed something, but how did it infect the whole system? The bloody file had been isolated.* Toby and his team were brain storming in front of the architecture diagrams spread out on the white boards. Each server that had been infected had a large yellow box drawn around it. For some reason two remained sterile. It was one of the old guard who came up with the possible solution.

"I bet that those systems only update once a week or every few days whereas the others update daily."

Toby could see his logic. "Go on..."

"Well if she had hidden a file on every server, and we did find other very small files that were anomalies, then when they update if they couldn't see the employee name on the HR file then they release a virus."

"So you're saying that the employee file that we think holds the critical data is a diversion to use up time and serve as a warning?"

"Yep, and some bloody warning it is, that girl can run rings round us." The virus was playing on a large screen behind them. "Here, isn't that picture the Minister for Education, that one in the bottom right hand corner?"

Chapter 29
The Committee

THE SCALE OF THE VIRUS BOMB and discussions as to the fate or whereabouts of Bridget Donovan led to a rapidly convened meeting of the Security Council which comprised many of the senior members of the Northern Ireland Assembly the Chief of Police, military figures, the UK's Minister for Northern Ireland, a special envoy from the Prime Minister's Office in Downing street and some shadowy members from the British secret service. Whichever way you looked at it the committee was full of heavy hitters who could make or break someone's career. Understandably Doug Schneider and Toby Trelawney were inwardly quaking sat outside the huge wooden doors leading to the committee rooms. Toby tried to distract himself by looking up at the ornate ceiling and oak clad walls; he shuffled on his seat trying to get comfortable, maybe they were deliberately built lacking in cushioning.

"Well Doug, It's been nice working with you. It looks like I'll be flipping burgers from now on."

Doug snapped out of his own melancholy realising that his young charge had probably never been in front of any committee or senior group before let alone one of the nation's most powerful. He mentally slapped himself. Toby needed reassurance.

"Sorry Toby, I've been wrapped up in my own thoughts. Don't panic, we've done everything that we could have done. There's bound to be a bit of shouting and blame thrown around but I'll take that on the chin. You just keep your head down unless questions are directed at you. You shouldn't be in the line of fire, that's my job. I'll do my best to protect you. You've done at great job Toby."

Toby's shoulders visibly relaxed and the timing couldn't have been better. The doors to the committee room swung open and they were ushered in to the room by a man dressed in charcoal grey striped trousers, a matching waistcoat, a black Jacket and a winged white shirt finished off with a black tie. He looked as if he was an undertaker - not good - Toby's mind wandered, the irony was not lost on him, an executioner, an old stuffy outdated room and a very modern problem to be discussed. The ushers dress code added to the level of intimidation as twenty five sets of eyes bore down on them. They were shown to two seats at a small desk located at the end of the massive U shaped table but nothing was said until they had pulled their papers out of the files and made themselves comfortable. The silence stretched out increasing their nerves until the meeting's Chairman formally announced the start of business.

"Gentleman, Ladies." He nodded to the two female members in recognition. "I'd like to introduce Mr Douglas Schneider our Chief Information Officer and Mr Toby Trelawney who led the team who managed to locate our rogue file. You've already been briefed on the threat from Miss Bridget Donovan and Mr Jack Fitzgerald or Jack Clements dependent on which name you know him by. Note that I still say threat despite some member's point of view that it is more of a passive defence by the pair. I beg to differ, however we look at things our government and that of the UK is under threat from the material that these two have possession of." He paused and stared over his half-moon spectacles scanning the room for any voices of descent "Now Mr Schneider, we have all read your preliminary report but would you like to frame this debacle in your own words. Everyone has already been briefed on the background to the problem brought about by Mr Fitzgerald's desire to retire."

Schneider was not a man to sit still and elected to walk as he talked much to the annoyance of some members. He put the problem into simple terms explaining the protection of a firewall as akin to a fireguard. Unless you could get round it or through the small holes then you couldn't get to the fire which he framed in terms of the operating systems. Donovan had found a way in which as yet was unknown. The systems came under attack from hackers daily but this was the first time in many years that their defence had been breached. He continued to paint pictures for the committee rather than using technical terms explaining how they first had to define what the needle might look like before even starting to look for it amongst fields and fields of Haystacks. He heaped praise on Toby and his team for their sterling work and put the blame for the proliferation of the virus squarely on his own shoulders. "The haystack was isolated in its own field, fenced off from all other systems but we think that every haystack had something much, much smaller hidden in it. Mr Trelawney is ready to implement a solution to the viral bomb but I'm afraid it won't leave us with a clean system."

"Well then Mr Trelawney, we are all ears." All eyes turned to Toby.

"Well, um, yes well, it's very simple really. We simply return the isolated server to the network and plug it in. We can either allow the system to run its normal daily and weekly updates or we can accelerate the procedures. If, I'm right then the rogue file being back on the system will result in the virus going back into dormant mode. As someone eloquently put it earlier the file has a passive defence based on it still being in existence, remove it and it starts to attack." He paused and pulled self-consciously at his collar. "Ummm this bit is a tad difficult... The virus seems to be deliberately degrading."

"Well surely that's good news isn't it?"

Toby swung his head side to side a bit like a nodding dog while trying to decide on the best answer. "Well it depends on your point of view. The degradation relates to the page full of bondage pictures. The pixilation is slowly disappearing and faces and therefore identities will eventually become clear."

The room erupted into chaos with questions been thrown at Toby and accusations of incompetence being thrown in the direction of Schneider. It took the Chairman some time to bring the meeting back to order.

"Gentlemen and Ladies...I expect people in this room to act professionally! The photos may well lead to the downfall of a number of our own but they will not bring down the government! If the information hidden by Miss Donovan gets out then only god knows what will be unleashed. We all need to keep our heads and work methodically."

"Mr Schneider, Mr Trelawney, you need to get the system back to the way it was as fast as possible. If those pictures get out we've got major problems. Get everyone working through the weekend and keep my office informed of progress every six hours, they have a direct line available to me. Thank you gentleman."

The final words were a clear dismissal. The usher in his funeral suit appeared at their side as they were clearing the desk and escorted them out through the doors. Toby could feel the sweat rolling down his back as they emerged into the cool outer corridor. Doug Schneider let out a long breath.

"Let's hope we don't have to go through that again eh Toby?"

"You can say that again, I could do with a drink."

"No time for that, we'll celebrate at the end, come on I'll buy you a sandwich for lunch and we can work out a plan to reinsert the file."

Chapter 30
Messages

DERMOT LEFT A MOBILE NUMBER with the message service asking for Jack to contact him urgently. Since getting the news from Joey he'd been on to his contacts at the ministry, the Royal Ulster Constabulary and within the Guardia. Everyone was confused. If Jack and Bridget were both on the untouchables list why bother having an alert on all borders? He had no intention of divulging more information until the Minster for Security called back in person. This was bad, very bad; he had to try to convince Jack that they weren't involved.

One of his many mobile phones buzzed on the table. He sucked in a huge lungful of smoke before stubbing his cigarette in the overflowing ashtray and answering. "Hello Jack; thanks for ringing back. I've had a message from Joey saying that Bridget has been kidnapped...tis nothing to do with us Jack, I swear it's so. I was sorry to hear the news....I've got a call into the minister as well but I don't believe they'd do anything either, you're both still on the untouchables list so you are."

"I didn't think you'd say much else Dermot, but words are cheap. You've got seventy two hours to get her back to me and then I start."

"Look Jack, it's nothing to do with us! The techie guys have been trying to figure out Bridget's virus bomb and they can't get round it so why would the ministry want to get involved, we'd all be losers." His anxiety started a coughing fit and Jack could picture him reaching for another shot of whiskey with his tobacco stained hands to help clear his throat. *How he'd like to have his hands round his throat now.*

"Shut the fuck up Dermot. No one else has the slightest reason to kidnap her. She was lifted from the streets of Rio at ten in the evening yesterday local time. Like I said, you've got seventy two hours and all bets are off." Click...the phone went down leaving Dermot furious. He lit another cigarette before trying the minister again, no luck.

He yelled in the direction of the kitchen in a foul mood. "Craig, get all the cell leaders together tonight at Mckinley's barn. Ten O'clock, no excuses, code red." Craig stuck his head into the smoke filled room.

"Boss? Did I hear you right? Code fecking red?"

"You heard me, code red!"

Jack was sat with Bashar at his London house. He came off the phone fuming. "The fecker expects me to believe that they've got nothing to do with it despite them having teams crawling over Bridget's programs... fecker must think I'm an idiot." His thick Irish accent came out heavily under stress making the last word sound more like eediot. "I've given them seventy two hours to get her back to me or I go to war with them. If they so much as harm a hair on her head..."

Bashar tried to be the voice of reason. "Calm down Jack. We haven't had any demands yet and we don't know who's involved. For the moment I agree all roads lead to Ireland but let's get some local intel first. Martin has already alerted Enrique Fernandez and he has an eight man team flying out as we speak. They should hit the ground running acting as muscle or fire power while Enrique's local boys provide the intelligence. Rio's underworld has no idea what's coming and someone will squeal Jack. Martin and his team can be very persuasive."

"What time are we leaving Northolt?"

"Three o'clock in the afternoon."

"Listen my friend, I know you're already providing a lot but could Ishmail take me to Tony's club? I've some business to settle."

"No problem Jack. Call me on the way back."

Jack sat in the back of the car in silence as Ishmail gunned the Bentley towards Basildon. His mind was swirling. *Why, why now, what would Bridget do? Argh you fecking dumb arse Jack, what was it I'm supposed to do? @EMERGENCY that's it.*

He pulled his Galaxy note out of his Jacket pocket found the email icon and sent a message to Bridget's private email account with the emergency tag in the title line. As he pressed send he hoped it would help, Bridget had told him to do it if she was uncontactable but he had no idea what he'd just set in motion. The email winged its way across to the server and sat waiting to be polled by Bridget's email account, when it arrived the tag line was immediately picked up and the message sent to a subfolder within her inbox, thirty minutes later a management subroutine scanned the folders and found the message sat in the account. The subroutine was simple. If the content of the folder equalled zero then no action was required. If the folder had a message in it then the value was greater than zero and a further sub routine would run the mail client and send a pre-planned message automatically to twenty people...the security minister, the head of the Guardia, the Chief inspector of Police for Northern Ireland and various other senior politicians and decision makers. Its message was short and sweet.

Warning!

An emergency code has been triggered due to Bridget Donovan or Jack Fitzgerald being unable to gain access to a computer. You are reminded of the consequences if they are unable to keep their data file safely locked away. All information held on people responsible for murders, locations of bodies, dates and times of clandestine meetings, payments to senior politicians and immunity letters granted by the UK government will become public in a pre- set timescale. You are encouraged to do everything within your power to find and release them before events become irreversible.

This is not an idle threat.

Bridget Donovan and Jack Fitzgerald

Ishmail craned his neck around from the driver's seat to get Jack's attention. "Jack...Jack, we're here, I'll wait for you in the car, call me if you need me."

"Thanks Ishmail, sorry, I was miles away so I was."

Jack opened the car door, picked up his pile of papers and started to stroll across the wide pavement towards the club doors. He stopped halfway and stared steadily at the entrance. It was hard to believe that so much had happened in the last eighteen or twenty months since the doors had a black Toyota car reversed through them and deliberately set on fire. Who could see the chain of events that would unfold? Who would have thought that he would find love and be on the brink of losing her?

Jack shook his head and continued on his way pushing the door open without knocking. As soon as the door started to creak Animal Frank was on his feet and heading past the bar. He strode up to Jack put his arms around him and hugged him before standing back and gripping his hand tightly in his own while staring into his eyes and giving a small almost imperceptible nod. The strength of emotion and determination that passed between the two men spoke more than words ever could. Their souls were bonded and about to set out on a common cause.

"Good to see yer Frank." He nodded to his brother in recognition. "Tommy."

"Would yer have any coffee on the go? Strong and sweet would be good if you have, black no milk, I need to keep me wits about me so I do."

At the sound of his voice Tony came bounding down the stairs. "Jack! I thought I heard your soft Irish lilt. Why didn't you call? I'd have laid out the red carpet for you." He closed the gap between them grabbed his hand and pulled his body into his own bumping chests. His eyes pooled with moisture as he spoke. "I can't thank you enough for what did for me Jack. We should talk. As he stepped back and scanned Tommy and Frank's demeanour and expressions he realised that something was wrong.

"What's up? Have I just gate crashed a funeral?"

"It's best you don't know Tony. I've got some business that Frank and Tommy need to take care of for me. Bridget's been kidnapped."

"Fucking bastards! I'm not going anywhere Jack, whatever you need I'll be there."

"I appreciate it Tony but it's taken months to get you back on the straight and narrow so it has...t'would be a shame to wreck all that good work. You'll have to sit this one out Tony."

"I'm not going anywhere Jack. You just don't get it do you? I owe you my life...fuck for me to say I'd lay down my life for an Irishman...you just don't get how big a deal it is do you?"

With a flick of Jack's eyes Tommy started to shuffle across to Tony ready to remove him from the discussions. Tony's eyes blazed with anger. "Don't even think about it Tommy or you'll end up in pieces. I'm as fit as I was in the forces, I'm running five miles a day, working out at cage fighting three times a week and I've got a vicious streak to match yours...back off big boy."

Jack interjected, the last thing he needed was fighting amongst his own. "Whoa, stand down; I get it Tony and I thank ye." He clamped his hands on his shoulders and stared at him intently. "Listen now, are you sure? The boys are going to war for me. It's not going to be pretty and it could screw with your mind big time."

"I mean it Jack, I'll lay down my life, get it into your thick Irish skull."

Showdown over the four of them sat around one of the lounge tables, the three foot soldiers were perched on the edge of their seats while Jack forced himself to lean back in a Chesterfield leather chair and to try to relax, more stress for his body was the last thing that he needed.

"Well, I suppose that I better start at the beginning... I'll try to keep it short I will." He took a deep breath ready to share his secrets. "This doesn't go outside these walls you understand." All three nodded. "Okay...about six months ago I retired from the paramilitary and drug running. Now normally there's no such thing as retirement other than a bullet in the back of the head and a burial on a cold beach or being fed to the pigs. You don't 'retire' in this game."

He paused gathering his thoughts. "But yer see I have one of those funny types of brains that remembers facts, figures, names, places...a bit like a photographic memory...that and I had a few key photos and bits of paper tucked away as an insurance policy so I did."

"How does that work then? I don't get it; surely they'd just top you if you knew too much like? Sorry I interrupted Jack." Frank looked like a naughty schoolboy who'd just spoken out of turn.

"You're not wrong Frank but that's where my wonderful girl comes into things. She's not just a pretty face....she's a genius when it comes to advanced mathematics, computers and the web and she worked it all out so she did. She came up with a plan to hide the files on the dark web in a way that needed us to be left alone in peaceful retirement, she explains it like this. All that information is stored away in a treasure chest and the chest is buried somewhere out in a featureless desert, no landmarks or anything, just sand as far as you can see. It's safe and stays safe as long as we both confirm that we're okay on a random basis. If we get killed or they try to torture the passwords out of us then the treasure chest jumps out of the sand and makes copies of itself which it sends to the press the security forces, politicians the works. And believe me the stuff that's in there will bring governments down."

Tommy being as slow as ever just couldn't get his head round things. "So where's the desert then? I f'ought we were going to Ireland? Plus I ain't got a clue when it comes to computers."

"The computing bit is all in hand Tommy, my wonderful girl had thought all of it through...apart from the fact that Dermot is such a fecking dickhead that he doesn't know when to leave well alone. There's nobody else that I could think of that'd be involved in kidnapping her. She's dealt with the brainy bit and we're going to deal with the brawn, an old school bombing campaign just to remind them who they're playing with... fucking bastards."

Frank twisted uncomfortably on his seat. "Me and Tommy don't know much about bombs Jack, I thought yer just wanted a few people shot."

A grin spread across Tony's face. "Well then, it looks like I'm in pole position then. I specialised in explosives for a short while when I was in the forces. Bombs are child's play...plus I get to blow up some scum....Happy days!"

Jack pulled out a sheaf of papers and laid them out on the coffee table before setting about explaining his thoughts. There were grid co-ordinates and maps for three stashes of C4 semtex, detonators and some Kalashnikovs and small arms. Everything had been wrapped in oiled hessian and should be good to go with a decent clean up that any competent person used to handling guns could provide. One stash was close to some farm buildings and the other in a small wooded copse both out in the small Irish back lanes but near enough to the border. The last was secreted in a church.

"How much C4 you got stashed?"

"There's plenty there Tony, yer won't need to fuck about with fertiliser and crap like that. There should also be a good few cases of detonators and other bits to help you out but you'll need a detonation source, a mobile, a battery and leads. You know the score."

They spent another hour or so going over plans and targets. Tony was in his element. He was keen to deliver Jack's message. They were interrupted by Ishmail coming through the door looking at his watch. "Jack, it's time to get going."

"I'll be there in a sec Ishmail...Well boys; I thank you for your support and for delivering my message...Good

Luck." He turned on his heel and headed straight out of the door, he hoped that Tony would cope with the pressure but he seemed to have no choice.

Chapter 31
McKinley's Barn

IT HAD BEEN MONTHS since Dermot had left the confines of his terraced house near the Shankhill road. He had no need, his whiskey and cigarettes were delivered, Seamus and Shaun cooked his meals, all he had to do was sit at the centre of the spider's web and control the twelve strands or cells by phone. For all intents and purposes he was an old man being looked after by his two nephews, at least that was the story if anyone ever asked but these days with the ceasefire tied up and the old leaders now treading the boards masquerading as responsible law abiding politicians, nobody pried into his business. Locally everyone knew who the three houses at the end of Banyon Street belonged to and generally if they had to pass them they'd walk on the other side of the street. He wasn't happy at leaving his home comforts behind and was as grouchy as hell as he got into the heavily armoured seven series BMW bought from an Arab Prince with Seamus behind the wheel. It was going to be at least an hour and a half drive to get to the farm and he'd sent a few boys ahead to act as lookouts and snipers in case anything got out of hand. Some of the newer recruits didn't show the respect that they should these days.

After a bumpy ride along winding country roads Seamus turned the car up a dirt track towards a solitary farm house with a selection of dilapidated buildings set in a sheltered square. Four or five cars were already parked in the concrete courtyard and Dermot scanned them carefully - O'Donnel, Connely, Heaslip, Park - He needed to watch Park, he was young, not schooled in the old ways, he'd over promoted him after a couple of unfortunate deaths; Too late now. Seamus tapped on the rear window of the car signalling the all clear. He pulled the door open for Dermot and a fug of smoke rose into the night air. He'd just stubbed his last cigarette, no point in making yourself a target for a sniper, mind you these days he was probably just as vulnerable with the technical advances to night vision optics. *Argh, if only I could turn back time.*

O'Donnel grabbed his arm as he walked through the side door of the largest of the barn's and steered him across to two hay bales set aside from the others. He offered him a cigarette and lit it for him. "What's happening Dermot? Fecking code red! We haven't had one of them in five years. Is it bad?"

"It's bad Rob, very bad. I'll explain it in detail when all the boys are here but I'm sure you've already heard about Jack retiring and taking up with the Donovan bitch."

"That I did; though his taste in women has to be admired."

"Hmm, that's debatable but the problem is that she's missing."

O'Donnel turned white. "Tell me it's those stupid fucks at MI5 and we can fix all this quickly." Dermot just shook his head. "Jesus mother of Mary."

Within ten minutes the rest of the cell leaders had arrived. Dermot stood and called them to order asking everyone else except Seamus to leave the barn... Seamus took the floor at Dermot's behest and explained the technical elements of Bridget and Jack's retirement plan, how it worked, how it was virtually impossible to find the hidden cache on the dark web and what happened if Bridget and Jack failed to verify that they were still alive and safe. The problem was that they had no idea when verification was required. It could be three months time; it could be in the next hour. There was bound to be some slack built in as a fail safe but nobody knew how much. With the rumours confirmed after an initial babble of questions asking for clarification about likely content and who would receive the files, the room fell silent. All eyes turned to Dermot as he stood and took to the floor.

"So, you all understand what Seamus is saying?" He looked round the room at the white faces. There's nothing we can do about the computer bits, the government have got teams working on trying to resolve the issue twenty four seven so they have." He laughed ironically. "I don't know if you've heard but one of their first attempts to crack the Donovan bitch's codes led to the whole of the assembly's back office system being brought down and some highly irregular pictures of senior figures hitting the screens." He puffed heavily before blowing the smoke out of his nose. "No doubt you'll all have heard that the education minister has resigned...not that he had a lot of choice to be sure; his was one of the more recognisable pictures."

With his cigarette burning down he motioned to Seamus for another and lit it from the smouldering butt. He inhaled hungrily. "Now to the other bit of bad news and the reason you've all been called here." He shook his head steeling himself to deliver the message. "One of our own...Jack no less, believes that we... " He waved his arms around the room dramatically. ."That we are responsible for Bridget Donovan's kidnap. You all know Jack and when I say that the conversation was calm collected and calculated you'll know what that means, you've all had your run ins with him and none of you have bested him." Park went to interrupt. Dermot reacted angrily. "Shut up Michael, you're not worthy of licking the man's boots; don't presume that you know him." The general murmur of agreement soon put him back into his seat although the anger at being publically rebuked still showed on his face.

"As I was saying, Jack was calm and collected when he told me that we." He waved his hands around the group again to emphasise his point. "We... have seventy two hours." He looked at his watch. "make that less than sixty hours to get Bridget back to him unharmed."

Park interjected again flashing a cocky smile not willing to be put down so easily. "What happens if we don't?"

Dermot shook his head, the stupidity and lack of understanding of some of the younger generation had him in despair. "Jesus ye thick shit Michael; do ye not have a brain in there?" He walked over and rapped him on the forehead. "O'Donnel, before I tell this whippersnapper a few home truths would you like to have a guess at the consequences? What do you say?"

"Well, as I see it Dermot we have two big and when I say BIG, I mean fecking HUGE problems. The first Seamus has explained, if Bridget isn't found then the information on murders, bodies, torture, drug running... basically the whole fecking caboodle of our organisation reaching right into the assembly goes public and we're all fucked including our politicians." Dermot nodded. "An accurate assessment of the first problem Rob, and the second?"

"Well if I know Jack, and I'd say I know him as well as any of you so I would, then he'll rain down holy hell on our heads and try to kill every last one of us if anything happens to his girl."

"Accurate again Rob." He turned to face the wider audience and raised his voice. "Jack told me we had seventy two hours until all bets were off." He stared pointedly at Park. "You don't have to ask what they means when you know Jack. He'll start a fucking war so he will; the streets will run with blood."

Park wasn't to be cowed so easily. "For fuck's sake, he's only one man! What can one man do against all of us?" He looked round the room desperately looking for support, there wasn't a sound except Dermot's forced laugh. "Seamus, shoot the fucker will you." Seamus pulled out a small browning thirty eight from his Jacket and put the gun to Park's head."

"Boss?"

"Agh, leave him Seamus, the mess'll take too long to clear up." He flicked his eyes as a signal and Seamus pistol whipped Park to the side of the head making him collapse from his hay bale seat.

Dermot once again raised his voice dramatically in volume. "Does anyone else here want to say that Jack is just one man?" He scanned the faces as Park got back up onto his straw seat clutching a handkerchief to the side of his head to stem the blood flow. "I didn't think so... You're an ignorant little shit Park. Jack is a legend, there are people in the streets that are loyal to him and him alone, they'd kill for him. As far as I know there might even be people here in this room who are loyal to him." He pinned Joey McCann with a stare. "Which side of the table do you sit Joey?"

Fuck, just the question I didn't want, I can't hide at the back anymore. "I've got to be honest Dermot. If I thought that one of our own had lifted Bridget it would be a tough call, I'm loyal to Jack, yer all know that...but if you're saying that her kidnap is nothing to do with anyone in this room I believe you Dermot and I'll do all I can for the cause."

Dermot and a few of the senior cell leaders were nodding their heads. "A fair and honest answer Joey. I appreciate your support so I do." *Shit that was close but it looks like I got away with it.*

"So the code red stands. All units are to be put on high alert. Seamus has pictures of the Donovan girl to give you; he'll email them as well so he will. You need to get on to every contact you've got in South America or with links to South America. Make no mistake SHE IS AND WILL REMAIN UNTOUCHABLE anyone with information leading to her being found will be rewarded. I don't need to tell you what we'll do to anyone found to be involved in her disappearance or withholding information. Get the word out to yer cells, keep a look out for unusual activity, ye all know how seriously we need to take Jack's threat...apart from this stupid fucker." He spat at Park.

Dermot motioned to Seamus and walked out of the room signalling the end of the meeting. As he got back into the car he leant forward. "Keep an eye on McCann Seamus; I'm not sure which side of the fence he'll be."

Chapter 32
SWAT Team

MARTIN'S SMALL TEAM ARRIVED AT RIO on the regular daily BA flight passing through passport control ostensibly posing as two sets of four ball golfers out to have some fun. If anyone asked they'd decided to travel light and hire their clubs locally, the only strange thing that may have been picked up was that four of them wore grey golf shirts with black trousers and the four other black golf shirts with black trousers. The more observant might also note the shaven heads and muscular bodies but it's amazing what a few golf hats and carrying golf magazines can do to people's perceptions. Once they picked up their luggage passed customs and worked their way through the scrum of arrivals they spotted two locals with their designated pick up sign "Smith Party - Golf collection Services."

Stretch held out his hand to one of the pick up team. "Stretch...Pleased to meet you. Can we get a shimmy on before anyone else asks me about poxy golf." The unlikely golfers headed outside and climbed in to two Mercedes vans with blacked out windows. There was no small talk, the guys were all nervy outside of their comfort zone; two of them had previously worked in South America as bodyguards and knew that life here was cheap. People were murdered for a watch, a few dollars, even for looking at someone the wrong way. Kidnap cases rarely had a good outcome; the key was not getting abducted in the first place.

The vans pulled away from the airport after the drivers handed out local intelligence packs with maps of Rio colour coded and marked up with the names of drug cartels and local gangs. There was a lot of territory to cover and a huge number of possible suspects. Gangs known to use kidnap as one of their techniques had a red star against them, those with links to the Escobar cartel had a yellow star. Stretch read through the pack cover to cover, he was impressed, he'd expected to have to work hard to get intelligence but he was pleased to find that the locals were organised and efficient; they could hit the ground running.

The team were taken to Enrique's lavish villa and compound where Julio teamed them up with members of his own crew to cover all options out on the streets. They were to have three hours rest and then start throwing round some muscle in the early evening to see what they could produce by way of information. Julio made it clear that the mission was dangerous.

"Listen up guys. This is new territory for many of you who've not worked in South America before. Be aware that all gang members will be armed, some with knives, some with guns, but importantly all members will be prepared to use them. The macho culture here and the desire to be seen to be brave and prepared to fight for the gang makes people unpredictable, anything could happen, be prepared. If in doubt the follow the lead of my guys they have the knowledge and are the ones who will be calling the shots."

Stretch looked round his boys and just shook his head while turning his mouth down. They wouldn't be listening to anyone, just their own gut instinct. Julio continued with his pep talk repeating everything in Portuguese so there was no room for mis-translation.

Stretch was to take Clarkey and two locals to Recife by private jet, they were already cleared through customs and would have a hire car waiting for them out on the tarmac meaning that they could transfer their hardware without upsetting the local police before they set about shaking the town up. As he was on a quick turn around he got his boys in a huddle and gave them his version of orders.

"Okay boys no heroics, I don't want anyone injured but make sure the bastards know we're here...I want to see trouble in the papers tomorrow." Julio had missed his speech and looked quizzically at him as he headed for the door. "Alright Julio! Hasta Luego...Oops sorry wrong lingo, ciao amigo." Julio just shook his head, at least he tried.

The three hours rest went out of the window as the boys were champing at the bit having been cooped up on a plane for thirteen hours. Julio was persuaded to bring things forward and set the teams loose. Rio and the surrounding area was huge and they had a lot of ground to cover; one final check that everyone understood the brief and they were sent on their way to instil fear in the underworld.

'Dog' so called because of his pug face and pitbull body had been teamed with Ricardo and Miquel. They were targeting two Favela (slum) hot spots dominated by drug gangs known locally as Militia. Gun fights with the local Police and rival gangs were common in the area with parts being virtual no go zones at night. Ricardo was keen to tread softly at first. "You understand Dog? Softly?"

Dog nodded while outwardly appearing calm, inside he was a mess looking to start a fight as soon as he could, he was a borderline choice for the operation but getting a team together in less than a few hours meant that a few compromises had to be made. He was known to have a twitchy trigger finger and was guaranteed to start a fight in just about any bar, a typical grizzled mercenary who would start a war if he couldn't find an outlet for his special services; Martin was hoping that his explosive nature might just come in handy and that no one else form the home team got hurt along the way.

As they entered the Cantagalo favela located on a hill near Rio's Ipanema and Copacabana neighbourhoods, it all seemed reasonably quiet. Kids kicking a ball around, a few men standing on corners shooting the breeze and the odd Mama getting her washing in off of a make shift line. Ricardo kept scanning the streets for known faces, stopping once or twice along the way and hanging out of the window to talk to people he knew. There was no news from his contacts but he had high hopes that this area might produce a lead. As they headed deeper into the slum, teenagers could be seen sitting out on balconies openly brandishing weapons, Ricardo began to feel uneasy, it was clear that news of their arrival was spreading, maybe he shouldn't have been so blasé about talking to people on the way in, the streets felt itchy, nervy even as if the slum knew that something was going down. He reiterated his speech about taking things easy. "Five minutes and we'll be outside their main site, everyone stay cool, follow my lead, the streets are hot, news of our arrival is spreading fast."

As the van slowed pulling up at the gangs café come club Ricardo went to open the van door and to greet the two huge guys standing out front. He intended on asking nicely for a meeting with the boss but was caught off guard by Dog bolting out of the back taking down the first doorman with a vicious punch to the temple and then putting his compatriot down and holding a gun to his head. A young stud lounging against the wall smoking weed saw his chance to make a name for himself and went to pull his gun, Dog shot him in the thigh, before kicking his gun away. It all happened in slow motion as Ricardo looked on. He pulled his gun and ushered his two other men into defensive positions beside him. "What the Fuck are you doing Gringo? You wanna start a fucking war!"

"What d'ya mean? I didn't fucking kill anyone, nice and softly just like you said." He cackled to himself. "Nuffing like letting people know we're here though is there, no point nancying about." He waved his gun at two tattooed young men. "Oi You! Chefe, now!"

Ricardo rattled off instructions in Portuguese. Dog made the mistake of removing his boot from the doorman who took it as an invitation to fight back. It was a huge mistake. In three moves Dog had him on the ground again although this time he was screaming in pain. He'd broken his arm and dislocated his knee; size didn't matter in Dog's book. The display brought about a slow hand clap from an older man stood behind the young studs who parted to let him get a clearer few.

"You either have big balls or no brains...which is it Englishman?"

Dog grinned showing one gold tooth and one missing. "My balls are fucking huge and my mates are even bigger. We don't play nicely when people mess with our property."

The man looked quizzical presumably struggling with Dog's Scottish accent which made him speak like he was chewing a wasp. Ricardo rattled off an explanation in Portuguese and handed over a picture of Bridget. The Chefe shrugged. "It's nothing to do with us."

"Well it will be something to do with you if we don't find her. We'll take this place out completely."

Ricardo explained again in Portuguese making the consequences clear and that Enrique fully supported the SWAT team's actions. He knew the English women personally and someone somewhere in Rio had crossed the line, he couldn't be seen to let a kidnap happen on his watch.

At the mention of Enrique's name the Chefe stiffened, he was not someone to upset, he flitted between the dark side and the establishment with ease and could have the neighbourhood crawling with police for months, making dealing and supply operations difficult. The Chefe lit a cigarette and slowly dragged on the tip, trying to make it seem as if he was completely unruffled.

"Like I said nothing to do with us but as a favour to Enrique I'll put the word out. We'll call if anything comes up." *And I'll call on the favour later.*

"Fucking right you will or I'll be back." The fact that he was using a famous Arnie line was lost on Dog if not on the on looking crowd. Pictures were passed around before they loaded up and drove warily out of the slum. Ricardo went for the jugular.

"You fucking stupid Scottish git, give me that fucking gun, you're out...you put us all at risk."

"You can have it if you can take it sonny boy; otherwise we're doing things my way."

The pattern repeated itself across the city. Violence seemed to be the first approach from Martin's team; Stretch had briefed them to upset as many people as possible and they were going about it with Gusto.

Chapter 33
In Control?

SCHNEIDER SAT BACK in his chair looking at the system map displayed on the huge flat screens attached to the wall in the team area of Toby's office; he'd been staring at it now for over eight hours whilst interacting with team members as each Masterfile was updated and subroutine run. They now only had five systems out of fifty six showing 'red' or 'infected', the plan was working quicker than expected. The irony of the dominatrix cartoon character appearing one final time on each screen before giving a one line all clear wasn't lost on him "There's a good boy, mummy's going to go back to sleep now" might as well have read - Do that again and all hell will break loose. He turned to Toby as he walked up with a can of soda in his hand.

"Hey, Toby, great job, you've almost got us completely clear now. How about you go home and get some shut eye, you look washed out and you need to be on your 'A' game if something else crops up."

Toby rubbed his eyes wondering when he last slept. "Yeah, thanks Doug, sleep and a shower would be great. If it's okay with you I'll grab a cab home."

"Nobody's going to query your expenses Toby after the mess you've got them out of, go on hit the road. I'll call you if I need you."

Toby could feel his eyes starting to drop as the taxi pulled up at his parent's front door. Before he'd even turned his key in the lock his mother was hauling the door open and fussing over him in typical mother hen mode.

"Good god son, when did you last sleep, have you eaten anything, have you been a work all this time?"

"Yeah Mum, I know I'm working too hard but it'll all be over soon, for now I just need a hot bath and some sleep. Once I've had some shut eye I'll tell you what's been going on but a lot of it is under wraps...Official secrets act stuff...You know." He pecked her on the cheek, dragged his body up the stairs and run a deep hot bath. Fifteen minutes later he was in bed and asleep, his mind trying to process the last twenty four hours of information to be stored away or used in dreams. God his bed felt good.

Five hours later he was vaguely aware of the phone ringing and his mother rushing to answer it so as not to wake him. He went back to his erotic dream involving two naked twins fondling their boobs and trying to entice him into their bed. His hand was round his rock hard prick and he was enjoying the sensation.

"I don't care if he's sleeping Mrs Trelawney, the car is coming to pick him up in thirty minutes and if you don't open the door the officer will break it down. Do you understand? We need him back here now!"

"But he looks so tired and he's only had four hours sleep and goodness knows when he last ate properly, you'll kill him, you're nothing but a bunch of slave drivers!"

"Twenty nine minutes Mrs Trelawney, and make sure he's carrying a suit with him just in case we get called in front of the committee again."

"But he needs some food; he can't go out not having eaten."

"I'll get the driver to pick up a bacon sandwich and a mug of tea on the way for him, now Mrs Trelawney time is ticking...Twenty eight minutes."

She slammed the phone down, she really wasn't sure about this new high powered job and the demands it made on her precious little boy but she knew what he did was important, she crept up the stairs and gently shook him from his slumber interrupting a highly erotic dream that Toby was enjoying immensely.

"Mmm, aww Mum, what did you wake me for?"

"Your boss called he's sending a car in twenty seven minutes precisely and you have to be ready. He's even providing a bacon sandwich. Oh and he said pack your suit in case you get called up in front of the committee." She sat on the end of the bed waiting for him to get up.

"Umm Mum, I can't exactly get out of bed with you there...I'm not wearing anything." *Anything but a huge boner that is.*

As she left the room he grabbed a dressing gown to cover himself as he ran across to the bathroom. He hopped in the shower washed his hair and dealt with the immediate problem in hand. His orgasm was intense and made him light headed under the hot stream of water running down his back. He didn't have time to enjoy it, a quick wash over and he'd have to be on his way. He just hoped that all the rush wasn't because his plan had failed; it was all too easy to go from hero to zero in a matter of days or hours in this game. His thoughts strayed; *I've really got to find myself a girlfriend, I'll go blind at this rate.*

Dead on time the car turned up at the door, Toby was just about ready but his mother was fussing over him trying to get him to eat or at least have a cup of tea before he went. "No time mum, I've gotta run, I'll grab something at the office."

As Toby slid in to the back seat of the car the driver handed over a Styrofoam cup of milky tea with sugar and a warm bacon sandwich wrapped in tin foil. "Hey, I could get used to this, thanks!"

"Don't thank me thank your boss...seat belt on? Let's go then."

By the time the car pulled up in front of the office Toby had finished his bacon sandwich and tea and was feeling decidedly perkier. As he walked through the door the spring in his step was in direct contrast to Schneider whose earlier optimism seemed to have been beaten out of him. He looked down and defeated. Toby's eyes flicked to the screens on the wall, everything showed green, surely that was good news.

"Hey Doug, where's the fire? The screens look clean; it all looks in control from here." He was puzzled.

"Well there's good news and bad news...the good news is that the systems have all been restored and the bug seems to be dormant again. The bad news is this." Schneider handed over an email that had been printed out on a sheet of paper and gave Toby time to read it.

Warning!

An emergency code has been triggered due to Bridget Donovan or Jack Fitzgerald being unable to gain access to a computer. You are reminded of the consequences if they are unable to keep their data file safely locked away. All information held on people responsible for murders, locations of bodies, dates and times of clandestine meetings, payments to senior politicians and immunity letters granted by the UK government will become public in a pre- set timescale. You are encouraged to do everything within your power to find and release them before events become irreversible.

This is not an idle threat.

Bridget Donovan and Jack Fitzgerald

"Well Spock, what's the analysis? Do we need to run more tests or have you reached a conclusion?" Schneider was a bit of a Star Trek geek in his spare time and liked to parody the lines from the show.

"Shit, I don't think Spock ever used this term but I've looked at the data Jim and my conclusion is that we're fucked...there's no way we're going to find the data vault and securely move it in the next year let alone with a clock ticking. Sorry boss, we can try but the best course of action is to do everything in the government's power to find Bridget Donovan and Jack Fitzgerald and get them in front of a computer."

"Yep, I've got to agree with you kiddo but it seems that a hastily convened committee would like to hear it from the horse's mouth. Suit up and let's go deliver the bad news."

"Have I got long enough to run a tracer on the email source?"

"You can try again but we've failed miserably so far, it's coming from an address called @EMERGENCY but the IP address is dynamic and the message bounces all over the place before it's finally delivered. The closest we can get to a location is somewhere in Russia."

The Committee were sat in the same room with the huge wooden doors and old fashioned wooden panelling. Once again Doug and Toby were sat outside waiting for the usher to come and collect them. The debate inside was heated and regularly getting out of control if the banging of the gavel and shouts of order were anything to go by. Toby despised it. Why did politicians have to act like a bunch of spoilt kids? If this was their reaction to a crisis god help everyone if the country ever went to war. His thoughts were interrupted by the doors being swung open. "The committee will take your evidence now Sirs."

How about that? This time I'm a sir.

The questions came thick and fast and Doug as last time took most of the flack without involving Toby and emphasising the excellent job that the team had done to date in getting the government systems restored and faces of ministers off of the screens. Despite the positive spin the crowd were not appeased.

A senior civil servant stood and virtually waved the printed email in Toby's face. "And what have you got to say young man, not so cocky now I see! A spark coursed through Toby's veins, he'd had enough. He stood and approached the Chairman pushing Doug's hand away as he tried to hold him back. Helga Iron pants was to the side of the Chairman as one of the stenograph operators recording the discussion word for word. She winked at him and mouthed "Go on, you tell'em." The Chairman raised an eyebrow but didn't tell him to go back to his seat.

Assuming that he had carte blanche Toby took a deep breath and stared the civil servant down. "Mr Sullivan, it's not my job to hold you to account for your past indiscretions but shouting and screaming at me because you're worried your rubber fetish will be spread all across the papers for all to see isn't helping matters. You've made your bed and now you've got to lie in it." Sullivan stood red faced about to release a tirade or abuse before the Chairman waved him back to his seat and indicated for Toby to continue.

"Doug and I have our teams working their arses off trying to find the data store and stop the information being released. I've had less than two hours to think about it but I'll give you the same answer that I gave Doug when he asked for my analysis. It's pretty simple." He paused for effect. "If you don't find Bridget Donovan and treat her nicely, many of the people in this room and many of our so called governmental leaders are fucked." He looked across to Helga. "Have you managed to get that Helga or would you like me to repeat it? Get every resource you have targeted on finding and releasing Bridget Donovan or your dirty secrets will be out in the wash and you'll all be fucked. That's F U C K E D for those hard of hearing. Now if you don't mind I've got work to do rather than standing around with my thumb up my arse shouting at people and achieving absolutely feck all." He walked out of the room and collected Doug on the way. You could hear a pin drop and Helga trying hard to stifle a snigger.

Doug and Toby walked back initially in silence until Doug could hold his tongue no more. "You know Toby, I think that was more Scottie than Spock, direct to the point and laced with emotion, just the sort of thing that he would say." His commentary and thought process was interrupted by Toby's phone.

"It's just a message... from Iron pants no less... Here listen to this...

Toby,

Way to go, keep telling it as it is!!

Wish you and Doug could have been a fly on the wall after your dramatic exit. It's one of the only times I've seen a bunch of politicians dumb struck. #Hilarious.

Helga. Xx"

"Well somebody enjoyed the show. I expect I'll get fired soon but who wants to work for such a bunch of tossers? Time to get back to the grindstone eh, Doug?"

Chapter 34
Preparation For Manoeuvres

WITH JACK SPEEDING HIS WAY towards Northholt Tony took charge of planning their trip to Ireland and working out which skill sets the boys had ,apart from being specialists in psychotic violence, that he could use.

"Right boys chip in with ideas at any time but these are some of the basics we're going to need. Firstly we need to find a model aeroplane shop, not the sort of crap little things that you see kids flying but one that sells the sort of semi-professional bits of kit that you see grown men playing around with."

A huge grin broke out on Tommy's face here was a question he could answer. "Here Frank, ain't there a shop in Barking that does that? The old geezer Barney from down at the allotments, he flies a mock up of a spitfire and a Lancaster bomber don't he? I'm sure he said he got the kits in Barking. What d'ya need Tony, we can swing by on the way home to get some gear."

"We need a top of the range quad band transmitter and receiver that can control up to twenty different models. It's a serious bit of kit and you'll need matching receiver units to go into the models. I'm guessing but I'd expect that you pay anything up to seven hundred quid. Tell the shop that it's a sixtieth birthday present for your uncle to upgrade his models with. Make sure you get ten matching receivers just in case."

"No problem."

"Right, transport, what are we going to do about transport? We don't want to stick out too much; we need to look as if we're going on holiday."

"Let's take the Discovery. If we chuck some golf clubs or fishing rods in the back we can say that we're doing a recky for a stag do later in the year."

"Good idea Frank."

Tommy looked set to explode. "You can fuck off Frank! You ain't blowing my Landie up."

"Don't be a fucking donut Tommy. We ain't blowing up our own cars we'll just nick what we need when we're out there. We need to take some false plates wiv' us that match up to silver Ford Focus cars, local plates as well as UK ones, there's always loads of Fords around and they're easy to nick. Fink you can remember how to do it Tommy, been a long time since you've done time for stealing cars." Frank laughed heartily knowing that a bit of goading would wind Tommy up no end.

"Fuck off Frank! I can nick anyfing and you know it."

"All right calm down boys. That sounds like a plan. We'll go over in the Disco, chuck a couple of fly rods in the back and take some plates that match up with silver Ford cars. Now what time can you get it all done so that we can catch a ferry? There's about four or five a day from Holyhead and we can work out our route once we're aboard. We also need to pick up some trench spades and metal detectors. Tell people we're going along the beach to find treasure. I'll get some from the local army surplus store. Time's a wasting boys, you get on the road and get the bits we need and I'll see you at your gaff in say four hours time?"

"Yeah, okay Tony, we'll see you then. You need the postcode?" He nodded "Write it down for 'im Tommy if you can remember how to write." Tommy's patience with Frank was wearing thin as he glared back at his brother.

With the boys heading back to London Tony looked more carefully at the information Jack had provided. The ordnance survey map had five separate stashes of explosives and guns marked on it. Helpfully he'd put them in order of risk or difficulty in retrieving them. He'd also written a name next to one of them at a church - Reverend O'Brien. The list of targets was equally clear. Stage one was all about causing collateral damage and setting a few hares running, stage two if Tony and the boys were prepared to go that far involved blowing up one or two specific targets. The decision didn't need to be taken now; they could see what the lie of the land was first.

Tony walked back to his house and phoned Freddie excusing himself from work for a few days. With his recent visit to rehab and his psychological problems Freddie wasn't expecting much from Tony, he'd even tried to persuade him to go away on holiday so was pleased to hear that he'd decided to take a short trip. He promised that he'd be hands on for the next week. Excuses made he set about pulling together some clothes to throw in a holdall, digging his fly rods and reels out of the shed and hopping up into the loft to pick out a few choice bits of kit left over from his army days. He laid everything out on the coffee table to check before setting off and could already feel the tension building and an internal argument starting in his head. *Dr Jones, where are the notes from Doc Jones? I'm going to have to do the exercises every day and try to keep things in check, we don't want more flashbacks and problems do we Tony? Nope, let's concentrate on the here and now. That's fine to say you stupid fuck but you're putting yourself back in the front line....But it's for Jack, we'd be dead if it wasn't for Jack.....We could end up dead all over again after this, when are you going to listen to me you stupid arse. I'm not listening, I'm listening to Dr Jones, go back to the dark recess of my mind, you're not wanted...*

By the time Tony started driving up the A13 past the Dartford Tunnel exit and up towards Silvertown the argument raging in his mind had been won. He was going to enjoy giving the Irish some of their own medicine. Bridget's kidnap just gave him an excuse. Maybe, just maybe this would be the best treatment he'd ever have....revenge....yes, revenge would help calm the voices, then he could hold his head high. The sat nav voice chimed out telling him it was time to turn towards the river, Joel might have graduated to the nicer Essex suburbs but the boys still lived on the tough streets that they grew up on. It wasn't a good area and the fact that the boy's Discovery, Range Rover and Mercedes sat outside their house untouched and unmarked was testament to the universal fear they engendered in the community. Thinking that it was all fear driven though was missing the point the Helsdon family supported the local community hall, the boys went to the boxing club whenever they could to give boxing lessons, they'd even go to the youth club and play the odd game of pool. It was all about building respect for your elders and your community. Nobody in Silvertown would dream of grassing on them. They were unlikely pillars of the community.

Frank and Tommy were packed and ready to go but insisted that Tony checked the kit that they'd bought from the model shop, there was a collective sigh of relief when Tony gave it the thumbs up. It would definitely do the job. Before heading out of the door Tony gave the boys a quick once over.

"Do you boys own anything but Levi's, Dr Martins and Ben Sherman shirts? You know something a bit more causal, even if you wore a puffa Jacket rather than the Crombie coats."

"There ain't nuffing wrong wiv the way we dress Tony. We'll chuck a couple of hoodies and trainers in the back just in case but trainers are for boxing and Doc's or Royal Brogues are for outside. Ain't you been dragged up proper?" Tony could see that he wouldn't win and accepted the concessions made.

Loaded up in the Disco they headed along the Limehouse link going against the heavy traffic of commuters starting to head home, Frank knew the roads well and cut up to the North along Grays Inn Road before hitting the traffic heading west just past Kings Cross Station. The end of evening traffic heading out of London was a drag and it really didn't start to get moving until they passed the Polish War memorial along the A40; Jack had departed from the airfield some two hours earlier and was now heading to Brazil via the BVI with Martin, Bashar, Lynette, and Millie with a cute looking nanny in tow to look after her while Lynette sorted out the business matters. Tony gave a small salute as he passed Northolt. *We're on our way Jack, revenge will be ours. Oh yes sweet revenge for all of our pain. Tony shook his head. Focus Tony, focus.*

The traffic didn't ease and it was getting on towards nine o'clock when they pulled over into the M6 services at Sandbach for a pee break and a burger. Tony had hoped that they would make better time so that they could get the very early ferry that left about two forty in the morning. They might be lucky if the traffic thinned out. After being ripped off for a greasy burger and luke warm chips served by a spotty kid who kept wiping his nose on his sleeve they got back on the road and started to make good time along the A55 regularly clocking over the hundred mark with Tommy driving.

Frank was getting agitated. "Slow the fuck down Tommy, we ain't supposed to draw attention to ourselves and you've set every fucking speed camera in the county off."

Tommy just grinned at him clearly pleased with himself. "Who's the clever one now then Frankie? Changed the fucking plates didn't I...someone'll have a lot of explaining to do, and they'll get a fine for the poxy London congestion charge." Tony was sat in the back and a smile spread across his face even though his eyes were shut as he tried to catch some sleep. The banter between the boys was comforting, the constant little digs and laughs took him back to his army days, it was just like being out on ops. He opened his eyes to see signs for Rhyl flashing by while glancing at his watch; there was a good chance with Tommy driving that they would make the ferry with time to spare and be at their rented cottage between Dublin and Belfast by lunchtime tomorrow. The cottage looked ideal and he just hoped that the pictures on the website hadn't been too doctored; mind you he had talked to the owner who seemed like a nice guy. He was going to make sure they had basic supplies including everything needed for a fry up left in the fridge. Tony smiled to himself. The preparation for manoeuvres had gone well, very well indeed.

Chapter 35
Riding To The Rescue

JACK BOARDED THE GULFSTREAM G5 which Bashar was considering adding to his portfolio as a new toy. With the ability to fly non-stop for six thousand five hundred nautical miles,-Singapore, San Francisco-Moscow New York and Tokyo were all in reach without the need to refuel that and the latest sophisticated technology made it a highly desirable plane. Then again for fifty million dollars it should be sophisticated. From his seat at the back he found himself looking on enviously at Bashar, Lynette and Millie all playing happy families. *It could have been me, I've found the woman of my dreams and she's been snatched away.* The rumble of the jet on the slotted runway as it taxied into take off position shook him from his melancholy. *He had to focus, rest then focus if he was to find Bridget.* As clearance for take-off came through from the control tower the jet took off on runway two five heading on a south westerly track towards the congestion of Heathrow airspace requiring the pilot to execute a sharp right turn at seven hundred feet almost immediately after take-off. The plane continued to climb as it tracked towards Henton and then on to Compton before banking left to head out across the Atlantic and attain its desired cruising height. It was child's play for the pilot and co-pilot with a heads up navigation display on the screen.

Captain Lockwood was a bit of a George Clooney lookalike and an annoyingly good sportsman able to pick up a bat, racquet or golf club and play with ease. His only impediment was his bizzare nickname of 'Lockcock' that had followed him round for years. He claimed that the name started after a trip to Singapore where the taxi driver couldn't pronounce his name but the cabin crew from his early flight days had an alternative story involving a young air hostess and a visible problem that he did his best to deny. With the plan now at cruising height and in relatively clear airspace due to its ability to fly as high as fifty one thousand feet Lockcock set the autopilot, double checked the routing and handed over to his first officer before walking in to the cabin to check on his guests. He'd flown with Martin a few times and knew not to ask too many questions but he was intrigued by the interaction between his passengers. A small happy family group, a young woman that he assumed was a nurse or a nanny and the big Irishman who seemed agitated or distracted. There was a strange bond between them all but he struggled to see the common theme or thread. He would have to tread carefully and ask a few questions out of professional interest after all as he was heading on to Rio tomorrow, it would be interesting to know why.

The strong headwinds over the Atlantic had slowed the flight slightly more than planned meaning that they were due to land at Road Town or Lettsome International airport Beef Island at dusk. The information for the airport was fairly explicit with a bold red letters warning- "Caution. Night operation should only be attempted by pilots familiar with the airfield." - Lockcock was unconcerned the G5 was very well equipped; he had his head up display and EVS (an enhanced visual system that gave him an infra red image of the runway). He was pretty confident that they would be able to fly straight in but after liaison with the Tower and his Navigation display showing red and magenta which warned of severe turbulence and precipitation he was forced to use the airports non directional beacon and follow the strange figure of eight configuration where you overfly the airport outbound before turning coming back over the runway by turning left and then banking hard right to line up with zero seven North West. It didn't matter what toys you had on board, the high ground all round rising up to seventeen hundred feet, a strong cross wind and heavy rain meant that you needed to be a skilled pilot.

Captain Lockwood's voice came over the intercom as calm and smooth although through the open cabin door Bashar could see him fighting with the controls and concentrating hard on trying to keep the plane as level as possible. "Could everyone make sure that your seatbelts are securely fastened and that Millie is strapped in tightly on someone's lap, I'm afraid we've hit a bit of a tropical storm and according to my instrumentation this is going to be a bumpy approach and landing. The tower have asked us to reroute but I've refused on the grounds of low fuel. In case you overheard that conversation I should say that it was a bit of a white lie I just didn't want you to end up somewhere where you didn't want to be. There's no need to worry, the plane is more than capable of handling the weather and Joe and I have been through far worse. Sit back and try not to worry. I would say enjoy the view but with sheet rain I'm afraid you won't see much.

The landing was indeed bumpy and the short runway forced heavier braking than normal but they were down and in one piece. When the door was opened the intensity of the storm shocked them all, the Captain had made it sound like a walk in the park. As usual Martin had chosen well.

Bashar, Lynette, Millie and Emma were ready to depart the aircraft while Captain Lockwood negotiated with the Tower to refuel and get a take-off slot. The Tower were adamant that the strip was closing for the night due to the weather. Lynette hearing the conversation looked up the number for Juan Rodriguez on her mobile and dialled.

"Juan? Nice to talk to you too. I'm sorry to cut in to your private time by ringing you at this hour Juan but we've just landed at Beef Island and some jobsworth in the Tower is refusing to refuel my plane to take a guest onwards to Brazil. He's not the sort of man I would want to inconvenience and I'm finding the whole episode very embarrassing. Are you able to pull any strings Juan, just for me? I really would appreciate it."

It was less than five minutes before the fuel tanker could be seen starting up and rumbling across the apron. A severely pissed off controller came on the radio and informed them that once they were refuelled they were cleared for take-off. Jack would be riding his metaphorical steed to the rescue in under an hour.

Chapter 36
Prison

THE BLACK VAN SLOWED in what Bridget assumed was heavy traffic, the effects of the formaldehyde were easing, she strained her ears trying to orientate herself, she knew she was no longer near to the sea as she couldn't smell the tang of salt in the air, the van bumped over a sleeping policeman or kerb and she could still hear cars and lorries whizzing past, maybe they were stopping. She could pick up the odd word being spoken by the driver and his accomplice from the similarities between Portuguese and Spanish. The van braked suddenly and she was flung forward landing heavily on her side. *Shit, that hurt...just wait until Jack gets hold of you bastards, your lives won't be worth living, huh, wait till you see how inventive my torture chamber can be....arseholes!*

Bridget's bravado waned as the rear doors were opened and heavy hands grab her arms, she kicked out with her feet hearing a satisfying grunt as she made contact. "Lady, you struggle you get hurt...you understand?" She kicked out again and was rewarded with a slap round her face that stung even through the heavy fabric hood. She winced. *That'll be one hell of a shiner.* "Okay, okay, I get it! I'll come quietly."

"Sensible Lady, stand!" The ropes around her ankles were untied causing a rush of blood to her feet, she couldn't feel them properly. As she was lifted bodily out of the van onto a hard surface she stamped them on the ground trying to alleviate the horrible sensation of pins and needles coursing through her veins. "Hey bozo, slow up! I can't feel my feet!" The goons took no notice of her protests and manhandled her along a path and up some steps. She could smell mint and sage as they brushed against plants, she could also hear the sound of water tinkling. *A fountain?* She cursed not being able to see with the hood blocking all light and disorientating her. It sounded like a heavy door being opened at the top of the steps and her nostrils picked up the scent of damp plaster and brick work. Her nose twitched, the place hadn't been aired in ages, it was musty. She hoped that if this was to be her prison that she would have a window.

"Sit!" She was forcibly pushed backwards, landing on something soft and sprung. *A bed?* The hood covering her head was ripped off by one of the goons causing Bridget to shut her eyes as light flooded in from an open window. She blinked. *This is not good, if I can see their faces and they don't care then they intend to kill me. Goodbye Jack...*

"Right lady...you listen good...you do as you told and no problem." He walked across the room to the open window and held his arm out. "See the window? They have steel bars. The door has a twenty four hour guard, he watch you even when you sleep. No window in the bathroom, no escape you understand?" Bridget reluctantly nodded her head.

"Now you give me your rings and necklace." Bridget shrank back against the wall. "Easy way or I cut your finger off with them."

He was strutting round the room like a cockerel, twiddling her diamond necklace around his finger while he examined her solitaire ring making positive noises. She smiled to herself, he'd be in for a surprise when he tried to fence them...both were Mossinite; the originals were safely stored in her safe at home. *What should she do? Talk? Stay quiet? He seemed too pumped up from the heist to start a rapport at the moment. She needed time to think.* As if reading her thoughts he grabbed her chin and pulled her face close to his. The Stench of tobacco and decaying teeth almost made her retch.

"You behave lady and maybe you get home in one piece, no funny tricks. You sit, you wait. The gringo pays a ransom and it'll all be over."

She kept her voice level and cool. "You're making a big mistake...You've got no idea who I am have you?"

He slapped her face away catching her eye again. "I don't care who you are, as long as the gringo pays up." He stomped out of the room and called for his compatriot to sit outside the door on guard. It was then that Bridget noticed that the room and the bathroom had no doors. She really would be watched twenty four hours a day. The thought left her cold. *Come on girl, you've been through worse than this, toughen up, think positive.*

For the next hour Bridget sat with her arms wrapped around her knees and her back against the wall. She rested her head on her thighs feigning sleep while actually keeping one eye firmly locked in the direction of her doorman who seemed to spend an inordinate amount of time scrunching his crutch while looking directly at her. She filed the thought away; maybe, just maybe she could use her sexuality to help her get free. She stood and headed for the bathroom to see what his reaction would be. As she pulled down her jeans and underwear he appeared at the bathroom doorway to watch. Bridget scolded him "Go away pervert, I need to pee!" He laughed and stared straight back at her grabbing at his genitals as she crouched over the pan and peed. She really didn't care if he was watching or not, the only difference was that he wasn't paying unlike some of her clients in her previous life where people regularly paid for her to pee all over them while pushing her stiletto heel into their most sensitive parts. She made a show of disgust and went to slap him once she pulled her jeans back up. He caught her hand in mid-air and squeezed her wrist hard making her yelp.

"You behave lady and maybe we'll have some fun eh? I like you European girls; I'll show you how a Brazilian makes a girl happy."

Inwardly Bridget smiled to herself. If she played this right he might be her way out of here. The night time hours passed slowly and the lack of a breeze or air conditioning made sleep difficult. The smell from the garden was pungent, Angels Trumpets and Dame de La Noche. Someone must have loved the garden at some stage, she was sure that she had read somewhere that the herbs and flowers were planted to keep the worst of the mosquitos at bay. Although her eyes were closed each time she heard a movement or the chair by the door scraping she looked out from between her arms, it looked like the guards changed every four hours and she was concerned that her target might have been permanently replaced but he appeared again for the early morning shift. She went to the bathroom to wash and made sure that he had a good view of her ample breasts as she soaped under her armpits and washed behind her neck. She could see he was getting aroused. *Don't over do it Bridget. Slowly, slowly catchy monkey.*

"Hey Bozo, did you enjoy the show? Bring me some shampoo and a nail file and you might get to see more." She covered up and sat by the window looking out onto the fountain. The traffic was still noisy and sounds of construction or fabrication floated on the air, it was a strange mixture, why would a once loved house now surrounded by roads and industry? Her train of thought was interrupted by a plate of refried beans, tacos and salsa being delivered to her bed. At least they were trying to keep her fed, they clearly needed her alive for a while not that she could stomach food, her appetite just wasn't there. *Come on Bridget, eat something and calm down. You're going to need your strength at some stage.* She forced herself to pick at the salsa and taco. Her captor came in to take the plate away and she decided to try to spark up some conversation.

"Thanks, hey, what's your name?"

"You don't need names lady."

"Okay, if you don't mind I'll call you Jackson, you know...like Michael Jackson the singer."

He moonwalked back with the plate in hand clearly pleased with his new moniker not realising that Bridget had chosen the name because he was always playing with his dick just like Michael Jackson dancing in his videos or performing on stage.

"Pretty cool Jackson, I'm impressed. Don't forget now, shampoo and a file for my nails." Bridget held up her hand and mimicked filing on her finger. "This one's broken." She smiled confident that she was getting somewhere. She hoped that Jack was having as much luck tracking her down. Tears welled in her eyes as she thought of her lover, the man she wanted to marry and hopefully if they were blessed have kids with. He didn't care about her past he had just as many secrets. *Would he remember what to do, to send an email to her address with* @EMERGENCY *in the title line? It would set off a chain of events that could only be positive for them.*

Chapter 37
Political Pressure

EVEN WHEN THINGS ARE URGENT the wheels in the political world turn slowly. A briefing document on the outcome of the viral mess needed to be produced to go with the updated request for political assistance in tracing Bridget, things only picked up when one of the Prime Minister's assistants remembered being asked to keep an eye out for any updates and to brief him immediately anything came in. The request was unusual but as he had previously been the minister for Northern Ireland earlier in his career she just put it down to professional interest but the reaction she got when she took the papers in to him late that evening was not what she expected, clearly the story was important, it was the first time she had ever heard him swear out loud and look panicked, he was normally so calm and collected, at least outwardly.

"Get me the Foreign Minister and the head of MI5 here as fast as you can and get the Brazilian Ambassador on the phone so I can see what his movements are later in the evening, oh, and you better get hold of Nick our press officer, call him in as well."

One hour later the four men sat round the table at Downing Street. Jon Barnwell from MI5 brought the meeting up to speed on the information his team had gleaned at the committee stage and produced a concise briefing note which included profiles of the key players in the whole debacle. The likely information that the data file held wasn't divulged but rather was dealt with by one catch all line. *We believe the information secreted by Bridget Donovan would have a catastrophic impact on National security if inadvertently released*

Barnwell read out the highlighted line to emphasise his point before continuing. "The best course of action is as suggested by an analyst who gave evidence to the Committee. He was a feisty young thing, one to watch. He suggests we do everything in our power to find Bridget Donovan and secure her release and by everything he means everything."

"Can't we just impose a news black-out Jon, invoke National Security or something."

"And how's that going to work when our dirty secrets are spread all over the web Nick?"

"Okay, I take the point, I'm just thinking out loud, you know, throwing out a few ideas....What about shutting down the web in the UK?"

The Prime Minister snapped. "Jesus Nick for a supposedly intelligent man you can be as thick as shit at times. One it's the Worldwide Web for a reason and two it would shut the whole bloody country down. Even if it was technically possible we couldn't do it."

"Well what do we do then, we have to do something or we're screwed. Can we deny the reports if they do come out?"

"That might work for a day or two but we believe that Miss Donovan has arranged for the data to post to multiple sites and multiple agencies around the world. Her first little virus bomb which almost caused political meltdown in Northern Ireland and the Irish Senate has more than proved her skill. We have to find out who's kidnapped her and get to her fast."

"What resources do we have?"

"MI6 have around thirty active operatives in Brazil with ten in the Rio area, we've already put teams at GCHQ on alert and they're monitoring all internet chatter, nothing has shown up so far. As you know kidnapping in Brazil is fairly common and there are lots of gangs with different affiliations looking to make some money. It's not going to be easy."

"Do we blitz the media over there; you know see if we can flush them out and get them to dump her?"

"That's the last thing we want to do Nick. If she's seen as a hot potato they'll definitely dump her but with a ninety percent probability that they'll kill her first. If she dies her program goes into overdrive and the government gets brought down. We can use the MI6 team and we need to get the Brazilian secret service on side as well." Jon turned to the Foreign Secretary. "How are relationships Keith? Do you think that they'll help us?"

"Relations are cordial, I'm pretty sure that they'll help. It's too big a tourist destination to have a kidnap spread all over the media. We can have the Ambassador here within the hour if you can have the briefing pack ready to go."

The Prime Minister stood and paced the room. "Okay, Jon get the briefing packs finished and alert MI6, Keith arrange for the Ambassador to meet us here in an hour. Nick, forget you ever heard this conversation, if I as much as sniff it in the press or some MP's biography the Tower of London will be open for business again."

A knock on the door interrupted his train of thought. He'd asked not to be disturbed so it had to be important.

His assistant came in with five sheets of paper and handed them out to each of the men.

Tick tock, tick tock, who's checking the clock???

Bridget Donovan or Jack Fitzgerald are still missing.

The emergency code that has been triggered moves to phase two in twelve hours unless Bridget Donovan and Jack Fitzgerald gain access to a computer. You are reminded of the consequences if they are unable to keep their data file safely locked away. All information held on people responsible for murders, locations of bodies, dates and times of clandestine meetings, payments to senior politicians and immunity letters granted by the UK government will become public in a pre-set timescale.

Tick tock, tick tock, it's time for action not watching the clock!

Events will soon become irreversible.

Barnwell vented his anger. "Fuck that's all we need, what a bitch; she's really thought this through. Let's all get moving guys, it looks like we've only got twelve hours before all hell lets loose."

As the four men filed out of the office the Prime Minister picked up his private line and phoned his solicitor. "Oliver? It's James, I thought you might still be at the office. I have a bit of an emergency on the horizon. Can you arrange to move all of my assets into a trust or Janine's name tonight? Yes, yes I know it's a strange request and that it'll be difficult but I need it done tonight and in the utmost secrecy, I can't afford for this to leak Oliver and believe me nor can you." The veiled threat seemed to work and after five minutes discussing some of the detail the wheels were in motion for documentation to be made ready for signing first thing in the morning.

Chapter 38
Ashes To Ashes

STEVE CARTER WAS PLEASED with the progress they'd made to date, building the show homes was the easy part, the difficulty was in getting the infrastructure correctly planned out and built to a robust standard. In the past week they had put in three bore holes using a combination of a drilling rig and compressed air. As the drill bored through the soil and down into the sand and gravel mix the compressed air brought the scalping or drill waste to the surface pushing it out through a waste pipe. At only twenty meters deep water gushed out of the pipe, a very good sign. The gnarled old drill foreman put his hand in the gushing stream and brought some up to his nose before swilling it round his mouth.

"Muito boa, água mineral macio sem sal." Carter's Portuguese wasn't fluent yet be he understood the huge grin and Aqua Mineral. This would save them a fortune on desalination, the next two holes came up exactly the same much to his delight, and the high water table would also help his arguments about the level of water recycling required. He hoped to get away with seventy to eighty percent rather than the ninety percent that the Regional government was currently insisting on. They still took the bores down to one hundred and fifty meters by sleeving them with reinforced plastic pipe as they went but there were clearly aquafers underground just as the old boy had predicted. Carter had been convinced that this close to the sea that the water would be brackish but was happy to have been proved wrong.

His joy at saving a large part of the budget was short lived when he got into work the following morning. He was walking the site checking the various areas where concrete was due to be poured later in the day when he saw a hand sticking out of sand at the bottom of what was meant to be the foundation for a pumping station. He jumped down into the hole and carefully examined the huge gold bracelet dangling round the wrist. He'd seen it before somewhere. *Juan Garcia? It couldn't be...* He followed the direction of the arm and scraped away the sand where he assumed the head would be, he jumped back as he was met by Garcia's lined and pock marked face and a pair of open eyes staring at him accusingly. It was the eyes that made him jump, that and gas expelling from his mouth, he knew he was dead but he still scrabbled backwards until his back hit the cool earth wall behind him. "Fuck, fuck, fuck!! Jesus what do we do now? Fuck!" Bracing himself and swallowing in an attempt to stop his gag reflex he scooped up sand to cover the face and pulled down on the eyelids to shut the eyes. Touching the body was too much and he emptied the contents of his stomach while hanging on to the earth wall for support, sweat was rolling down his face even though the morning air was still cool and the sun was still low in the sky.

He hadn't signed up to deal with bodies and murder, *where was Paolo when he needed him?* He phoned his mobile willing him to pick up, *he'd dealt with the local mafia, surely he'd know what to do, at worst his language skills would help with the local officials.*

The screen icon turned green indicating that the phone had been answered and Steve immediately started to babble. "Paolo, its Steve, we've got a problem, a huge problem...you've got to get up here now...get the next plane."

Paolo was still sleepy. "For Christs' sake it's not even seven o'clock...It can't be that urgent Steve, call me at a sensible time...I didn't get to bed until four."

"I don't care a shit about your party lifestyle Paolo, we've got a problem, what's not urgent about finding Juan Garcia dead at the bottom of a hole that's about to have concrete poured in to it! What the fuck am I supposed to do?? Once the police get here then the whole place will get shut down... Bashar's team will go fucking mad."

Paolo was suddenly very awake. "Shit, okay, okay. Give me five minutes to make some calls and make sure nobody sees the body. Someone will get back to you."

"What do you think I am an idiot? I'll make sure that it's covered with a tarpaulin but as soon as the sun gets up it'll start to cook and the smell will get people talking, that and the flies that are starting to take an interest."

With the call disconnected Steve pulled himself together and walked back to the site office. It was coming up to half past six and some of his keener workers were starting to turn up. He grabbed two cups of coffee and walked over to his foreman handing him one as the guy pulled on his prized steel toe capped leather site boots. "Xavi, I just want to check out one or two things before you start pouring concrete. Don't start without me, keep the trucks at the gate and hold the boys off of the site until I say so." He hoped he'd bought himself enough time and that Paolo was pulling his finger out.

His mobile buzzed in his pocket and he headed into the office away from prying ears to take the call.

"Steve Carter?"

"Yes."

"This is Martin; I have the advantage that I know everything about you as I did the security check on you before you joined Bashar's team. We've met once briefly in London, you probably don't remember."

Steve searched his brain trying to focus. *Martin... Martin was he the balding wiry man he met at his final interview? I think so.* "Did I meet you at my final interview along with the big Irish guy?"

"Good memory Mr Carter. Now I understand that an operative has been sloppy and that you have a body on site. Correct?"

"Yeah, um yes, did Paolo call you? What am I supposed to do?" His thoughts took a while to catch up. "Umm sorry umm rewind a bit what do you mean by an operative being sloppy?"

"The operative comment is irrelevant. Now focus Steve you need to do your job... Pour the concrete and forget what you've seen. Make sure that nobody else sees the body, your workers are starting to turn up I assume."

Steve's voice went up an octave. "Yes, yes they are but I can't let them start pouring, the guys probably been murdered, I'd be an accessory to the crime."

"Exactly but it's preferable to joining Mr Garcia." Picturing him wavering Martin pressed on. "You are very well paid for what you do Mr Carter and you know that this is a money laundering operation...where else do you think your bonuses come from? Without even seeing the body I can predict that Mr Garcia was indeed murdered and as I said you wouldn't want to join him now would you?"

"No, no...I'm just paid to do my job...I know enough not to ask where the finance comes from. I'm straight up and down and I like to keep it that way...we'll have to call the police."

Martin shouted down the phone in his best drill sergeant voice shaking Steve to the core. "You're paid to do what you're fucking told Carter! Now man up and get with the program. You'll pour that concrete before eight o'clock this morning and you'll make sure that nobody else sees the body. If you fail, or if you crack up and call the police you'll be next along with your brother and Mother living at twenty seven West Street, Worthing. Do you understand me!?"

Carter sounded like a lonely little boy. "But, but what about the police?"

"Fuck the police. They're busy drinking coffee somewhere; it's too early for them to be up and about. Garcia fucked up. He crossed the line. Which side of the line are you on Carter? Our side the side of the living, or their side where you and your family will join the dead?"

Bile rose in Steve's throat and he just made it to the sink where the coffee he'd just drunk came back up, Martin could hear him retching; he'd clearly got through to him.

Fifteen minutes later the first cement truck pulled up and Steve made sure that it poured the first load making up the pump room floor straight over the tarpaulin. They were short on labour this morning, the local police and army reserves had all been called up by the Mayor, his foreman told him that something big had gone down five miles outside town. The rumour was a mass slaughter, a drugs gang war. As the depth of the concrete increased and the hand sticking up under the tarp was covered he said a little prayer...

"Ashes to ashes...dust to dust....."

Chapter 39
Paranoia

AS THEY DEPARTED TORTOLA late in the evening and reached cruising speed Captain Lockwood left the confines of the cockpit to talk with Martin.

"How we doing Captain?"

"Pretty good thanks Martin."

"I meant the predicted flight time?"

"Oh sorry, that's what I was coming back to tell you. With one or two small kinks that air traffic have put into our flying route and the strong headwinds we're encountering we've got around seven and a half to eight hours flying time before we're on the ground at Santos Dumont."

Jack opened an eye and sat up. "Can't we go any faster?"

"Sorry, unless you can change the wind direction the time is what it'll be. I'll update you nearer to Rio so you may as well try to get some shut eye. Landing is going to be around six thirty to seven in the morning."

Jack shook his head. He was struggling cooped up unable to do anything to save Bridget. He'd make sure that Dermot paid in full.

One hour out from Rio the co-pilot came through and gently shook Martin on the shoulder. Jack was wide awake, he must have slept at some stage but he felt like he'd been staring at the ceiling all night. "One hour to go guys, keep a look out, you should get a full view of the Guanabara Bay, Sugar Loaf Mountain and the Rio-Niterói Bridge today. You've got about fifty minutes to get yourselves together...coffee anyone?"

Captain Lockwood's timings were accurate and the co-pilot was right about the view. He'd also placated Jack slightly by telling him that by going in to Santo Dumont Airport he'd be arriving right in the center of Rio de Janeiro giving really fast access to the main hotels and tourist attractions; not that Jack had any interest in the sights, all he wanted to do was get on the ground and start doing something practical. *I'm coming sweetheart, I'll find you or die trying.*

The landing was smooth and efficient and Jack was craning his neck out of the window to see where arrivals were sign posted but much to his dismay the plane continued to Taxi by the transparent green arrivals and departure structure towards the far end of the airfield towards a waiting grey Range Rover sport which was pulled out onto the apron and had a customs officer standing beside it, clipboard in hand to check them through. Jack was elated; more time saved meant more time on the ground. Martin shook his head...*the old fox*...he was amazed at how Enrique had managed to get airside given the strict entry and insurance requirements; as usual somehow he'd managed to pull strings. He was first off the plane and walked down the steps with his holdall in his hand heading towards the car. As soon as his feet touched the concrete apron the car door opened and Enrique closed the gap to embrace him in a bearhug.

"Martin my friend, it has been a long time and we're both still breathing eh?" They held each other at arms length eyes locked together recalling their joint experiences and common bond before hugging once again. Jack held back recognising brothers in arms reconnecting after a time apart. As they broke their embrace Enrique turned to Jack and shook his hand.

"You must be Jack, I've heard a lot about you. You have all of my resources at your disposal to try to find your woman, any friend of Martin and Bashar is a friend of mine."

"Thanks Enrique, I've heard a lot about you too and I know if anyone can find her in this urban jungle it'll be you. I'm keen to start roughing up the local gangs to take my mind off things so I am. I take it you'll be able to provide some intel and equipment."

"Ah, straight to business...but to be expected, we can talk after we find her...Yes there's a small armoury in the back of the car, when we're away from the cameras you can fight over who gets what toys." He chuckled knowing that they would be like little boys in a sweet shop.

Enrique chatted rapidly with the customs officer before palming a pile of dollars in a handshake, the officer radioed ahead providing clearance from the airfield out of a side gate which brought them straight into the early morning traffic and workers heading to the tourist hot spots for another day of squeezing as many dollars as possible out of the holiday makers. The traffic although heavy was moving well but they had barely covered two miles when Martin picked up on Enrique checking the mirrors almost continually.

"Problems?"

"My friends, we seem to have a tail, he's sitting between six to eight cars back driving what looks like a white rental Chevy compact. Are either of you expecting company?"

Martin pulled the rear view mirror across to get a view of the car following them. "Are you sure Enrique? It seems odd given that we came in on a private flight. How would they know which airport we were coming into or what time we'd land? You're not being paranoid are you?"

"No, I'm sure he's tailing us, he's not that good at it either. Watch him while I make a few moves and see what he does." Enrique pulled out in to the outer lane and increased his speed. Five cars back the white Chevy accelerated to keep pace and mimicked the Range Rover. A switch to the inside lane saw the Chevy drop back two more cars and match the reduced pace.

"Looks like he's acting alone to me Enrique, I can't see any other vehicle playing tag with him. Stupid really, one on one you nearly always give yourself away."

Jack was getting antsy. "Stop the fecking car in a side road and I'll beat the shite out of him to find out what's going on. I haven't got time to play games no I haven't."

Enrique tapped the sat nav screen bringing up his phone directory. He scrolled down and selected a number. "Ricardo, fifteen minutes Calle Lima, at the back of the Hospital in Benfica, near the railway tracks where we have the lock up; have the stinger and an extract team ready. We have a white Chevy compact car on our tail with a single male occupant. I'm going to lead him on a little dance before we arrive, make sure you don't kill him Ricardo. We need him alive."

Ten minutes later they had entered the Benfica district and the tail was still with them. The traffic generated by a major hospital made it easy to stay a few cars back and the driver was blissfully unaware that he'd been spotted. His focus was solely on keeping Jack in his sights. The traffic thinned as Enrique took the right turn forced by the railway track dissecting the city, the Chevy was still with them but it looked as if he was being a bit more cautious maybe he was conscious that keeping under the radar was going to be difficult on the quieter streets. As the car followed Enrique let out a his breath that he'd been holding worried about the lack of traffic; they were too close to lose him now.

"Come to Daddy, just one more turn, don't give up now...Bingo he's hanging back but I'm pretty sure he's going to take the bait, I'll accelerate to give him some room."

The street had a mixture of cars, vans and trucks parked down one side and a number of small workshops and garage lock ups spilling out onto the pavement on the other. They passed two small garages, a pump repair business and a small carpentry store making bespoke cheap furniture expertly out of pallets by the looks of things. While not a salubrious area it was by no means dead beat and the fact that he might be driving straight into a trap didn't even cross the driver's mind. He concentrated on keeping space between himself and the Range Rover Sport ahead which seemed to have picked up speed pulling away from him into the industrial zone. He was focussed solely on the car ahead and as he drove past one of the garages although he was aware of someone kneeling down between parked cars he never saw the stinger with its three inch nails deploy. As the steering became heavy and the car started to handle poorly, things became clear all too late. An old VW pick up van with a huge bumper had trapped him from the back and the Range Rover was reversing up to him at speed. He looked around frantically, he had nowhere to go. Glass showered over him as the driver's window was smashed from the outside and a nine millimetre pistol was shoved against his head.

"Keep your hands on the wheel in plain sight and you won't get hurt." He was tempted to fight but as the passenger door opened he was greeted with a twelve bore pump action man stopper shotgun favoured by the American security forces held by a young punk. He'd see what a mess they made of people and his bravado quickly evaporated, surrender was the best course of action.

He raised his fingertips but kept his palms flat against the wheel hoping his captors would see his supplication. "Okay, okay, take it easy, I give up... my wallet's in my Jacket pocket and I've got a Browning pistol in a shoulder holster, take what you want just don't shoot me." The pressure from the pistol held against his head relaxed as the driver's door was pulled open and he was unceremoniously yanked out by his collar while his head was being pummelled by a big Irish fist. Martin had to pull Jack off of the guy before he did too much damage.

"Ease up Jack; we need information, not a body, get him inside, the streets have too many eyes and ears."

A young punk grabbed the man wrenching his arm up behind his back forcing him to walk with a stoop in through the up and over roll up door which was quickly closed behind them. The driver noted the concrete floor which had a mixture of oil patches, bits of metal and broken pallets strewn across it and what looked like a half dismantled car in one corner. He driver was forced to the back of the lock up come workshop where he was forced to sit on a plastic backed chair with blood dripping down his white shirt from the cuts around his eyes and his spouting broken nose. Martin searched through his Jacket pulling his passport and wallet out before inspecting them. His face lit up with a wry grin and he had to force himself not to laugh. "Hmm, Nigel Smith, not very original is it? Who do you work for Mr Smith? Freelance or government?"

The driver remained tight lipped as martin walked slowly round him in a circle forcing his eyes to try to follow him. "Whatever they've taught you about torture and being able to hold out for a day at least, forget it, we can do this the easy way or the hard way."

The driver shook his head which made Jack lunge forward, he was on his feet looming over the man and about to strike him again. "I'll not be listening to speeches Martin, if he knows where Bridget is he'll be telling me now." Jack hit the guy twice before standing back and lighting a cigarette. He dragged hungrily on it making the tip glow before ordering two of Enrique's men to help.

"You...hold his head and you keep his fecking arms out of the way." The man's head was pulled backwards roughly so that he was looking up at the ceiling. Jack sucked on the cigarette again and flicked the ash before pushing the glowing butt into one of the cuts at the side of the eye causing the driver to scream with pain. He threw the butt down and lit another cigarette before holding the glowing end less than an inch from the man's Iris.

"Now then sonny boy...you don't need your eyes to talk and I'll burn them out one by one unless you start talking. Why were you following us and what do you know about the whereabouts of Bridget Donovan?"

Smith gritted his teeth in defiance. "I've nothing to say and even you're not that much of an animal. I've got diplomatic immunity, my real passport's in the lining of my suit, you can't do this, you'll start an International incident."

"Oh, will I now....Do you think I give a fuck?" Jack took a deep drag and flicked the ash again before ramming the burning end into the corner of the man's eye searing his tear duct and blistering the eyeball but leaving his vision intact. Smith's body went stiff as the shock tore through him, sweat ran down his face and he was panting loudly. Jack now had his full attention. "I don't care a fuck about Diplomatic immunity. You'll tell me what I want to know or you'll be blind and castrated in the next twenty minutes. What's it to be?"

Martin was wincing, the smell of burning flesh assaulting his nostrils. Jack was a man in a hurry; subtleness didn't appear in his dictionary. He stepped in as the voice of reason to encourage Smith to talk placing his hands on his knees and leaning in to him in a conciliatory manner. "My pal here is mighty pissed off and he's going to get the information out of you one way or the other. I'm guessing he didn't blind you deliberately because he'll make you watch as he chops bits off you, always keeping you alive, never going so far as to cause your body to shut down or to cause a heart attack. It's not a subtle technique but it's effective, and believe me he is a master." He stood again signalling that the nice guy talk was over. "Now let's start again shall we....Are you freelance or Government?"

Pain continued to sear through Smith's eye, he took a deep breath and thought rapidly, it wasn't as if he would be giving away National secrets. He reached his decision quickly not wanting to suffer more pain. "Government... I work for MI6 and was asked to tail you from the airport to see if we could get any leads on who has Miss Donovan." He paused hoping he'd given enough until Martin motioned with his hand for him to continue. "The whole network is on alert and the Brazilian forces should be joining the manhunt some time tomorrow. That's all I know, nothing more, I promise....please, please some cold water for my eye...save my eye."

Martin was not impressed. "Ah fuck! That's all we need a bunch of toffs playing at being spies, you could end up getting her killed. Is Barnwell still at MI5?"

A glass of cold water was tipped over the burn reliving some of the burning sensation. "Yes, he heads it up."

Martin moved towards the front of the lock up and indicated for Jack to come with him. "I think he's telling the truth Jack but give me a few minutes to make a call."

He dialled a number on his cell that put him through to Thames House in London, as soon as the operator picked up he started talking. "This is Martin; Delta, Foxtrot, two nine two zero Whisky. Patch me through to Jon Barnwell immediately please."

There was a slight delay before the operator came back on the line. "I'm sorry Mr Martin but your code is not showing as active, can anyone else help."

"I'll hold, contact his PA, he'll take the call; tell him the life of an agent depends on it."

Martin walked up and down listening to the piped music being played whilst he was on hold. It seemed to take an age until it suddenly stopped and a gruff voice could be heard at the other end. "Martin, this is highly unusual. I'm only taking the call as our intelligence says that you were heading for Brazil and I don't believe in coincidences."

"I'll get to the point Barnwell. Some dipshit toff from MI6 claiming to be Nigel Smith followed us from the airport and is currently bound to a chair enjoying the delights of having his eyes burnt out. Now tell me straight. Do you have any information as to the whereabouts of Bridget Donovan or do I just let the locals kill him?"

"I'm sorry Martin; I didn't know that they were going to tail you or that you were even involved, I assume that someone's hired you to recover Miss Donovan... they must have deep pockets." He paused expecting a response but Martin remained silent. "Look Martin, MI6 have been put on alert and are actively trying to trace Miss Donovan, the Brazilian services will hopefully join in on the search later today. It's being kept as a news blackout but as you can imagine we have to be seen to be trying to do our best."

"Call them off Jon, your amateurs will just get in the way. I've got one of my teams here and I have excellent local support, the best there is, I don't want the waters muddied."

"I wish I could call them off but the order comes from the top."

"Well don't blame me if you end up with collateral damage, you've been warned." He terminated the call and turned to Jack. "He's telling the truth, they haven't got a clue and were just following you hoping to get a lead. I've told them to keep out of our way." He raised his voice and shouted to the other end of the garage. "Enrique, can you get one of your boys to deliver Mr Smith to casualty at the Benfica hospital, we don't really want to damage British Government property unless we have to." He was walking down towards the driver who was breathing easier having heard the news. He leaned over him and spoke quietly. "You've been lucky today Mr Smith. We're here for less than seven days and I suggest that you and your Public School colleagues keep out of our way. We'll deal with it far quicker than you can. Now, just remember to answer the questions next time and you'll end up with a lot less damage. One of the guys will take you straight to casualty and they should be able to repair the burns enough so that it doesn't bother you too much in the future. Just remember keep out of my way unless I call you...you are now mine... you owe me your life and I will call in the favour."

Chapter 40
Playing The Fish

TIME WAS PASSING SLOWLY for Bridget, she'd been here for two nights now, the food, if that was how you could describe it, was crap, the company was dull and staring out of the window hoping beyond hope that Jack would come for her was all that was keeping things together for her. Jackson hadn't been around for a whole day and she was beginning to doubt her plan. *What if he didn't come back? The other guards don't seem to have any interest. Could I over power them? If there is a god out there I know I've never been a believer but I promise I'll be good, just spare me and I'll be good.*

She could hear raised voices in the other room. From the tempo and from catching the odd word she was pretty sure that it was an argument about her but she couldn't get any detail, her Portuguese language skills were non-existent. *Why couldn't they speak Spanish or English?!!* She could recognise Jackson's voice, the boss and one other, she thought that money was being mentioned, that they weren't getting enough but she wouldn't pin her hopes on it, she could be entirely wrong. *Would it be worth offering to pay them more?* The argument ended as quick as it started and Jackson appeared in the door with his boss.

"Well pretty lady. The boss man he have some questions...you answer good then no problems. .you no answer..." He held his hands out to his side and shrugged. "He have a very bad temper, not possible for me to save you."

Stench breath strutted across the room pulled back his hand and slapped the side of her face sending her sprawling on to her side on the bed, it seemed to be his standard mode of operation. She gritted her teeth and sat back up staring straight into his pock marked face, she wasn't going to flinch or cry it would give him too much satisfaction. Hitting women seemed to get his rocks off. As she stared back at him she could see anger and hate in his dark eyes, making her flinch and feel less confident. *Is he going to kill me now?*

"You think I'm a fool?!" He raised his hand again... Slap. *Ouch, that one hurt?*

She couldn't stop the wise crack. "I've never said that but if that's what you think."

He wasn't impressed grabbing her hair as a lever he pulled her face close to his causing her to gag at the smell of his halitosis. "You think you funny girl eh? Palm off fake diamonds on me." He threw her back onto the bed. Things were not going well.

With her arms covering her head expecting the next strike she spat out her words. "I didn't say they were real!" The expected strike didn't come; instead he took a few steps back and spoke in a softer voice.

"Who are you lady? Why we have people asking questions trying to find you?"

Bridget's heart leapt with the mention of people asking about her. *Jack, you're here, come find me my darling.* She took a deep breath and sat back up composing herself to talk evenly and without emotion. "I told you that you had no idea who you were messing with. You need to let me go before all holy hell rains down on you."

"Ha, not without my money bitch, maybe I ask for more...they pay more for you now eh? Lots of people asking questions, what your gringo expect...he think I forget that he owes lots of money?"

Bridget flew to her man's defence. "Jack doesn't owe money to anyone; he's his own man, a proper man who would never hit a women!"

Confusion flitted across Stench breath's face. "Who the fuck is Jack? Your gringo owes the money, your gringo with the big beach development. Why he no pay!?"

Bridget was deeply confused. "Which Gringo, Jack Fitzgerald?"

The man had heard enough and spat on the floor. "Don't play games lady."

The dismissal of Jack's name made Bridget feel sick, she started breathing hard. *Oh no, no...please let him be wrong...how could she be mixed up with someone else's mess.* Things were worse than she thought. *God help me.*

As a final thought she shouted as he was about to leave the room. "I work with the Irish and British Governments. They'll be trying to trace me". *Please Jack... please god you've sent the @EMERGENCY email.*

He seemed unimpressed. "Fuck your Governments. Your Gringo pays up or you die..." He turned on his heel leaving Bridget with tears of desperation running down her face. *How could she have been kidnapped in error, surely they meant to kidnap someone else. They must be wrong, it had to be Dermot, he had all sorts of investments in Brazil, he had to have issued the order. It had to be Dermot.*

Once Stench breath had left the room Jackson walked over to her with a face cloth soaked in cold water. She took it from him and held the cooling material against her rapidly swelling face. “Thanks Jackson, I appreciate it.” She looked up into his eyes and fluttered her eye lashes at him while licking her lips making them shine. As he moved towards her she turned away timing it perfectly

“Pretty lady, your man needs to pay...” He wandered out of the room before coming back with a small bag that he placed on the bed. “Present.” Bridget opened the bag and her spirits lifted...shampoo and more importantly an emery board nail file, she couldn’t use it as a weapon but she could fashion one from it. By the time she’d looked up Jackson was gone replaced by a cocky youngster who clearly thought that guarding a woman was beneath him. The shower would have to wait until Jackson was back but she could start on her nails once she’d freshened up and wiped away her tears.

Come on Bridget, your stronger than this, you can do this.

Chapter 41 Play-doh

DEPARTING THE FERRY at Dublin Frank drove the car along Terminal Road while Tommy played with the sat nav trying to get the cottage address to register without much luck. He handed the unit over the back seat to Tony who found the village and stuck that in as the destination address, he was sure they could ask and get exact directions once they were in the locality. It took them a while but eventually they got onto the M1 heading North past Drogheda before turning off at Dundalk and heading for the railway station car park. It was an ideal hunting ground for what they wanted, a pay and display car park with most of the cars belonging to commuters which, with luck, meant it would be six or seven hours before a theft was reported. Frank drove up and down the car park as if looking for a space before dropping Tommy off next to a silver Ford Focus. He pulled a tennis ball cut in half out of his pocket placed it over the lock and hit it with the palm of his hand. The door locks made a satisfying "Pop" sound as they cycled open. Tommy opened the door, slid inside and set about starting the car by ramming a stubby screwdriver into the lock, finesse was not something he knew much about but he had cut his teeth on older Fords and knew how to get them running quickly. One adjustment on the lock barrel and the engine turned over leaving him plenty of time to stick his false UK plates over the Irish ones and drive away.

Tony and Frank were sat in a layby on the A37 road heading towards Castleblayney. The green fields and dark grey lochs coupled with a stark blue sky had a serene effect on every traveller and Frank was no exception. It was his first time in Ireland and having never taken much notice of the years of terrorism to him it was idyllic; a massive contrast from the grey drab streets that he'd been brought up on next to the Thames and industry in London.

"It's lovely Tony ain't it? Why would anyone cause trouble living in a place like this?"

Tony shrugged and shook his head. "It would be lovely if they hadn't spent the last fifty years blowing the shit out of each other all over their religious and nationalist ideals. Now it harbours too many ghosts and grudges...then again I say fifty years but it goes back even further if you read the history books. But keeping it simple the Catholics wanted a united Ireland and an end to perceived discrimination from the predominantly protestant government and authorities in Northern Ireland and the Protestants wanted to keep things as they were, remain part of the UK and keep control. It's always the same shite Frank...people are never happy with their lot in life. Anyway it wasn't long before it got bloody, so yeah it's pretty but it has a very dark underbelly." *Fucking bastards, it's time to get even Tony, they killed your mates, it's time to put up, do your bit. Shut up I'm not listening to you... not, not not...*

Tony took a deep breath and focussed on the exercises that he'd been given by the Doc. Maybe it was a mistake putting himself back in the firing line but as far as he was concerned he owed it to Jack, debts had to be paid his Dad had taught him that at a young age. He started to focus. *Breathe in breathe out, breathe in breathe out.* As he pulled himself back to the present his mind flitted to a conversation from years ago. He turned to Frank to share his wisdom.

"You know what a builder told me once Frank? Irish guy he was living in England next door to me for a while. Showed me a picture of his place in Ireland, bloody fantastic it was with a lovely view over one of these lochs that we're passing. I asked him why he left such a beautiful place, so he turns to me all serious like and he says...'You can't eat the view'...Now that was deep and it's still a problem today despite all the wealth created by joining the European Union. Ironic in't?"

A small silver Ford car pulled in behind them and flashed its headlights. Frank put his thumb up so the driver would see. "Looks like Tommy remembered how to do it then...better get the map out Tony, I don't trust this sat nav over here...right then onwards and upwards as they say."

As they drove Tony was monitoring the sat nav and reading the local map while still chatting about Ireland, despite multi-tasking somehow he managed to spot a sign coming up. "Hang on Frank, there's a sign to the village; turn right here, it should be a couple of miles up the road just across the border, slow up and make sure that Tommy's still on our tail or the donut will end up back in England."

Ten minutes later they were parked outside the local store which was typical of the small shops you found in the small villages of Ireland doubling up as the pub, post office and local café. Frank wandered in for directions and was soon hanging out of the door waving at the guys to come in. The owner had insisted that the trio had a pot of tea and some toast slavered in thick melting butter. "Rory'll be along in a minute to show you to the cottage so he will. Anything you need you can get from here, I've even got some flies and fishing gear out the back if you want to try your hand at the trout or pike." He disappeared and came back with a weird looking fluorescent pink lure with a massive head and large hook which he wiggled in front of them. "See...the Pike love 'em, you have to learn how to cast them though but I'll teach yer if ye hire me as yer ghillie."

Rory they were told was the local farmer who'd branched out into holiday let's to supplement his income from his dairy herd. When he appeared at the door was exactly what they were expecting, a big guy with ginger hair wearing a boiler suit with god knows what spread down it and wellington boots that definitely needed a wash. Thankfully he left them outside with the tractor while proceeding to enjoy the craic with his new found friends so much so that it still took them the best part of an hour to get out of the store. The hospitality was wonderful but they really wanted to get on, Tony's inner demon was getting twitchy, he'd spent too many nights as a sniper hidden close to the border and too many nights on patrol where he was the target; memories were starting to wash over him. He needed to take action, to get moving, tonight was his plan if possible. *Breathe in, breathe out, relax Tony, breathe in breathe out...We'll sort it Jack.*

The cottage was great, three double bedrooms, a big open kitchen diner and a cosy lounge with a huge wood burner and a full length window looking out towards a small loch. Frank was in raptures.

Tony was becoming decidedly grumpy and had to have a little dig. "Just remember Frank, you can't eat the view."

An hour later the boys were unpacked and ready to hit the road. Frank and Tommy were heading off to see

Reverend O'Brien and Tommy was nominated to ride one of the cottage bikes back in to the village to get a few more supplies. He could have taken the Disco but when in Rome as they say. The lanes all looked the same as they drove along the bumpy roads trying to find the church. Tony had deliberately chosen the cottage as it was less than six miles from the first store but he hadn't reckoned on the twisty turning lanes. It took them a good fifteen minutes to get there what with stopping to get their bearings on a regular basis. The church was stone built and surprisingly large given that there weren't that many houses in sight. Someone years ago must have paid for its construction. As they walked through the gates along the path to the front door the gravestones gave away some of the history with dates back as far as the fifteenth century and common surnames repeating over time. The heavy oak door creaked on its hinges as they pushed it open acting as a doorbell for the vicar who stuck his head out of the vestry. He was short, spectacled, and had thinning grey hair swept back over his head. There was a softness to his demeanour and the care he had for humanity shone from his face. Tony wasn't convinced that he was in the right place. *What would a man of the cloth be doing hiding an arms stash?*

"Good morning gentlemen, can I help you or have you just come to seek solace?"

"We're looking for Reverend O'Brien."

"Well, you've found him so you have, what can I do for you."

"A friend sent us." Tony paused at the vicar's quizzical expression. "Jack Fitzgerald."

The seemingly frail old man suddenly lit up. "Ah, you must be his friends; Jack called me and told me to expect you but you're not local are you? No matter, no matter, this way, this way...Jack always told me it was best not to know too much." He beckoned and scuttled along to an old arched wooden door at the back of the church, fumbled for the light switch and picked his way carefully down the heavily worn stone steps into the crypt.

"This is what you're looking for." They'd stopped at the end of the room but Tony couldn't see anything of interest. He looked up at the wonderful brickwork forming the ceiling in an array of interlaced arches... nothing, he looked at the walls...nothing..."Where exactly?"

"You're standing on it."

He looked down to find himself standing on a memorial slab of some kind with Celtic markings. The slab was old, worn smooth in places by years of feet walking backwards and forwards across the floor. The transcription pulled at him although he couldn't make head or tail of it because it was written in Gaelic.

"What does it say?"

"Roughly translated it says in times of need I hope to provide. It's one of Jack's ancestors, Finley Fitzgerald; He was famous for his charity works hereabouts as was Jack... a great man...do you know him. No, no don't answer that, the less I know the better." The vicar looked troubled. "I pray that I'm doing the right thing but Jack has never failed us before and in his time of need we all must answer, may the lord forgive me."

Tony raised his hand to his forelock as a sign of respect. "Amen to that Father."

"Look carefully now....see the gap? It's hard to tell that the stone's been reset. The boys added the small indentations at either end to allow a crowbar to be slipped in to place to lift it. You'll have to be careful now, it has to go back exactly the way it is, we don't want any snoops now do we."

The vicar produced two steel crowbars from a recess in the corner and handed them to Tony and Frank. They carefully lifted the slab and were met with a void much larger than the slab itself that was filled with small two wooden crates and four good sized grab bags. They pulled each of them out and examined them carefully.

"C4 plastic explosives, Kalashnikovs, some handguns, detonators and what's this? It's bloody heavy."

Frank pulled off one of the wooden planks from the top of the box and pulled out a six by four inch plain white coloured cardboard box. He opened the lid carefully expecting more explosives. "Ball bearings? What the fuck use are they?"

"Collateral damage Frank. Pack them into the explosive and they act like multiple bullets, think of a shotgun cartridge with a wide spread."

"Shit...that's a bit heavy in'it..."

Tony ignored the comment and turned to the vicar. "Thank you Reverend, we won't take the Kalashnikovs but we'll load up the rest and be on our way if it's okay with you."

The vicar stood silently while the boys put the slab back in place clearly struggling with his conscience. "You'll not be targeting innocents now will you? I don't want to know what you're taking but I wouldn't want to be seeing the troubles restart, it wouldn't be good now would it?"

"No father, the targets on Jack's list are anything but innocent...misguided maybe... but they all have blood on their hands...besides mostly it's going to just be about shaking a few people up. I promise we'll look after the ordinary people Reverend."

"No, no, no...don't tell me anything. All Jack said was that you needed access to the crypt...I don't want to know anymore, no I don't. I'll not be seeing you again boys." It was a statement that he hoped would prove to be true.

Back in the car heading towards the cottage Frank had sweat across his brow and was clearly very nervous gripping the steering wheel so hard that his knuckles were white. The car hit another pothole and Frank cringed pulling his neck down into his shoulders. Tony laughed heartily. "For fuck's sake Frank, cringing ain't gonna make any bloody difference is it? If we're gonna go boom they'll be picking up pieces of us in Dublin and Belfast given the amount of gear we've got in the back."

"It ain't funny Tony, I don't wanna die yet."

"You daft git...I'm laughing because there is no way that the plastic is going to go off...its inert...like play-doh...you can throw it at the floor, at the wall, play with it in your hand, do whatever you want with it, it's only when you add a detonator and a firing source that it becomes dangerous. During the troubles they used to cherish the stuff just using small amounts in with salt peter...fertilizer to you and me soaked in diesel. The detonator blows the plastic and then the boom from the C4 sets off the fertilizer. It's why they used to use big vans... the fertilizer isn't that great so you need large amounts...more bang for your buck if you like, we're not going down that route, Jack won't need more explosives so we'll just use more of this stuff...It's gonna be fucking great Frank, fucking great."

Frank was starting to get nervous; the change in Tony was worrying. He was going about the job with relish; he was enjoying it too much, Play-doh was a very apt tag for the game that Tony seemed to be playing.

Chapter 42
The BVI Connection

THE LATE LANDING at Beef Island didn't give them much time to enjoy Island life before they would be heading to bed. The small boutique hotel had everything they needed and after an enjoyable meal revisiting the excellent fresh fish and lobster available in the British Virgin Islands, Bashar and Lynette elected to stretch their legs leaving Emma to look after the baby. Bashar was in a melancholy mood as they strolled barefoot along the beach on the edge of the surf glinting white as it was lit by the lights from the bars and hotels.

Lynette squeezed his hand. "Want to tell me about it Baz? You're deep in thought...something's troubling you."

Baz stopped turned to her and took both hands in his staring intently into her eyes. "Lindy, I know we have our differences from time to time but I've tried really hard to alleviate your concerns and I was wondering if you've considered my proposal of marriage?" He paused before continuing to babble. "I've got to be honest sweetheart recent events and the kidnap of Bridget makes me all the more worried about losing you again. I'm like a cat on a hot tin roof...I couldn't bear to be without you and Millie...Marry me Lindy...Please."

Lynette caressed his cheek while trying to let him down gently. "Baz we've been over this, you know I love you and I'm not going to leave you, but I'm also not having Millie treated as a second class citizen in your country or excluded as a sibling just because she's female, when we can resolve that issue then I'll marry you straight away and yes I do want more babies and only with you my darling." She stopped and kissed him staring into his eyes as the surf washed over their feet. "I mean it Baz, I love you and your quirky ways which brings me onto thoughts about tomorrow...Just remember I love you and only you...Play nicely with Juan, I don't want an alpha male pissing contest to break out...remember I'm yours not his." Baz pouted. He hated having to behave.

The following morning the meeting with Juan went well mainly due to the fact that it was managed by John Lynton who had all of the documentation laid out in rows on a huge boardroom table together with beautifully crafted fountain pens and each company seal at the ready. As they signed each set of documentation and applied the relevant company seal John had Juan Rodriguez sign the minutes recording the pertinent facts of the meeting. In the short time available somehow he had even managed to get a banking licence and name approval for Sterling Eco Finance. Things were looking good.

John coughed looking slightly uncomfortable. "Urm, MKS next but it umm, you've asked for me to be the director on it Lynette." John Flushed red.

"Yes please John...If that's okay with you Juan." She raised an eyebrow and flashed him a toothy grin.

He didn't move from his reclined position. "Whatever you want Lynette. I'm sure you have your reasons."

"Well, John will still be around when Millie grows up...Millie Kaddouri - Smythe or MKS for short. You Juan will no doubt be chasing young ladies around on a beach somewhere enjoying your retirement." He shrugged and laughed a little the explanation was accepted without a second thought.

With the paperwork completed Juan insisted on the group celebrating with some champagne. Bashar saw the more relaxed atmosphere as an opportunity to bring up Jack's problem as suggested by Lynette earlier over breakfast, the man should have relevant contacts. She noted that he was trying hard to be on his best behaviour and talking in crystal cut public school English.

"Senor Rodriguez I would like to thank you for your help in getting clearance for our guest to continue on his journey last night, it was extremely important to us." He paused hoping he would ask why but Juan sat back and waited. "He uh, he has an urgent mission...a terrible turn of events...you see, unfortunately his wife to be has been kidnapped in Rio something that I understand can happen there quite often. South America is not a continent that I am that familiar with, we have a few investments in property and ...more interesting areas...but I still don't really understand the culture. Presumably you have connections there?"

Juan nodded and sat forward the phrase 'more interesting areas' had sparked his interest. "Yes, yes, many connections. It is as you say a difficult culture to get to understand. Poverty is rife and life is of little value. Kidnapping is quite common but normally a ransom demand is received quickly. Has one been received?"

"I wish it were so simple. Despite concentrating significant resources and the involvement of two governments we are currently drawing a blank. The local gangs have been encouraged to 'cooperate' but still no word. Do you have any suggestions?"

"I'm sure it's not news to you that we have a number of the major cartels as clients so to speak. If you have a photo and information I would be happy to forward it to them with a request but you realise these things do not come for free."

Bashar had to stop himself from smirking. *Lynette said that you were a wily old goat.* "Of course if it led to her recovery then we would be deeply indebted." He gave a small bow to emphasise the point. *No result no debt - checkmate I think.*

"You do realise that too much attention could result in her death."

"Yes in normal circumstances but I understand that we have begun to make our point with local gangs and cartels that the consequences of her death would be catastrophic, we have found a number of pinch points including inside the government but the more the message is reinforced, as it will be from your kind offer, the better." *No backing out now Senor Rodriquez. You'll also see just how far our influence reaches.*

"Talking of which it is time for us to go. I have promised we will be in Rio before nightfall."

"Ah, but not before I see your beautiful daughter, I have a present for her....You are such a lucky man Senor."

Chapter 43
Dynamite

WITH NIGEL SMITH DELIVERED to hospital Enrique headed to his villa to rendezvous with Martins' team to see if last night's foray into the Rio underworld had produced any leads. The fact that his phone hadn't rang suggested that as yet nobody was talking, it was worrying, somebody somewhere should know something even if the rival factions just blamed each other, silence was the last thing he expected.

The teams were milling around in the main compound area swapping a few stories and ideas before Martin called the meeting to order. Each unit reported back and the list of suspects on the white board was slowly whittled down. In some ways the night had gone well, nobody had been killed and the gangs knew that they meant business, one of Martin's team had a minor knife slash on his arm but his Kevlar vest had stopped any damage to vital organs, his bruised pride was the most visible wound. The heavies had broken a few arms, broken a few noses and jaws and threatened worse if people didn't talk. The local gangs had been given twenty four hours to come up with a name but unusually even though they were rattled they weren't accusing each other despite Enrique's reach and power was well known.

Enrique paced the floor. "It's too quiet; we've covered most of the main drugs gangs and nobody seems to know anything, it has to be a small group, focused on the bigger picture." He stopped and turned as he reached the end of the room recounting his steps..."Or...or, it could be mistaken identity...maybe just maybe they meant to kidnap Rachel or someone else completely, stranger things have happened."

There was a knock on the door and stretch together with his four man team walked through with one member using a crutch and another wearing a sling. Martin noted that his boys were uninjured but it was clear that they had been in a serious fire fight. Despite the wounds he didn't cut them any slack. "Where the fuck have you been, you're late!"

"Sorry boss, things got a bit messy up at Vistamar and I had to patch the guys up before we got to the plane. We might have a lead though." His eyes scanned the room before focussing back on Martin. "If you don't mind boss a private debrief would probably be best."

"You know how we work Stretch, all information is shared."

"I know boss, but I wouldn't ask unless it was important."

Martin stared at Stretch trying to decipher the hidden message before taking his decision. "Okay team, let's break for thirty minutes and then we'll share the relevant details." He emphasised the word share and locked eyes with Stretch making a point to all in the room.

There was a little bit of grumbling about special treatment and a few good natured jokes made about the state of the team but it didn't take long for the room to clear leaving Stretch, his three bedraggled men, Martin, Enrique and Jack. Martin was straight down his throat. "You were uncontactable Stretch, it's not acceptable, and to compound matters you were late...I take it from the injuries to the team that it was unavoidable. This better be good."

Stretch stood to attention as if he was being bollocked by his sergeant major. "Sorry Boss, you've always told us to take decisions in the field as things changed and I thought we were doing the right thing."

Stretch had been with Martin for over ten years and he knew that he wouldn't go AWOL unless he really had an emergency, his eyes wandered over the four man team; he needed to ease up on them. "Sorry to be hard on you guys, I need to listen to what you have to say, I'm sure that you took the decisions that you had to, get a hot drink or a beer and let's talk about it." The change in approach and the more mellow body language being displayed by Martin took the tension out of the room. All four of the guys opted for coffee, two with a dash of rum. Stretch started their story.

As planned they had flown up to Recife and hired a car to drive to Vistamar and seek out Garcia. To start with everything went smoothly until they were told that Garcia was holed up at his Finca and that sometimes he didn't come to town for days, it forced them to change plan. They drove out to the countryside, hid the car away by covering it with banana and palm fronds before making their way to the Finca on foot to check out the security and the opposition. So far so good, a few dogs, two armed guards, nothing they couldn't handle.

Stretch continued feeding information as concisely as he could. "So we took down the guards and locked the dogs round the back pretty efficiently. Garcia didn't look like he was expecting visitors. He'd just put the phone down in his office when we picked him up and started to interrogate him. He wasn't playing ball so I used my old favourite."

Martin winced and could smell the burning in his nostrils even though the torture site was hundreds of miles away. He'd seen Stretch in action before and it wasn't pleasant. *Maybe they could skip that bit...crap Jack just had to ask the question.*

"I need to know what you did Stretch, I've got to be sure that he wasn't lying."

"Trust me Jack, he was telling the truth. I had him strapped to a chair with his shoes and socks off." He grinned manically enjoying recounting the tale. "I always start with the little toes either slicing them off with a chisel or a bowie knife, whatever's to hand really. Anyway to make sure they don't bleed out too quickly I seal the flesh with a blow torch, normally they pass out so it's a bucket of water to wake them up and we start all over again working inwards on both feet until you get the truth. It normally doesn't take long."

Jack was completely unfazed by the revelation. "And? ...what did Garcia say?"

"He started singing by the time we cut off the third toe. He wasn't so tough. He claimed that the Ruskies were involved, something about a hundred grand, I reckon we lost some of it in translation but he said that Paolo owed the money, he was probably just blabbering. Anyway he starts to change his mind and point the finger at his brother and then bang we get hit by his drugs gang, we estimated fifteen to twenty guys with small arms and shotguns. Thankfully they weren't too good and we picked off most of them without getting too shot up." He looked over at his two wounded colleagues. "We managed to dig the bullets out of the leg and arm and fix them up enough to get them back here but they really could do with seeing a good doctor."

Enrique opened the door and barked out some orders in Portuguese. "Go on guys, Fidel will take you to our doctor. He's good when it comes to dealing with bullet wounds."

Jack's temper was starting to fizz. "Are you telling me that Paolo's involved in this?!"

Stretch held up his hands. "Hang on Jack. Let me finish....Once the fire fight was over we decided to move Garcia in case anybody had heard the shooting. We loaded up in one of his cars and drove to the development on the grounds that only the night watchman would be around and we could bribe him to disappear to town with a few dollars. It took an hour or so to patch the boys up and get them stabilised before I started working on Garcia again." He paused. "Mind if I get another coffee and rum?"

Martin nodded his head towards the drinks on the side. The fire fight had taken an emotional toll on Stretch. He gulped deeply before topping the coffee off with more rum and collecting himself. "Okay...so we went back over the same ground. Garcia confirmed that Paolo owed the Russians over a hundred grand and then claimed the debt had possibly been sold to his brother or cousin. The story was slightly different so I pressed ahead, maybe a bit too quickly and the fucker died of a heart attack." He looked over to Martin. "Sorry boss, I pushed a bit too hard because of the time constraints with two injured men, it's my fault."

Martin shook his head. "No Stretch, you did what you had to do, maybe he just had a dodgy ticker."

Relieved at his reprieve he continued his story. "So we left the two injured guys laying up in the bushes and covered Garcia's body with sand in one of the pits that were shuttered off for concrete pouring. If he does get found then hopefully they'll just think it was a local drugs feud when they count up the other bodies...It was a bad one boss...I did all I could."

Jack went to leap in with questions but Martin held up his hand to silence him. "Go get a hot bath and a few hours sleep stretch, your team is off detail for twenty four hours you need a rest."

"I'll be ready to go again in six hours boss as will Clarkey." His compatriot nodded. "Enrique's boys need the recovery time...not us."

"Okay, eight hours, don't argue...and Stretch." He turned back as he was heading out of the door. "Thanks for insisting on a private de-brief. The news about Paolo could be dynamite."

Chapter 44
Boom Boom

TONY, FRANK AND TOMMY headed out onto the road in convoy with Tony driving the Ford Focus, both of the boys were still nervous about the C4 despite Tony throwing it at the floor and ceiling in the cottage to prove that it was inert. The passenger seat had two manhole covers, acquired along the way the previous night, rammed against the side cushion. The door card contained far too much C4 and a mass of ball bearings. It was targeted, the car would explode but more importantly it would explode mainly in one direction spraying whatever or whoever was on the passenger side with a lethal dose of ten millimetre steel balls, it was a vicious concoction.

The drive to Belfast was uneventful. They headed in to the centre cruising while looking for a suitable target car for Tommy to boost. It needed to be the same model, not the same year but definitely the same colour. It didn't take them long, a quick drive around the Cathedral Quarter and Queen's Quarter where young and old were revelling in the various Irish water holes and they had a choice of two cars, they sat watching the favourite of the two parked away from too much action and away from the light. Decision taken Tommy worked his magic and he was soon behind the wheel on false plates. They stopped short of the Shankhill road in a dark area where they could swop the UK plates from Tony's Focus, it was a minor detail but if anyone in the village had clocked the plates it could set a hare running. Back on the stolen Irish plates Tony hoped that his car would blend in on the fiercely loyalist estate, there was bound to be others He knew that planting the car was a risk but it had to be balanced against all of the others, missions were never simple, as long as he wasn't rumbled by Dermot's foot soldiers.

"Okay Tony, the cars are ready but are you sure this fucking airplane model kit is gonna work?"

"It'll work Frank, the days of Electronic Counter Measures or ECM units are long gone. Huh, I used to carry forty pounds of kit on patrol and a good chunk of it was made up from counter measure stuff...you know... things to jam signals so that they couldn't set off a bomb as you walked by...Not that it made much difference, they'd just use two wires sit the other side of the hill and arc them across a battery...and boom we'd be fucked up yet again....Bastards!" *Time for revenge Tony, maim and kill, maim and kill, haha, revenge will be mine.*

Tony pulled up in front of the three terraced houses at the end of the row and engineered a breakdown on the car. He pulled the bonnet, walked round the front and lifted it up before looking inside with a confused expression on his face. As expected a young gun opened the door and immediately told him to move. "You fix it mate and I'll move it, I dunno why it's stopped." He couldn't afford for the guy to see that the ignition had a screwdriver rammed in it so played things carefully. Seamus stuck his head out of the door to see what was going on and Tony was instantly on the charm offensive.

"Hello mate, sorry to break down here. I'm over visiting one of my mates who works in London sometimes, brickie he is...and a bit of a part time mechanic...if you don't mind I'll walk round the corner and go get 'im, I ain't got a fucking clue when it comes to electronics, it's not the engine that's for sure 'coz it's turning over okay. I'll just be a couple of minutes and we'll push it out of your way...sorry mate...when it rains it pours eh?"

Seamus flicked his head at the other young gun to come back inside. "Keep an eye on him lad, ten minutes no more." He'd bought the story...Why would an Englishman blow up someone on the same side?

Dermot was less convinced, his wily old foxes nose sniffing the air and not liking the odour. "We'll sit out back in the kitchen until he's gone Seamus."

"Argh, he's not a problem Dermot, just some guy over from London that's broken down."

Tony walked round the corner picked up the model control system from the back of the Discovery and poked his head round the cold brick wall searching down the street to make sure that no innocents were nearby. The front door was still open...the young gun was still hanging around...*Perfect...* He flicked the control to the right as if dipping the wing on his model aircraft; the actuator on the control system closed the circuit and the street lit up. Flames leapt into the sky and ball bearings fizzed from the side panel destroying the front door and penetrating the laminated windows where Dermot would have been sitting. The young gun had just shut the door in time but was still hit badly; the burns were superficial but it would be touch and go whether he would keep his right leg, Seamus also suffered damage akin to bullet wounds and would be in hospital for at least six weeks, Dermot being the old fox that he was had sat himself in the corner of the kitchen protected by two solid brick walls. It would be a while until his hearing recovered but otherwise he was unscathed.

He slammed his fist into the counter top angry that they had been caught out. "For feck's sake Jack, you said seventy two hours it's not been half that time. Seamus, Seamus, here hold this on your wounds, I'll call an ambulance for you, the boy's in a bad way as well, hang in their I'll call for help."

Frank slowly pulled away and Tony selected a CD on the audio system...John Lee Hooker...Boom, Boom. He laughed manically as they drove away. "Fucking brilliant eh Frank, Boom fucking Boom, I fucking love it! I hope we got a couple of the fuckers."

An hour and a half later they were back in the cottage and Tony insisted that Tommy took them down to the shop come bar. "It's time for a session boys, create a perfect alibi...I can feel a few pints of Guinness coming our way."

"But you're on the wagon Tony...no booze no drugs."

"Fuck it...I'd forgotten that, ah well, maybe not then." *Who needs alcohol when we can have revenge? Boom fucking Boom!*

Chapter 45
Tick Tock

DOUG SCHNEIDER AND TOBY TRELAWNEY were burning the late night oil trying to find a solution to the pressing problem of publication when the next email pinged up on their screens.

Tick Tock, Tick Tock, still watching the clock?

The first mouse is off and running with the following information has been sent to four national newspapers.

Press Release: A former government MI5 officer today revealed the existence of immunity letters for known terrorists

A former MI5 officer revealed today that known terrorists and on the run prisoners from within Sein Fein and the Provisional IRA have been given letters promising immunity from prosecution. No such scheme exists for the Loyalists. Our source has indicated that there could be as many as two hundred letters of assurance in circulation that were given to wanted IRA members as part of a deal between the British Government and Sinn Féin during negotiations aimed at securing IRA decommissioning, and republican support for new policing reforms and the restoration of devolution.

The existence of the scheme is a closely guarded secret but it is believed that the Northern Ireland Office (NIO) have pulled a number of high profile potential prosecutions due to the letters providing a potential get out of jail free card which they have not wanted to reveal in open court. It leaves a bitter taste for families of the victims who have always suspected that prosecutions were not being pursued to the full extent of the law.

Names to follow within twenty four hours

Tick, Tock...Stop watching the clock

Doug got to the end first and sat back in his chair letting out a low whistle. "Well Spock, it looks like the shit is about to hit the fan. I've never heard of immunity letters and I've worked here for years. You come across them Toby?"

"Nope but I bet a lot of people out there are pretty happy that they've got them. Incredible isn't it... commit multiple murders and never get called to account. Even soldiers these days get prosecuted for war crimes if they act outside of the Geneva Convention don't they? Wasn't there a recent case about prisoners in Iraq or something?"

"Yeah I remember reading about it recently, they even get court martialled for bullying and humiliating prisoners... where's the logic? This lot murder, maim and terrify people throughout their own communities and all they'll get is a slap on the wrist. I tell you what though Toby...one things for sure, there's going to be a lot of very scared politicians out there."

Doug was certainly right. The press office at number ten was under siege from half a dozen different reporters who had been tasked with digging out whatever information they could to verify the story. To the editor of the Belfast Times and the Editor of the Telegraph it felt right. It wouldn't have normally landed on their desks but luckily they had some grizzled old hacks working their news desks who just like their editors worked on gut feel. If they dug fast and deep maybe just maybe they could get a headline out with the second morning edition. What a coup that would be, rumours all these years finally confirmed.

The Prime minster was sat with his Lawyer James in their swanky London offices moving things into trusts and company holding accounts. If he was going to be brought down there was no way he wanted his assets visible to the world, especially side line dealings carried out in his wife's name, he'd already had enough press heat for property dealings. The more things could be hidden away the better especially if he avoided tax.

James probed him with a few questions. "Look, my team have worked all night to carry out your requests but I have to advise you as a friend that everything that you're doing here contravenes the whole ethos of your party and is border line as to whether it constitutes tax evasion. What's happened Robert? Things don't change that quickly...we've known each other since university and you always championed the working man and taxing the rich...I just don't get it...If anyone finds out you're going to be toast...the press will have you for breakfast and what about the members register of interests? Half of these links haven't been declared."

"You'll have to trust me James. I take it your team understand the consequences and that you've made them all sign the Official Secrets Act."

"Of course they bloody have but none of them are dumb enough to think that your personal information would be covered by it. Stop playing games Robert what's up?"

"I really can't say at the moment. I just need you to promise that none of this will leak. Events are underway that I can't stop and I need to make sure that my family are protected."

"Oh don't bullshit me Robert...I've been up all night, I've read every page and I know damn well that this is all about self -preservation in case of a catastrophic event. Tell me...will it affect all of us or just the political arena?"

"You'll be fine James, there's no need for you to worry."

"The only thing that I'm worried about is how you'll live with yourself...you've fudged your ideals...you're more of a capitalist than Thatcher."

The remark stung causing the Prime Minister to pick up his coat and briefcase and head for the door. "When I need political advice Robert I'll be sure to ask for it...now if you don't mind I've got a busy day."

Chapter 46
The Russians

THE REVELATION THAT THE RUSSIANS might be involved set Jack thinking. Joey had offered him whatever help he needed on when he left a message for him the only question was whether Joey was still loyal to him or whether he had turned to the dark side and Dermot's ways. He slapped himself. *How could he even think that Joey wasn't loyal? He needed help, joey was a friend and friends help friends. Yer fecking idiot Jack... pick up the phone.* He flicked through his mobile and dialled the number for the office in San Pedro talking briefly to the owner Carlos before he was handed over to Joey.

"Jack! Are ye all right? Have ye found Bridget yet? Is she safe?" Joey had a stream of questions.

"Whoa slow down there Joey. No she's not safe yet but I'll die trying to make it so. You offered yer help Joey...does the offer still stand?"

Joey was slightly affronted. "Of course it fecking stands Jack, I gave yer me fecking word, you're the closest thing to family I've got. You shouldn't have to ask Jack."

"I know Joey, I know, but you realise the consequences...siding with me or working with me could be terminal if you know what I mean."

"That's fine Jack, we all know the risks, by the way have you seen the news? Dermot's place has been bombed, one guy's critical and one stable. Dermot's been moved to a new safe house so he has, so there'll not be a lot of prying going on."

A huge grin spread across Jack's face. *Tony you bloody beauty! Strike at the heart.* Despite feeling elated he was careful what he said. "Tsk, tsk, now isn't that a shame, have the IRA admitted responsibility yet?"

"Everybody's denying it Jack. The news feeds are saying it could be the start of a new war, there's also a rumour about immunity letters handed out to politicians and the fecking bog dancers, but I'm sure you already know that."

"It's good to talk Joey but I need to get to business. We have a lead. Apparently Paolo owes more than a hundred grand to the Russians and the debt might have been sold to the locals down here. I need you to get the truth from Rasvan and make a point of teaching him not to fuck with me or my family. It's asking a lot Joey, just do what you feel's right, don't put yourself at risk now... yer hear me?"

He smiled, typical Jack, ever the fatherly figure. "I'll call your message service as soon as I have news."

Joey walked back to his booth and flicked through his mobile for Rasvan's number. He hated the way the slimy Russian looked down at him as some sort of upstart. Maybe this would give him a chance to get his attention. After a few pleasantries Joey asked the question about Paolo and outstanding debts. Rasvan just laughed.

"Joey, Joey, Joey...Why would I tell you who owes us money or if I've sold the debt to the South American's; It's none of your business now is it?"

Joey could feel the bile rising in his throat; Rasvan didn't give him the respect that he deserved. "Yer might not like the fact that I run the operation now Rasvan, but you'll show some respect so you will. I've asked the question nicely and I've promised Jack an answer. Now we can do this the easy way or the hard way, the choice is yours."

Rasvan openly laughed. "Such big threats Joey. Jack is no longer the man. Dermot wields the power." The remaining smirk in his voice was evident.

Although Joey was furious he played his bluff. "You're behind the times Rasvan, haven't yer seen the news? Dermot's pad was blown sky high last night..." He deliberately waited leaving the 'by who' unsaid. "You've got two hours, I want answers or the trouble starts." Joey slammed the phone down on the table so hard he broke the screen. He turned to his minions "Fuck it! Get me a new phone and get two of the boys ready in one hour to start a barbeque." *Rasvan would show respect one way or another.*

Joey sat brooding for just over an hour...*Fuck the Ruskies, action that's what Jack would expect...*" Boys, go set light to Annabell's club...I want a proper blaze, plenty of petrol, give the girls some warning but feel free to fry any Eastern Europeans."

The surprise on their faces was evident. "You sure boss?"

"Don't fecking question me! Just do as I say...plenty of petrol!"

Carlos brought another Spanish coffee to the table and hovered briefly. "You'll be alright Carlos, there'll be no trouble here. Jack just has a bit of a problem that needs sorting out." Without a word but seemingly placated he wandered back and began polishing glasses earnestly behind the bar.

Thirty minutes later Joey's phone pinged. He'd received pictures of the fire at Annabel's via whatsapp.

He laughed out loud. "That'll get your attention." He forwarded the photos to Rasvan with a short but sweet message.

I see one of your clubs has a problem. It would be a shame if it spread. I will not ask again.

Two minutes later a number flashed up on his screen. An evil grin spread across Joey's face as he answered and put the phone to his ear.

"What the fuck do you think you're doing McCann? You've set fire to one of my best clubs, people die for less...Are you trying to start a turf war?"

"Argh, stop your fussing Rasvan, I asked nicely, I told you it was urgent and I see that I've got your attention so I have...Now I'll ask nicely again...Does Paolo Williams owe you or your organisation money? Yes or no."

"Yes."

"And have you sold the debt to the South Americans?"

"No but we have had a few talks with them. Olaf has dealt with it directly. Paolo has promised the money in the next ten days but understand McCann, this is none of your business, if he fails to pay it's our choice whether we kill him or not."

"It is my business when you step on Jack's toes. His girls been kidnapped and anyone found to be involved will meet a grisly end Rasvan. I swear to god so I do."

There was a moments silence as Rasvan digested the news. "Are you sure Bridget's been kidnapped?"

Joey rolled his eyes. "Of course I'm fecking sure."

"It's nothing to do with us Joey, we're not that stupid."

"Well if it's nothing to do with your crowd then yer won't mind putting the word out through your network that she's untouchable...I'll text you a photo."

"I'll do what I can to help but we need to talk Joey. Games like yours can start wars."

It was Joey's turn to laugh. "War? People are about to find out what happens when Jack Fitzgerald wages war... believe me it won't be pretty."

Chapter 47
Secondary Damage

TONY HAD BEEN FIDDLING with batteries some wires and a test tube half filled with mercury all day, swearing regularly at the difficulty in getting the mercury switch to behave the way that he remembered and the way that he wanted it to.

"Fucking fing's a nightmare...we could all get blown up." He turned to Frank and Tommy. "I don't like it boys but we're gonna have to be around for the next two bombs. I was hoping to use a mercury switch on Park's car but it's too unreliable. We'll just have to let one bomb off outside Dublin and then drive back to Belfast to sort Park out....sorry mate but it's better than ending up brown bread if you know what I mean."

Tommy was getting twitchy. "Ain't we done enough already Tony? I don't wanna end up brown bread, that weren't the fucking idea....I fought we were just gonna shoot a few geezers...normal stuff like...this fucking play-doh crap scares the fuck out of me."

"Enough? We haven't even started yet. Jack has given us an address on a council estate outside Dublin, he says it won't be an easy target coz there's a drug dealer on every corner and a network of young lads riding bikes or bareback on horses that keep an eye out for strangers. Its tight knit but it's important that we make some noise there...getting frightened Tommy? I thought you'd love this...tell you what, you can fly the plane this time...how about it eh?"

The boys packed up their supplies and headed for Dublin early in the evening driving the Disco and the stolen Focus in convoy, Tony was a bit more nervous than he'd like to admit, he wasn't worried about the explosives but what if they got stopped by the Guardia? He pulled in to a burger joint on the edge of Town and was about to park when he realised that the place was full of cameras. *Best not be seen together.* He flicked his indicator and headed for the drive through hoping that Frank would cotton on and make it look like it was just two random cars coming in. He barked his order at the huge plastic boxed menu and drove forward to pay for his food. Once he picked it up he deliberately pulled away slowly as if hunting for something in his car to allow Frank to catch up before joining the traffic. A mile or so down the road he pulled in to a side road to enjoy his meal with Frank and Tommy.

"Well done Frank, you switched on quicker than I did there...I forgot about the cameras...best if the cars aren't seen together if you know what I mean."

He spread a map of the area out on the bonnet of the car as they munched their way through their burgers pointing a greasy finger at a densely populated area to the North of the city. "Right, this is where we're going. See this street here?" Tommy nodded. "I'll take the Focus in and park it up in front of one of the houses, number forty five which should be this end." The greasy paw print indicated his chosen spot. "There's a green in front which leads across to the dual carriageway. Now all you've gotta do Tommy is push the switch to the right as I get into the car and Frank can get us out of there. Got that Tommy? You push the switch before and I'm a gonna, fucking fried along with the Mick's...and believe me Tommy I would not be happy."

A familiar manical grin spread across Tommy's face. "If it goes right Tony will yer teach me to build me own bombs?"

Against his better judgement Tony heard himself agreeing. "Yeah of course mate, sure I will."

Ten minutes later as Frank parked up at the edge of the green and Tony drove further into the estate they could hardly believe their eyes. East London was rough, Silvertown the boys hailed from was definitely no picnic but the Ferndale estate looked like a war zone...Burnt out cars, busted bikes and mattresses littered the road, kids as young as nine or ten stood around a large fire openly smoking and swearing at each other. They were feral. Tony was shocked at the state of the place. What had happened to all the European money that flooded in to Dublin? Clearly it never found its way here. A young kid tapped on the window. "Looking for a girl mister? My sister takes it from behind, don't cost much." He grinned showing missing teeth before Tony waved him away. *Best get this over with.*

He parked up in front of the house, the car was prepped just the same as last time, a passenger door packed with C4 and ball bearings braced with a steel drain cover. To make a bigger bang this time he'd gone heavier on the plastic and eased up on the ball bearings, this one was more about the noise. He ripped the wires from underneath the steering column before stepping out and walking back up the road. The same kid on a bike came back to him. "You ain't from round here are yer mate. You sure yer don't wanna shag my sister? Fifty euros what d'ya say, yer not queer are yer?...Okay a special for you forty euros."

"Piss off kid, my cars broken down; I need to go get my mate."

As Tony padded across the green the kid kept circling him on his tatty bike. Tony was getting nervy and decided it was best to talk. "What house number kid?" His face lit up. "Number twenty five second road down."

"Here, thirty five euros, I'll be there in ten minutes."

The kid grabbed the money and sped off laughing and waving the notes in the air. "So long sucker."

As he approached the Disco Tommy's grinning face appeared at the window, he wound the window down and made a big show of pushing the actuator to the right. Boom! The kid was three hundred yards up the street but the blast made him wobble and fall off his bike. Tony noted that he didn't drop the euros.

Tommy was animated. "Fucking great fun....can I do the next one as well?"

The house was a known drug den and unofficial office of the Provisional IRA and the bomb hopefully would set hares running. As the boys headed back to Belfast they could hear the wail of sirens in the distance. Jack's aim was to cause confusion and set the sides against each other. The morning papers should be interesting.

Chapter 48
Party Time

PAOLO WAS DOING WHAT HE DID BEST; ignoring his problems in life and partying. His phone had been buzzing with demands about Bridget but he hardly knew her, what did they think he was going to do? *Time to run and hide for a while.* He'd left Max and Rachel in his apartment in Rio and headed back up to Turtle Bay in Vistamar to clear his head and enjoy life and he was certainly enjoying it now...He sprinkled a liberal amount of cocaine between Belinda's huge breasts stuck his head into her cleavage and snorted for all he was worth. *Man I could happily die like this.*

"Not too much Paolo, I still want you to be able to fuck me."

"Always willing to oblige my darling."

Paolo sat up and dipped his hand in some coconut oil sat on the side table before liberally applying it to Belinda's prize assets, shoulders and chest. He kneaded her gently working down her body before taking her sex in his mouth and teasing her with his tongue. She groaned loudly as she got she got close to orgasm before Polo stopped and entered her, riding her slowly before building a steady pace. He pinched a small amount of coke and placed it under her nose balanced ready for their crescendo. As he could feel his juice's rising and Belinda heading for another climax he grabbed another handful and snorted, the rush to his head and body was almost too much to bear, he rolled to one side closed his eyes and passed out.

Jack was fuming as he prodded the intercom to Paolo's apartment. "Rachel? It's Jack open up." He skipped the lift and headed for the stairs taking the steps two at a time with Martin following closely behind him in the hope that he could stop him doing anything stupid. He burst through the door catching Rachel by surprise sending her stumbling into the hallway.

"Sorry Rachel. Where's Paolo?" Rachel could see the fury in Jack's eyes and was dumbstruck; all she could do was shake her head. Max came round the corner at the sound of the commotion.

"Jesus Jack, and hello to you too... nice to see you. You've only got to knock there's no need to break the door down you know. What's your problem?"

"Your brother's my problem. Now where the fuck is he?"

Max was amazed that there was no remorse or recognition from Jack that his behaviour wasn't acceptable. He clearly wasn't going to get through to him with sarcasm. He stood his ground uncertain what to do before averting his eyes against Jack's stare which was steely, unsettling even.

"I don't keep him on a leash Jack. He headed back up to Turtle Bay to take care of business; at least that was what he said; personally I think he was just trying to give me and Rachel some space. Have you called his mobile?"

Martin piped up. "He's not picking up. Sorry if we seem a bit heavy handed but it's critical that we talk to him now, not in a few days, today, not in a few hours but now!"

"Well I think he took a private plane with him so I suppose he could be back in a three, four hours, you'd know better than I do how long it takes. He could just be in a meeting...Have you tried Steve Carter's phone?"

Martin kicked himself. He should have thought to ring him. He flicked through his contacts and pulled up the number walking out to the balcony to improve his signal and to get some privacy.

"Steve? It's Martin. We talked earlier today. I assume the concrete has been poured without any problem."

"Yes...but do you know how many other bodies there are? You've turned this into a fucking war zone!"

Martin's voice was as cold as ice. "Seventeen bodies and if you don't want to be number eighteen you'll find Paolo Williams and get him here in the next three hours. Do not tell him anything, no phone contact; it's critical that he gets here as soon as possible."

Steve was close to breaking point. "Where the fuck do you think he is? In the whorehouse as usual! He's probably passed out by now, he won't come round until tomorrow. Can't you do things by phone in the morning?"

Initially Martin didn't reply but when he hid the tone in his voice conveyed a deep threat. "Don't be stupid Mr Carter remember what I told you. Now, is the pilot and plane at the small strip rather than Recife?"

"Yes."

"Well get him to help you bundle Paolo up and get him here. I don't care if he's naked with a girl still wrapped round him; believe me your life depends on it. Find him and call me. Many lives depend on it not just yours." Martin terminated the call and looked directly at Jack, now he just had to find a way to keep him calm until they tracked Paolo down.

Chapter 49
Claws

BRIDGET SAT ON HER BED, pulled the emery board out of the bag and began to file her nails. The young upstart looked up momentarily and craned his neck to get a better view, satisfied he went back to reading his magazine, he normally only lifted his head out of his book when she went for a pee. *Pervert.* Thankfully she'd never succumbed to the fashion for false nails or shellac. Living in the sunshine of Spain for most of the year meant that her system was pumped with vitamin D and produced large amounts of keratin making her nails grow fast and strong. She concentrated on her right hand fashioning the nails on the thumb and first three fingers into wide sharp points, if they were too thin and snapped her plan would fail. Satisfied she continued to finish off the other hand using the polishing edge to buff them up. Now all she had to do was wait until Jackson was on shift again.

She must have dozed off looking out of the window into the scented garden as she was woken by raised voices with Stench breath screaming down a telephone. He stormed into the room looking directly at her as he carried on the conversation. She wasn't sure but he thought he was describing her to someone on the other end of the phone. He held the phone away from his mouth and barked at her.

"You! Lady! Who are you really? What's your real name lady?"

Bridget tried to calm her nerves with a deep breath. "I've told you before my name is Bridget Donovan and I work with the governments of the UK and Ireland. People will be looking for me."

He spat directly at her. "Bullshit. Why every drug gang in Rio look for you? It's no just Policia."

She opened her mouth to reply but it was clearly a rhetorical question as he slapped her across the face before she could get a word out and went back to screaming down the phone. *Something about paying more? Big risk? Damn her language skills.*

The four man team were now all together in the room watching their boss carefully for a reaction or order. They knew that when he started screaming things were bad. He put the phone down and rattled off information to them. The young gun was the only one who spoke. *Oh no, he wants to kill me?*

"The governments will pay money for my release. If you kill me believe me you'll die in the most brutal way you can imagine."

Stench breath stared at her before spitting in her direction again.

"Vamos rapido."

He stomped out of the room with his Cuban heels clicking on the tiles. Jackson was left behind to guard her. She heard the sound of the van revving up and the gates creaking open before it pulled out with a screech of tyres.

"What's happening Jackson? Your boss isn't very happy, he scares me."

"You have a lot of important people looking for you lady. Big names...gangs...drug lords...the police...he goes talk to big boss maybe ask for more money." He shrugged his shoulders. "I don't know but he not happy lady."

Shit. I've seen their faces. Jack must have sent the email and the pressure's on. Why didn't I think this through? Because you never considered kidnap that's why dumbarse...They'll kill me. It's now or never.

"Hey Jackson, you got anything to drink? Alcohol? I'm gonna take a shower if you know what I mean." She pouted at him and slowly pulled off her top allowing her ample breasts to bounce.

By the time Jackson had returned with a bottle of rum and two glasses Bridget was down to her underwear provocatively pushing her breasts together and upwards. "You like these Jackson?" She grabbed the bottle and poured two large shots drinking hers in one before sashaying towards the bathroom. "Sit back and relax where you can see the show Jackson. I've gotta have a shower first."

Bridgette breathed in deeply before unhooking her bra and sliding her panties down her legs. She could do with a bit of gardening down below after being held captive for so long but the audience didn't seem to mind. Jackson rose from his chair and made towards her. "Uh, uh Jackson." She waved a finger at him as if he was a naughty school boy. "Sit back and enjoy the show, we've got plenty of time haven't we?" He headed back to his seat and gulped greedily from the bottle.

She turned the shower on full force soaking her hair whilst playing with her nipples to keep Jackson interested. The scented shampoo in her hair and the suds running down her body felt fantastic making it difficult to focus on the show. She faked playing with her self noting that Jackson had stripped off his shirt and was clearly getting very aroused. *You've got one chance at this girl, don't fuck up...You need his trousers round his ankles to give you an advantage. You're running low on time.* Bridget rinsed her hair quickly and wrapped a towel around her body before soaping a small face flannel and beckoning to her prey.

Jackson was a lamb going to his slaughter. She run her left hand down his chest grazing his nipples before tugging at his belt and making short work of the buttons freeing his impressive erection. Pants must have been optional she thought finding him commando and ready for action. Bridget knelt before him all the time looking up into his eyes and telling him not to touch...not yet anyway. She grabbed his member and teased his tip as she washed his balls and penis before taking him in her mouth. He groaned loudly as she sucked greedily while he enjoyed short lived ecstasy before it was suddenly replaced with searing pain.

Bridget bit down hard on his bulbous tip whilst simultaneously clawing into his scrotum has hard as she could feeling the soft skin yield to her sharpened nails. Jackson had grabbed her hair trying to lever her off but his grip began to loosen as she managed to get one finger through the skin and force in another. His screams were those of a prey animal snapped in the jaws of a lioness, blood curdling but his strength wasn't yet quite sapped. *Sorry my friend this is gonna hurt but it's me or you.* She circled one testicle with her two fingers and pulled with all her might, her prey was still screaming in agony as he dropped to the ground, the pain presumably too much to bare. She gagged on the blood in her mouth, she was appalled at what she had just done but quickly pulled herself together hitting him over the head viciously with the chair trying to ensure that he didn't come round. Still naked but clutching the towel to her breasts Bridget ran down the corridor to a small kitchen opening and closing drawers looking for something to bind him with. *You're wasting time Bridget....Come on girl.*

Panicking slightly she ran back to the room that had been her cell for what seemed like an eternity and pulled the belt from her victim's trousers whilst dragging him to the edge of the iron bed. Forcing his arms behind him in a sitting position she wound the belt through the frame and buckled his arms in place, hopefully it would buy her enough time. She picked up the testicle that was sitting grey and lifeless in the middle of the floor and placed it on Jackson's lap. She had no idea if it could be repaired but it seemed only right to reacquaint them.

As the danger and need to fight started to subside the adrenaline surging through her body was making her pant and clouding her judgement, she was starting to shake. *Come on Bridget come on!* She went to put her clothes back on wanting to flee but common sense kicked in. *I've got to get some of this blood off, it makes me stand out.* She turned the faucet to cold and stood under the freezing water for a full minute while trying to force herself to breathe deeply and not to rush head long out of the door. *Okay Bridge, come on girl...Move, move! There's no time for tears, no time for regret.* She pulled on her underwear and clothes over her wet body not bothering to dry off...*Damn no shoes.* A groan from Jackson made her jump and she checked his pockets quickly before he came round.

A few Reals, and three dollars, it's all I need. Run Bridget run!!

Chapter 50
Going To War?

THE YOUNG GUN walked through the fug of smoke and approached Dermot, he was nervous, normally Sean or one of the other lieutenants would deal with the boss. He'd heard some really bad stories about him having a short fuse and felt uncomfortable, out of his depth, he'd not seen much action, just a shooting or two abroad when the network needed someone disposed of but now it was happening back on his own turf, happening around his family and friends.

"Err, Boss erm..."

Dermot's eyes flashed. "Spit it out boy!"

"Erm I've had a request for you to make a phone call....to talk to the other side so to say..erm."

"I don't talk with Republican bastards...that's for the politicians. Tell 'em to feck off, go wank in the Senate or whatever else it is that they do...away with yer, fuck off now."

Dermot turned back to the amber liquid in his glass and continued staring out of the window. *How the fuck has it come to this? Two of my best critically injured... Jack fighting his own? Didn't I give him enough? He would have been the next leader....What was it he said now? It's not what I signed up for, things have changed... huh!*

The young gun sidled back in to the room disturbing Dermot's thought process. "I thought I told ye to feck off so I did."

"Sorry boss but my contact says it's too important for the politicians...Gerry Malone's place in Ferndale has been car bombed and he's fucking furious...he wants blood...says it could start a new war."

Dermot stood shook his head and raised his eyes to the heavens. "Holy Mary mother of god...What have yer done Jack, what have yer done?"

As Dermot was cursing his luck the boys were sat parked up in the Discovery outside of the Vegas Casino. Four cars in front they'd spotted the silver BMW they were looking for and now it was a case of planting the bomb followed by a waiting game. Jack's intelligence was as usual spot on and Park was a creature of habit, he liked his cards, poker or black Jack, he always thought he could beat the odds. Jack had sworn he would be there and that he'd leave around midnight. *Patience Tony my boy patience and you can have another Irish fuckers notch on your bed post...It feels good doesn't it Tony...revenge... ha...yeah revenge is sweet.*

Tony went to the back door of the car and pulled out a small briefcase sized package a roll of duck tape and some instant grab adhesive. Tommy stood on watch as he rolled under the driver's side of the car and wound the tape round the exhaust pipe close to the driver's seat. Grab adhesive was liberally smeared on top and the box secured with the rest of the reel. There was no way it was coming off. Two loose wires dangled down and Tony ran back to the car to get a smaller piece of C4 which he stuck to the side of the petrol tank before inserting a detonator and connecting the wires. Park wouldn't know what hit him.

Time passed slowly particularly as Tony insisted on no smoking in case it drew attention, instead Tommy sucked noisily on a kojak style lollipop which was annoying the life out of Frank. "For fuck's sake Tommy...stop fucking slurping or I'll tell mum you eat like a pig!"

"Easy boys easy, it's almost midnight, our mark should be out soon. You ready to fly a plane again Tommy?" His face lit up in a grin and the sweet was forgotten.

Michael Park came out of the door with a couple of guys shook hands as they said farewell and headed towards his car, he had a swagger to his walk, tonight had been very lucrative. *Who fucking needs Dermot and his bunch of Jackasses; I make more money from protection than the rest of 'em.* He patted his pocket stuffed with Euros notes...*This time it's one for me one for you Dermot, I'm fucked if I'm paying it all over.*

With the apparent indestructability of youth on his side he jumped into the car turned the key and the engine roared into life idling while the Bluetooth connection to his phone went live. Even though there was a code red meaning that he should be checking things first he didn't think it would ever reach him. He blipped the accelerator waiting for the Bluetooth link up. It didn't take long before music blasted out of his speaker and his heavy bass box locked away in the boot. He selected his favourite tracks to drive to...power rock and roll, put the car in gear and made the wheels squealed as he spun in reverse before flicking the paddle gear stick forward and slamming the accelerator causing him to fishtail out of the car park.

"Now Tommy, now....fucking now Tommy!"

Tommy was pushing the paddle as hard to the right as he could but there was no reaction. "Left Tommy fucking turn left!"

Park was now a good few hundred meters away but as Tommy dipped the left wing an almighty boom rang out in the night, flames jumped in the air, shop windows shattered, the car was a mangled flaming wreck. It would take a long long time to piece together whoever was inside. Park had just about vaporised.

"Oops, maybe used a bit much plastic." He turned to Tommy smacking him playfully over the head. "Fucking donut Tommy, I told yer we had failsafe detonaters if the first ones didn't go off."

"It ain't my fault Tony."

"No, no I guess you're right, they were pretty old, some of 'em were bound to be dodgy." A huge smile cracked across his face. "Anyway....boom fucking boom eh? Home James; back to the cottage."

It didn't take long for the news to filter through to Dermot that Park had been murdered. "Fucking Gerry Malone! Argh I should have called him...Boy get me Malone on the phone before we all go to war."

Chapter 51
Bodies

TOBY AND SCHNEIDER had predicted the timing of the next email, things were accelerating on a pre-planned scale which Toby had managed to decipher, it had been ten hours since the last communication; the next would be in either eight or six. There was also the problem that the emails were starting to contain threats that could prove devastating. As it rolled up on the screen they jointly hit print, somehow the written word on a piece of paper made it all the more sinister.

Tick tock, tick tock...still watching the clock?

Either Bridget Donovan, Jack Fitzgerald, or both, are still missing.

The emergency code that has been triggered has now moved to the next phase. It is essential that Bridget Donovan and Jack Fitzgerald gain access to a computer. You are reminded of the consequences if they are unable to keep their data file safely locked away. All information held on people responsible for murders, locations of bodies, dates and times of clandestine meetings, payments to senior politicians and immunity letters granted by the UK government will become public.

In eight hours time details of where to find the bodies of innocent Catholics murdered by the 2nd Battalion C Company buried on a beach in County Lough will be revealed. Six hours later the names of the persons responsible for the murders will be published. Presumably without the convenient immunity letters handed to IRA members prosecutions will result. The dates relevant to the first burials are January 1991 to June 1992. More will follow.

The movement's motto is "Quis Separabit", or more simply "Who will separate us?"

We have now been separated and will have our revenge. Tick tock, tick tock.

Schneider read the email out loud. "Jesus this girl knows how to build the pressure. Man the phones Toby the calls will start coming from on high although there's nothing we can do."

Jack sat back at the apartment with time to kill picked up his messages from the ITT service in London. The female voice leaving the messages was soft and easy to listen to.

A Mr Joey left a message: Bridget now on Russian untouchable list, debt confirmed, not sold. Call at the office for more information. End of message one.

A Mr Dermot: Called six times, please ring on this number. End of message two.

A Mr Jon Barnwell: Please reconsider your actions and call him. Martin has the number. End of message three.

He turned to Martin and handed him a post it note where he had scribbled down Barnwell's message. "You can talk to him Martin. I'm going to call Joey then that shite Dermot."

Joey was sat in the office when the phone was delivered to his table by Carlos. "It's Jack."

"Thanks for calling Jack...Any news?"

"No, nothing Joey, although with luck we should have Paolo here in an hour or so to question about his potential involvement, what else do you have to say to me, me old mucker, I'm hungry for news so I am."

"Rasvan is an unhappy man but has a bit more respect for us now. The boys saw a fireworks party near Annabell's and one of the rockets must have gone astray. He should be able to reopen in a few months. Anyway he confirmed that Paolo owes them more than a hundred grand and that the debt still belongs to them. Olaf had talks with the South American's but didn't sell it on as Paolo promised the money within ten days."

"He could never fecking raise that much so quickly, something smells."

"Argh, I agree with ye Jack. He's involved somewhere, I can feel it in me water."

"We'll see in the next hour or so, he'll soon start talking, what else?"

"Someone's been very busy over in Ireland. It looks like the troubles might be starting up again so it does. Gerry Malone's place in Ferndale has been bombed and Michael Park, god rest his soul, has been vaporized in his car...none too professional...someone used enough explosive to take out a tank let alone a BMW. Maybe Gerry is sending a message to Dermot but it's getting serious that's for sure."

A smile spread across Jack's face. *I owe you Tony.* "I'll be calling Dermot next. Thanks for the update Joey. I'll keep in touch. Have ye got a direct number for the next twelve hours?"

Joey flipped his mobile over and read the number from the sticker on the back. One of the problems of changing the Pay as you go SIM every few days was that he could never remember it. Jack read it back and punched it in to his phone before comparing notes with Martin who was sat at the breakfast bar drinking a black coffee while talking to Rachel and Max explaining the importance of time when it came to getting a kidnap victim back in one piece and asking what they'd be prepared to do if it was one of them. The discussion was sobering. Max's mood mellowed dramatically, he felt for Jack with all his heart. *If it had been Rachel?*

Ever the military man Martin recapped what they thought they knew. "So...Joey has confirmed that Paolo owes the Russians serious money and he's confirmed they swear that they've got nothing to do with the kidnap. Do we believe them Jack?"

He was pacing up and down on the tiled floor holding his chin, deep in thought. "I think we do. Joey got their attention by torching one of their best clubs and Rasvan has confirmed that a notice has gone out placing Bridget on their untouchable list...Not that it's doing her any fecking good. She's on three government untouchable lists and a number of drug gang lists and we still haven't found her." He shook his head in frustration. "So help me if they've harmed a hair on her head."

"Focus Jack. The Russians are out. My discussion with Barnwell suggests that the UK and Irish governments aren't involved either. I don't trust Barnwell but you could hear the stress in his voice. Whatever it is that Bridget has released on their technology systems is causing blue bloody murder and could bring the governments down, they're as desperate as we are to find her. So who does that leave?"

"Fecking Dermot! Otherwise we're looking for some random unconnected person."

"Random doesn't happen Jack, I never believe in coincidences. You best ring Dermot and I'll update Bashar, his flights due in the next few hours."

Jack walked out onto the balcony overlooking the busy street below and the tourists lazing on the beach enjoying the golden sands and azure blue sea. *It should be me with Bridget frolicking in the surf. Don't give up sweetheart, I'll find you. Time to ring the dirty old bastard.*

As the phone rang Dermot jumped from his chair. "Jack! What the fuck are you trying to do! Start another war? Get us all sent to prison? Come to your senses man, I swear on my mother's life and my own life we've nothing to do with Bridget's kidnap and Gerry Malone swears the same."

"So you're friends with Malone now Dermot? You always were the slippery one so you were but I'd have bet against yer being cosy friends with the other side." Dermot winced at the spoken words, they cut deeply. *How was he going to get through to the man*? "I've told ye before Dermot your words are cheap, I couldn't care a shite whose life you swear on."

"Do you think I'd be so stupid as to go to jail over Bridget? I've been careful not to get caught all me life and now you and your girl are about to try and pin a murder or two on me by telling them where to find the bodies and who did it. For feck's sake Jack I'm not that stupid. See sense man! You'll bring us all down."

"If I haven't got Bridget then it really doesn't matter does it. We'll all be judged at some point. If what you say is true then you better redouble your efforts to find her. Goodbye Dermot."

Jack stood staring out to sea mulling over the conversation before updating Martin.

"You know Martin, Dermot has always been good at one thing...looking after himself...He's panicking, he thinks he's going to jail." Jack paused collecting his thoughts. "Which he will if we don't find Bridget...It hurts but I'm inclined to believe him...He wouldn't risk going to jail if he knew where she was..."

"But that leaves only one line of enquiry...Paolo and whoever he owes money to but why would they kidnap Bridget? She hardly knows him and doesn't have any real connection to him? Hopefully he'll have some answers."

"If Dermot's out I better call Joey before my boys bring Ireland back to the dark days. Anything else I need to do Martin."

"Just try to stay calm Jack, stay calm, we're getting to the short strokes."

Chapter 52
Heading Home

THE DRIVE BACK TO THE COTTAGE was uneventful and Tony slept better than he had in years. The voices were placated, his buddies were at rest. He mulled things over in his mind. *Can I now rest, is revenge all I needed?* He picked up the notes from the bedside table that Dr Jones had given him and started repeating the phrases and exercises. *No more funny business Tony... Straight and narrow.* Even though it was only seven in the morning Tony decided to get back to his regime. He pulled on a T shirt and shorts before setting off on a five mile run. He returned for breakfast feeling brilliant and in control.

"Right boys. We're going home, let's pack up and wipe down all surfaces that might have prints on them."

An hour later Tommy was left to carry out the final wipe downs while Frank and Tony headed back to see Father O'Brien; he hadn't been expecting them and was clearly flustered. After a lot of talking eventually Tony persuaded him that the safest place for the unused explosives would be back in the crypt, he relied heavily on Jack's influence saying it was what he would have wanted.

"I hope the good lord can forgive you boys for what ye've done. We could be going back to a very dark period so we could, I hope Jack is happy tis all I can say...Now do you have any news on Jack or the Donovan girl."

Tony shook his head. "Best to keep things in separate compartments don't you think Father. I'm sure Jack'll be in touch soon enough."

Frank's ears suddenly pricked up. "Whoa back track vicar...what was that you said?"

"I'm not sure I know what you mean, I was just asking if ye had heard from Jack."

"No...You asked about the Donovan girl...We haven't said any fing to you about her." He reached out with his bear like hands and grabbed the vicar by the throat. "Now who've you been talking to you piece of scum? Call yourself a man of the cloth? Fuck you! Start talking or you'll find out how persuasive I can be." Frank gave him a back hand slap just to make things interesting.

The vicar coughed immediately. "MI5 were here asking about Jack and Miss Donovan. I didn't say anything about you. I swear so strike me down god if I'm telling a lie....It wouldn't do for me to admit that I store arms for the cause now would it?"

Frank looked across at Tony for direction. "Hang 'im up on the cross upstairs Frank, see what he thinks of his god then. He can die on the cross like his hero."

"No, no boys, you've got me all wrong, I'm loyal to Jack so I am. I'd never breathe a word that would put you in trouble. I just listened; I didn't tell them anything new." Being held a foot off the floor against the wall and thinking his time was about to come to an end his bladder gave way causing a spit spat splatter on the floor. Frank let go and father O'Brien dropped into his own pool of urine.

"For the love of god you've got to believe me."

"Leave 'im Frank, he ain't worth it. We'll let Jack decide his fate. But know this you piece of shit...If you tell anyone about us your god won't be able to save you. We'll hunt you down and exact our own form of retribution."

The discussion at the shop come bar was much easier. Rory, although disappointed not be taking the boys out pike fishing could understand their concerns about the recent resurgence in violence.

"Argh to be sure the summer bookings will all be cancelled. The Americans won't be coming now the bombings have started again. I understand why you're leaving early boys but I hope to see yer back. Thanks for the business now."

As they drove to Dublin to catch the ferry Frank and Tommy were still arguing about the pistols. Tommy had wanted to take them back to London to sell on but Frank had refused on the grounds that security might be tight on the way back. He just hoped that it was too soon for the border forces to be checking cars for traces of explosives.

"Listen Tommy. As soon as we're back in London these false plates are getting dumped in little pieces along the motorway, and me old mucker as soon as we're home this motor is going through the auctions."

"I ain't giving up me motor Frank."

"You will Tommy...sooner or later people will remember a black Discovery near the scenes of the bombs and we won't be owning it then. I know that everyone on the estate will swear it never moved but there's cameras bloody everywhere these days."

Tony rarely got involved in their arguments but interjected. "He's right Tommy, it's got to go. We'll chip in to help you change it won't we Frank."

Frank's face was a picture and he muttered under his breathe. "Fucking hell Tony! Then again he's always been a spoilt brat."

Sat round Frank's Mum's table with a pot of tea and a Victoria sponge cake Tony's mobile pinged.

Ring Joey McCann on this number when you can talk.

Tony was among friends shared the message and rang back immediately. After some small talk Joey got to the point. "I've been talking to Jack and he asked me to get hold of you. He says thanks for all your help, it was much more than he expected, if you could stand down until contacted he would appreciate it. I hope it makes sense to you Tony, he wouldn't tell me what you'd been up to but I've got an idea in me head so I have. I hope the Guinness was good...shit, sorry Tony, I forgot you're on the wagon."

"Yeah, I'm on the wagon and happy Joey. I've exercised a few demons, it's the straight and narrow for me now."

Chapter 53
Letter Bombs

"PRIME MINISTER, PRIME MINISTER, have you seen the headlines?" Nick rushed into the PM's office ignoring the secretary's pleas that he was busy. "Look at this front page of the Mirror...'Letter Bombs'...its believed that the recent resumption in bombings and attacks in Northern Ireland are linked to the revelation that dissident IRA members were given immunity from prosecution as part of the peace process deal."

"And the mail is just as bad...'Bombs linked to IRA concessions'...The broadsheets are also covering it but as you would expect they look for a bit more proof first. It hasn't stopped the tabloids talking about an unnamed Civil Servant confirming the existence of the letters and that there could be fifty or more in circulation...We must have a leak... it needs fixed fast."

The Prime Minister sat back in his chair stretching his neck from side to side to relieve the knots while looking skywards for divine intervention.

"Jesus Nick. Where have you been the last few days? Of course we've got a leak...Bridget Donovan is leaking more information every twelve hours and so far we still haven't found out how to stop it or found her!" He grasped the edge of his desk his knuckles going white in contrast to the angry redness showing on his face. "Do something useful, manage the papers, call the editors...do what you're paid to do! In the next twenty four hours this government could be brought down and we'll all be looking for jobs. I don't want to know about the papers Nick, not unless the headline is Bridget Donovan found... get it?!" He sat back down and went back to reading the files on his desk blanking his press secretary...Hopefully he'd take the hint.

When he heard the click of the door closing he stood and paced round the room. *No matter what happens I will be secure. Time to stand down and appoint my deputy? Health concerns? Hmm...Possibly a good option... Conflict of interest...maybe...We'll talk over dinner tonight.* After consulting the cabinet whereabouts list he called his secretary. "Jenny, can you set up a private dinner with the Chancellor tonight at Rules, tell him it's strictly confidential and extremely important that we talk.

Sat in a quite back room at Rules the oldest surviving restaurant in London the Chancellor didn't know whether to believe the Prime Minister or not, there was no love lost between them and they only kept a coordinated front for the sake of the party. In his eyes the PM was a puppet for sale to the highest paying lobbyist, a slimy snake who wriggled and turned to get the best publicity or more importantly the best for himself, the two generally went glove in hand. The man lacked morales, he'd cosy up to anyone if it filled his pockets. A change was needed, prudence was needed but could he believe what he was hearing? Could it just be yet another trap to try set the party faithful against him?

He took another mouthful of his Steak and Kidney pie wondering how many calories it would add to his waistline, the PM loved the place but delicacy wasn't their watch word...*tradition that was it traditional British food, superbly cooked but most definitely calorific.* How ironic given that the man in front of him had destroyed many a great tradition since his election to the head of the party. Indeed the faithful no longer knew what the party stood for they had moved so far into the middle ground.

As he swallowed he probed with another question. "And how long have you known about these health problems?"

"It's been a while now but the last meeting with my consultant really brought things home. He said I was a ticking bomb and that if I didn't change my lifestyle that it could happen at any time.... You're the only person in the cabinet I've told. If I go it'll be a done deal that they'll agree to you taking over so we may as well prepare the ground...of course I'll recommend you for the position."

On his way back to Downing Street the Chancellor was running the night's conversation through his head. *Could it be true? Finally he'd get to be Prime Minister and do a proper job? He'd have to check up on the PM's health problems on the quiet...the PM couldn't be trusted... was he missing an angle?*

Chapter 54
Collection

STEVE SPOTTED PAOLO'S CAR as he pulled up outside Paco's bar in Vistamar. He turned to the pilot. "I swear I don't know how the guy does it. He snorts so much cocaine and shags so many different women it's amazing that he isn't dead yet. I could be wrong but I bet he's passed out upstairs somewhere."

As they walked into the bar Paco's sixth sense picked up that they weren't here just to pass the time of day or for a coffee. He said nothing but flicked his eyes and head towards one of the doors in an unspoken communication. Carter nodded back and headed straight to the room to retrieve Paolo from his stupor. The scene that greeted them was pretty much as expected. Paolo was still passed out on his back having not moved since his exertions. His nose and mouth were smeared with the remnants of the drug fuelled party. Belinda had pulled a sheet around herself at some stage and was curled up in the foetal position breathing heavily and oblivious to the world. Steve grabbed Paolo's arm and shook him. No response.

"Grab a glass or two of water and chuck 'em over him."

The pilot complied with Steve's instructions but it didn't even illicit a groan. "Oh shit, he's totally out of it, let's grab his clothes, stick them in a bin bag and wrap him in a blanket for now. There's no way we'll get him dressed when he's this out of it. Here give me a hand to wrap him up and get him over my shoulder."

With the pilot's help Steve balanced Paolo using a classic fireman's lift. His dead weight made carrying him much harder than he expected as he grabbed the rail on the stairs to steady himself. Paco motioned his disgust as they passed the bar, given recent events voicing an opinion seemed like a bad idea but he was sure his body language and facial expressions conveyed his thoughts. His bar was set up for people to enjoy themselves but he abhorred the excess of the gringo but then again it didn't stop him taking his money. Steve bumped Paolo's head against the frame as he tried to negotiate the door to the garden outside.

"Oops, sorry Paolo."

No response. *What did he expect?* "Just a few more yards Paolo and we'll put you down in the back of the pick up." As Steve manoeuvred him into position the pilot held his head and stuck it on a pile of old cement bags before Steve unceremoniously dumped the rest of him into the back. He tossed the keys from his pocket to his compatriat "You drive, I'll call ahead."

Shit I've gotta get out of this job no matter how much it pays. Sooner or later we'll all end up dead. He pulled his mobile from his pocket and called Martin as the pilot gunned the pick up towards the small airstrip.

"Martin? I've got your package but I want to make it clear that I'm not a delivery boy and I want out of this operation as soon as possible."

A smile spread across Martin's face. "Ah, well done Mr Carter and nice speech, but you will be delivering him back to Rio in person. As I said before your life and your family's depends on it."

"Go fuck yourself! He's comatose as predicted. I've wrapped him in a blanket and I'll load him into the plane and that's it."

"No Mr Carter, that's not it! You will accompany Mr Williams to Rio or you will suffer the consequences. If you wish to resign it needs to be done through the proper channels and Mr Kaddouri will be here to talk with you in person. I will excuse you telling me to go fuck myself this once, repeat it and I'll kick the shit out of you. Are you listening Mr Carter?"

Steve's bravado evaporated in the face of Martin's cool collected manner. "Okay, okay, we'll see you in a couple of hours."

The lightweight six seater Cessna took a bit longer to make the journey than the fast jet but a pre cleared landing into Rio Galeo International helped them save fifteen minutes or so. Steve was impressed with the pilot; he was totally focussed on what he had to do and didn't seem to be at all fazed that he had a comatose naked man wrapped in a sheet tucked in behind the seats. It wasn't an everyday occurrence but flying in Brazil he'd seen stranger things and from the groans coming from the back at least he knew that his cargo was alive.

Enrique had arranged collection in an unmarked van with no windows by two forgettable faces. Jack had wanted to collect him in person but common sense prevailed, there was no point putting himself in the line of fire. Steve went to get in the back to keep an eye on Paolo but was pushed away and handed a piece of paper by one of the goons. It was a slip for a hotel on the front at Copacabana beach with 'Room booked, meet at breakfast' scribbled across it. He shrugged walked back to the plane and grabbed his holdall. The pilot stopped him for a signature on his flight sheet and offered him a lift into town. *Why not maybe they could go for a beer, he seemed like a decent guy.*

Paolo felt like someone was hammering his head with a pick axe as his eyes tried to force themselves open. He gagged as strong hands held his jaw and poured warm coffee into his mouth. "Come on Gringo, we need you awake." Yellowed teeth stared back at him as an eyelid eventually held open. His mind wandered and he rolled back onto his side trying to cuddle up to Belinda. *Where's she gone? I'm cold...* The effort was too much and he drifted back off as the van zipped along the motorway back to the warehouse district. The bump as the van backed up the ramp into the workshop brought him out of his stupor momentarily and once again sweet warm coffee was forced down his throat. He coughed and mumbled "fuck off" at no one in particular. When he next came round he was under a stream of cool water sat on the floor of a filthy tiled shower area, he shook his head. *Fuck where am I?*

A glass was forced into his hand. "Here drink this, you'll feel better." Paolo took it without thought and chugged it back. A towel was thrown in his direction. "Dry off."

Standing was still a bit of an issue and he decided that staying on all fours was currently a better option while he tried to towel dry his hair. "Where am I, where's Belinda? Ah, Jesus my head, anyone got some rum?" His momentary focus lapsed and he tried to curl up on the floor and go back to sleep. He was vaguely aware of being lifted under his arms and a scratching sensation on his right arm as a cannula was inserted. The drugs pumped through it suddenly coursed through his system bringing him instantly back to the present.

"Fuck, where am I? Where's my clothes?"

He was strapped into an upright wooden chair. He could feel a concrete floor under his feet and from the echo of his voice he could tell that he was in a large room. A bright light shone directly at him making it difficult to see. His reddened eyes smarted and he found it difficult to keep them open.

"Turn the bloody light off I can't see, it's killing my eyes. If it's about the money I told you I'd pay in ten days and it's only been three. What do you expect bloody miracles?"

Max and Rachel were sat at the back of the warehouse being forced to watch as Paolo struggled to adapt. As much as she hated him Rachel felt sorry for Paolo, yes he'd brought this on himself but he was being treated like an animal, he didn't deserve this, surely he hadn't harmed anyone. Yes he tended to run fast and loose spending money that wasn't his but he couldn't have sacrificed Bridget could he?

"What the fuck is this?" Paolo bucked against his chair nodding in the direction of the cannula and tube hanging out of his arm.

Martin responded from behind the light. "Settle down Paolo, it's just a cannula to make it easier to get you rehydrated and in a fit state to answer some questions. We've pepped it up with some amphetamine so if you give it twenty minutes you'll be feeling fine, well I say fine but that depends on your answers to some tricky little questions.

Chapter 55
Out Of The Pan...

DRESSED IN HER DAMP CLOTHES and with wet hair Bridget looked out into the garden to check for the van. The gates were still closed and there was no one in sight. *C'mon Bridget, time to move.* She padded down the corridor and opened the door into the hallway conscious of the creak from the hinges as she pushed on the heavy door, no one came running. *You can do this Bridge.* The front door was open letting a light breeze from the gardens and fountain into the hallway, the smooth stone steps were cool on her feet before she trod on the gravel path. It was uncomfortable but not painful, living in Spain she was often barefoot around the house and gardens and always on the beach, her skin was tougher than most. *Thank goodness I didn't get a pedicure.* The scent of mint and sage jumped up to meet her as her legs brushed against the plants making her recall the time that she was brought here but also making her feel alive. She headed directly towards the huge gates but as she reached them her heart sank. There was no pedestrian doorway and the gates were electronically controlled with no override button in sight. She would either have to climb and jump or try to find the control box. *You haven't got time Bridget, climb!*

There was a silvery leaved tree with a purple blossom to one side that reached up to the top of the wall.

Unsteadily she grasped a branch with one hand and placed one leg high up the trunk while pushing off with her other leg and grabbing for the next bough. She caught it by her finger nails and clung on for dear life as she slowly straightened her legs and made herself secure. *Hard part over, now just get to the top.* Five foot above her she could see the top of the wall and made it to the summit in three moves. The view was not what she expected. She gave herself a quick speech.

"Oh fuck! Breathe Bridget breathe, c'mon girl it's not that high..."

She didn't think she was doing a very good job of convincing herself, heights weren't her thing and the gardens were three foot higher than the other side of the wall, she had to be twenty feet up. There was no going back, she had to jump. She slowly lifted her legs onto the outer side of the wall and balanced herself on her stomach before letting herself down as far as she could with her arms. She was committed but still was a good ten to twelve feet off the ground. She pushed away but failed to let go with her left hand and clattered down the face of the wall grazing her nose and face and landing in a crumpled heap at the bottom instantly rolling on her back and grasping her ankle while letting out a muffled scream.

"Oh god, please don't let it be broken, please..."

As she tried to stand her ankle wouldn't support her weight and a piercing pain shot up her leg. She mentally screamed at herself. *C'mon you've got his far!!* Using a hand against the wall as support she hobbled away from the gates. Across the busy road she could see industrial units but she had to try and get further away before asking for help, her kidnappers surely had friends and eyes and ears locally. *Two or three streets Bridge, for Jack, don't let him down.* She dabbed at the bloody graze on her nose and face with her sleeve. *So much for being inconspicuous, fifty yards done, keep going. Fuck my ankle hurts!*

Two hundred yards on and two streets further back there was a sight for sore eyes, a tatty café with a sign up for the internet, she hopped unsteadily on one leg across the road hoping beyond hope that it was true, if she could get to a computer she could summon help. As she got to the shopfront she clattered unsteadily into one of the white steel tables outside, all eyes turned to look at her. *What was a tourist doing in this area?* She straightened herself up and walked as best she could through the door using the bar for support. A gnarly faced middle aged man looked back at her impassively.

"Hi, can I get a coke and use a computer?"

He shrugged and pointed to the back of the café while pulling a cold bottle out of the fridge. Bridget had hobbled to the seat and was trying to work out which coins she had to put in to the computer to get it to work having emptied her pocket onto the table beside her. The old man appeared with a tray placed the coke and a glass on the table, picked up one of two of the dollar bills and headed off back to the till. Bridget was cursing.

"I'm so close and I can't work out how to use a fucking coin machine!!!!"

Everything she tried to feed it rejected. The owner appeared at her side again put two coins into the machine and hit the front with the flat of his hand. The coins dropped and the screen slowly came to life. He looked carefully at Bridget who was thanking him profusely before handing her a wet towel and motioning to her face and nose with a wiping motion.

"Yes, thank you, thank you."

The machine was incredibly slow as was the internet connection. She just needed to get to the dark web and one of her emergency caches. Her eyes scanned the room in constant panic. *Was the barman watching her?* She was sure he kept glancing in her direction. As her page finally opened she clicked over to the C:\ prompt, old school using DOS commands would be much faster. As the screen blinked she typed in three commands

Run locator

Post locator

Post medical B

All three set off subroutines and once the commands were received by her server messages would ping off at high speed. The locator programme identified her ip address and translated it into an address and location, the post command instantly sent the location out to a list of ten people, some she could trust, others that hated her but all with a vested interest in finding her alive. The medical B post went out to the same list.

As she stopped typing she was aware of shouting out in the street and the owner was now openly staring at her. He walked calmly out from behind the bar before flipping the notice on his door to closed and making towards her with a piece of paper in his hand, there was nothing she could do, her ankle prevented her from running and she wouldn't stand much of a chance against his bulk.

He stood over her and placed the sheet of paper on the desk, her face was staring back at her with the word 'Reward' and something indecipherable in Portuguese underneath, it couldn't be from her captors it was too quick. She looked up at the big man and made an assessment. *He's got kind eyes...you're gonna have to trust him Bridge...there's no escape.*

"Quick lady, out back." He helped her up and took her through to a storeroom where he kicked over a few boxes and opened the back door before lifting a floor hatch which had steps heading down. He motioned to the stairs. "You hide, I tell them you run out back."

Was it a trap? Had she just jumped out of the frying pan into the fire? Please Jack come get me!

Chapter 56
All Hands On Deck

TOBY AND DOUG were beavering away at their desks trying to trace the source of the last email without much success. They'd set up a monitoring system to capture the next communication and run an instant trace which hopefully would get them past the servers in Russia that seemed to be blocking their progress. Simultaneously both of their inboxes flashed red.

Tick Tock...

Bridget Donovan or Jack Fitzgerald are still unable to gain access to a computer.

Action required: Send armed help immediately!

Last known location: Ciudad de Deus, Rio de Janeiro, TV Judas or TV Lais.

IP Address: Exact IP unkown

Bridget Donovan has sent a distress call with her location. All recipients of this notice are requested to respond immediately.

Tick Tock stop watching the clock.

Schneider picked up the phone and called the head of security in Ireland while patching in Jon Barnwell. Toby checked the email over for embedded commands or viruses, gave it the all clear, and forwarded it to the 'need to know group' giving Doug the thumbs up indicating that the file had been sent. As he brought his hands back to the keyboard his screen flashed red again;

Tick Tock...

Bridget Donovan or Jack Fitzgerald are still unable to gain access to a computer.

Action required: Bridget Donovan needs urgent medical treatment. Send medics now.

Last known location: Ciudad de Deus, Rio de Janeiro, TV Judas or TV Lais

Blood type: O rhesus negative

Allergies: Penicillin

Known medical issues: Asthma/Breathing difficulties

Additional information: [None]

Tick Tock stop watching the clock.

"Shit, this could all be over Doug, she needs medical attention. I'll clear the file and forward it to the need to know group. Fuck this could be bad."

Thirty minutes later outside number ten a paramedic arrived on a motorbike and rushed in to the Prime Minister.

"Are you ready Sir?"

"Yes, yes." He turned to his new MI5 temporary press officer. "Are you ready with the press release?"

"It's typed up and ready to go. We won't release it until you've been in hospital for a least an hour or so."

The PM turned to the paramedic. "Is there anything I should be doing? We've made my face up so that I've gone pale and got dark rings round the eyes. Anything more dramatic needed?"

"It would probably help if you were seen to be clutching your chest Sir. I'll get in the back of the State car with you and we'll blue light it round to King Edwards VII's hospital. We have a consultant waiting, an operation room set aside, and staff that are all secret service as am I. It should be smooth Sir."

"What does the press release say?"

"Downing Street confirm that the Prime minister was rushed to King Edward the VII's hospital today suffering with a heart condition. He is receiving treatment and is expected to undergo a minor operation to resolve issues. Given his ill health the Prime Minister has decided to hand control of the government to the Chancellor until the cabinet are able to formally elect his successor to continue the good work that is returning the UK to economic growth and social equality. The Prime Minister has also confirmed that he will stand down as an MP at the next election.

No further information is available at this time.

We've also added a second page with a biography and key achievements so hopefully the tabloids will be singing about your achievements and lamenting your departure rather than digging up crap about the peace settlement."

"Good, good, well then, let the show begin. Oh, before I go make sure Barnwell is on the case and keeps everything under wraps."

The Paparazzi hanging round Downing Street for the chance of a saleable photograph hit pay dirt as the PM emerged from number 10 aided by a paramedic to a waiting car which received a police escort. The photos were uploaded to the news agency and within minutes had been snapped up by the main news channels who broadcast them as 'breaking news'...Prime Minister rushed to hospital.

In the back of the car the PM was sure that he had chest pains...*was he over acting or was something really wrong?* "I didn't think this would happen for a least a week...Damn Bridget Donovan...Ouch...Jesus my chest... I'm struggling to breathe...help me."

Chapter 57
Confession

"YOU DON'T NEED to do this...I'll answer whatever you want to know...I've told you that I'll have the money in a few days, I'll pay, I promise, my life depends on it."

"What money Paolo?"

Paolo's drug fuelled brain and hangover was making it difficult for him to think. *Who is it? The Russians or Gomez trying to enforce his gambling debts?"* He stalled. "Yer know, the money I owe you, I said I'd pay, I was going to talk to my brother Max today to get him to lend me the money; he's got the cash not me."

At the back of the room Max let his head drop onto the back of the chair so that he was looking up at the ceiling, Rachel clamped a hand over her mouth shocked at what she'd just heard. She grabbed Max's thigh and squeezed making him look at her before slowly shaking her head and imploring him with her eyes and speaking quietly. "Not this time Max, not again..."

Paolo picked up the different voice but couldn't place it. *A women? Could it be Bridget? Maybe it was Gomez behind the light.* "Whose there? Is that Bridget?" No response.

"Listen, Gomez, I'll pay okay, I'll pay but I've gotta get the money from Max...I don't own the development up north...he does. I told you that you'd kidnapped the wrong woman."

Jack was ready to explode and it was all that Martin could do to keep him quiet and let the confession come naturally. The mention of Bridget's name had him lunging forward and Stretch trying to hold him back along with Clarkey. Martin motioned him into a corner and spoke in a whisper.

"For fuck's sake Jack...Ease up, he's talking, we're getting information quickly. As soon as he dries up then you can torture the rest out of him. Don't be impatient now; we're close to getting real answers." He turned and walked back to stand behind the light and continue with his gentle prodding.

"Why do you think Bridget is here Paolo?"

Shit, it must be the Russians, no it can't be, it's gotta be Gomez. "I thought I heard a women's voice and you did kidnap her didn't you. I told you that you had the wrong women Gomez and I told you that it'd cause a heap of trouble but you wouldn't believe me. I told your bozo's that phoned up, you've got the wrong girl and I don't have the money yet anyway. What am I supposed to do Gomez eh? I can't pay you strapped to a chair." He slumped forward exhausted with the effort of stringing so many words together. Rachel winced realising that she was supposed to be the kidnap victim... *How could he do that to her?*

Martin questioned Enrique with a look. He nodded his head, he knew who Gomez was, small time, retired, this wasn't his normal style but it had to be checked. He pointed to two of his men teamed with two of Martin's and circled his hand with one finger in the air signalling them to load up and go find him. "Keep in phone contact, bring him back here alive."

Paolo heard movement and made a final plea. "Listen Gomez, I'm sorry I'm late with the cash, I'll make it up to you, I just need a bit of time."

Jack couldn't stand the whinging and whining any longer, he had to know the truth... "Stretch give me your blow torch."

Rachel leapt from her seat. "No! That's barbaric."

Jack fixed Max with a steely stare. "I've told you once Max...I won't tell you a third time...Keep Rachel out of this." He grabbed the blow torch and walked out from behind the light much to Paolo's relief.

"Hallelujah Jack! Thank fuck you're here...get me out of this... that fucker Gomez has got me trussed up like a turkey for Christmas."

Jack didn't say a word. He turned the gas tap on the side of the burner and clicked the electric spark generator, a huge yellow flame burst from the front and he adjusted the flow to get a neat triangular concentrated blue flame. Paolo's face was a picture of confusion.

"What are you doing Jack? Stop mucking about and cut me loose."

He didn't waste time with explanations stepping forward and applying the bright blue flame to Paolo's face bringing up a huge blister on the right cheek that burst as the flame went deeper. He then moved his attention to his nipple. His terrified blood curdling scream echoed round the warehouse and was followed by the smell of burnt hair and singed flesh. Rachel gagged and brought up her breakfast in the corner with Max holding her head and trying to keep the contents of his own stomach down. A bucket of cold water was thrown over Paolo to bring him back round.

Jack loomed over him torch at the ready. "Now then Paolo, you were saying something about Bridget, where is she?"

"Fuck, fuck, why did you do that? I don't know Jack...I promise I don't know..."

"Wrong answer." Jack applied the blow torch to the other nipple but this time made sure that he didn't cause him to pass out. Once again Paolo let out a heart rending scream.

"No, no, no more...I don't know where she is but I know who's got her...Gomez and Pedro took her."

"Pedro who?"

"Garcia's brother or cousin, the local drug guy up north...please let me go Jack, I'll tell you everything I promise...aghhh for fuck's sake...no!"

Jack applied the heat to his manhood singeing the delicate skin. "I know you will Paolo, I know you will. I'll ask you again where is she?"

By now Paolo was going into shock, his body was shaking. Martin stepped forward and upped the dose of drugs to keep him stable and talking. "Please Jack, please, I don't know. I owe them a quarter of a million dollars and the Russians over a hundred grand sterling....I was supposed to win at cards but they tricked me...please Jack."

"Stop whining and finish the story."

"I told them I couldn't pay but they wouldn't believe me...they thought I owned the development...they must have confused me with Max and kidnapped Bridget thinking she was Rachel...please Jack no more."

The mention of Bridget's name brought out a sadistic streak and he turned the blue flame onto Paolo's penis once more causing him to pass out. Another bucket of cold water doused him.

"I don't know anymore...I don't know anymore... please..." Paolo was sobbing, tears were running down his face.

As Jack was about to start again his phone vibrated in his pocket; at the same time Enrique received a phone call. He read the message.

Tick Tock...

Bridget Donovan or Jack Fitzgerald are still unable to gain access to a computer.

Action required: Send armed help immediately!

Last known location: Ciudad de Deus, Rio de Janeiro, TV Judas or TV Lais.

IP Address: Exact address unknown

Bridget Donovan has sent a distress call with her location. All recipients of this notice are requested to respond immediately.

Tick Tock stop watching the clock.

Relief washed over him and he went to turn to Enrique who was trying to tell him he had a lead when the second message pinged through.

Tick Tock...

Bridget Donovan or Jack Fitzgerald are still unable to gain access to a computer.

Action required: Bridget Donovan needs urgent medical treatment. Send medics now.

Last known location: Ciudad de Deus, Rio de Janeiro, TV Judas or TV Lais.

Blood type: O rhesus negative

Allergies: Penicillin

Known medical issues: Asthma/Breathing difficulties

Additional information: [None]

Tick Tock stop watching the clock.

Jack's face filled with pain. "Get a medic there Enrique, she's injured." He pulled out a nine millimetre

Glock from the rear of his waistband and turned to Max and Rachel pointing the gun directly at them before spinning on his heel and squeezing the trigger placing a neat bullet hole through Paolo's right knee before spitting on him. At the sound of the gun Rachel screamed and Max fell to his knees losing the battle to keep the contents of his stomach. He forced himself to look, Paolo was still alive but for how long and would they be next?

Jack placed a huge hand on the back of Max's collar and forced him back into an upright position so that he was face to face. He handed the gun to Max. "This is for you; he doesn't deserve the easy way out. I could keep him alive for days and believe me I will. You've got a choice. You can kill him with a bullet to the head or I'll finish what I've started when I get back."

Jack walked up to the chair and kicked Paolo's firmly in the chest making the chair topple over backwards into the blood soaked mess on the floor. "Fuck you Paolo, she's worth ten of you. You've got off lightly if your brother has the balls to finish the deed. Max! Finish him!"

Enrique was barking orders into his phone mobilising troops and telling them in no uncertain terms to kill anyone who got in the way. "Julio, get your bike, here Jack take an M10 and some clips, Julio will get you there quicker on his bike; we'll follow in the trucks and car, she's in Ciudad de Deus, out in the Western suburbs, it's one of the more modern slum areas." He grabbed Jack to get his focus. "Go Jack, go, may god be with you."

Chapter 58
Double Cross

STENCH BREATH AND THE BOYS were screaming at Gomez. They were desperate to know who they were looking after. The heat on the street was too much and they wanted double the ten thousand dollars they'd been promised for the job. Gomez and Pedro Garcia consulted in the main drawing room. It had been planned as a quick deal but was turning messy; news had reached them about the disappearance of Pedro's brother and the massacre at his Finca, they needed to distance themselves from the kidnapping as quickly as possible and dispose of the girl; if their teams died at the same time so be it. Neither of them were above a double cross or two.

Gomez walked to his household safe hidden behind ornate panelling and took out five thousand dollars before walking back into the hallway. "Here, a little something to keep your men happy and your fee will be doubled when we conclude."

Grins spread across their faces. Real hard cash not just promises. "Garcia will arrange some reinforcements for you. Go back to the house and they should be with you in say thirty minutes, everything is in control."

The mood in the van on the way back to the house was jubilant. Little did they know that Garcia's reinforcements were being given orders to shoot to kill; the girl and her captors must all die in the shoot out. As the van pulled into the driveway through the big gates the team were laughing and discussing how they were going to spend their money, they were all swigging from cans of cold beer and were jubilant as they walked through the doorway calling for their compatriot to come and join the celebration. Rounding the corner they found him with his trousers round his ankles, bound to the iron bed frame sitting in a pool of blood and groaning in agony; the euphoric bubble burst...

"Where is she?"

Jackson responded with a groan and few words. "Escaped...Help me..."

Panic set in. The team pulled the house apart while Stench breath rang round for reinforcements to search the neighbourhood, ten minutes later they had eight men starting to comb the streets asking questions. They soon got leads; the girl had been seen, she was injured and had hobbled north. If they hadn't been out on the streets searching they would have been sitting targets for Garcia's hit squad which arrived at the house minutes after they had left. Jackson had been left tied to the bed as the sacrificial goat in case the failed to find her. It made things simple for the hit squad, as soon as they had the information required they shot him, things were getting messy but orders were orders...none were to survive and if people got in the way, so be it.

The team spilled out onto the streets and spread out across the various shops and small industrial units seeking intelligence, they were pointed in the same direction as the men that were there ten minutes before. The owners of the shops were bemused, what was the fuss about? A stray tourist with a limp; what was so important?

Garcia had just put down his mobile having received an update that his team had finished off one member and were in hot pursuit of the girl, he smiled; things were going well. Less than a minute later the smile was wiped off his face as the front doors burst open. A man dressed in black was pointing a gun directly at Gomez and two back up men had a gun trained on him. The man in black motioned with the barrel of the pistol.

"Move, outside. In the car." The tables had turned. The hunter was now the hunted.

Chapter 59
Darkness

BRIDGET COWERED in the dank dark cellar straining her ears to hear what was going on. She'd heard footsteps running through the café and out onto the concrete of the street out back but now she could hear glass being broken upstairs and shouting. *Please Mr Barman don't give me up...not yet...Jack's coming I can feel him...I know he's coming.* A gun shot rang out, there were more heavy footsteps, she wasn't religious having seen the divides and problems it could cause in life but if there was a higher being out there then she was willing to prey. *Please save me; let Jack find me, one last kiss together.* Tears began to stream down her face, her resolve was breaking. The staccato sound of an M10 lightweight machine gun barked out, whatever was happening was serious. There was a thump as a heavy object landed on the trap door. *Boxes? It sounded heavier.*

Above ground Garcia's team and the original kidnap gang were having a shoot out in the street outside the bar. The trail had gone cold not long after and Stench breaths guy's had soon doubled back to the last confirmed sighting running in to the kill squad at the bar. Wisely the barman had made himself scare. He'd done all he could, he'd telephoned his contact not knowing that he had a direct link to Enrique. The information had been critical. He picked up his phone again and sent a text.

Girl hidden in cellar, gun fight in street by bar, come quickly.

He was hiding in the fabric shop next to the cafe with the old lady who did most of the sewing. They'd locked the door but knew it wouldn't help them. His apron had been discarded and he tried to look like any normal customer cowering in the corner. A stray bullet hit the front window causing it to shatter and the old lady to let out a piercing scream. A gunman's eyes bored into them but dismissed them instantly as bystanders. Sirens could be heard in the distance. Police? Ambulance? He couldn't tell... *Why had he decided to help the girl?...*He admonished himself. *Soft hearted old fool.*

A motorbike roared around the corner. The pillion passenger had a machine gun in his hand and was scything through the ongoing battle outside. Bodies were dropping everywhere, the rear tyre was hit but the rider was experienced and laid the bike on its side sliding to a halt and using it as a shield against the spray of bullets. Jack would not be cowed. He pulled a pistol from his belt, put a new clip in the machine gun and launched in the direction of the battle; he sprayed an upturned table with bullets and watched as the hidden gunman jumped up dancing like a marionette as a second dose of bullets riddled his body. Julio was covering his back and had taken out two more; the street was beginning to fall silent apart from the distant sound of sirens.

Julio's phone rang, time was short, no hello's just concise information. "She's in the cellar under the café, get her straight in the car as soon as we get there then back to the villa as soon as you can, we have the Doctor on standby."

"Jack! Jack! The cellar in the café."

He ran for the doors oblivious of the blood seeping down his arm from a minor bullet wound. Julio signalled the all clear for the bar area. A man groaned in the rear, Jack pointed the gun at his head and squeezed the trigger, the single shot from his Beretta was placed perfectly. He ran into the storeroom and shouted at the top of his voice. "Bridget! Bridget! It's me Jack."

He didn't need to identify himself Bridget would recognise those dulcet tones anywhere. "Down hear Jack... Jack down here!"

He pulled the body slumped across the trapdoor away with one hand throwing the cadaver out through the rear onto the street. He tore at the handle almost ripping the trapdoor off of its hinges. Light flooded down to the cellar and Bridget's bedraggled tear streaked face appeared at the bottom of the steps. She held up her hands and Jack lifted her up through the hole and in to his arms as if she were as light as a feather. Bridget sobbed unable to speak pushing her tear streaked face into his neck and gripping him round the waist with her legs.

"Don't ever leave me again my beautiful girl."

Julio broke up the party with a stern command. "Jack! Move! The car's out front the Doc is at the house. Hurry, the police are starting to put up road blocks."

He scooped Bridget up, ran to the front of the café and placed her carefully in the back seat before sliding in beside her. Enrique was up front barking orders to the driver, the car snaked up the road as he floored the accelerator. Enrique leaned into the back of the car with wads of padding and bandages in his hand. "Bridget, talk to me, where are you hurt?"

Bridget was a sobbing mess; her face buried in Jack's shoulder, the mixture of blood and tears making it impossible to see who was injured or how serious it was.

The car lurched to the right up a side street throwing Enrique into the window as the driver spotted two police cars heading straight down the road towards them. Two further fast turns and the police cars were nowhere in sight, he had no way of knowing that they had continued straight on.

Jack held up a hand, and Enrique relaxed. "She's fine, just drive."

He cradled Bridget's head against his chest running his hand through her hair and talking softly to her. "C'mon my beautiful girl, it's over now, I've got you, I've got you."

Chapter 60
The Warehouse

MAX CRASHED BACK TO THE FLOOR as soon as Jack let him go, he stayed on his knees looking at the Glock pistol cradled in his hand. He hated guns, he hated violence. Rachel walked up behind him and cradled his head against her. "Come on Max, Paolo needs help."

"You don't get it Rach do you...if I don't kill him then Jack will torture him for a week to get his own sick kicks and revenge." He stood feeling the weight of the gun in his hand. "How have we ended up here Rach? What do we do?" He took heavy steps towards Paolo who was bleeding profusely from his right knee; still tied to the chair and looking up at the ceiling, the right side of his face was a mess from the blow torch causing him to squint from his right eye. He was groggy where his head had hit the floor and his speech was slow, blood loss and shock were starting to affect his ability to function.

"Max, Max...get me out of here. I need to get to a hospital, hurry Max, hurry."

Max pointed the gun at his head. The barrel was shaking from side to side mimicking the movements of his body. Rachel grabbed his arm.

"No! It would make us as bad as them."

"I thought you hated him Rach...Let's be honest he sold you down the river, he wanted you to be kidnapped to pay off his gambling debts so why are you defending him now?"

"I'm not defending him, I'm defending you. You'd never be able to live with yourself."

Max snorted. "What choice do we have? Jack will make him last for days and let's be honest he's caused us nothing but trouble."

"Who are you! It's your brother! You can't kill your brother Max!" Rachel was close to hysterics.

Paolo was slowly taking in the conversation and started to babble. "Get me out of here Max, I can sort everything out, I can....I promise Max, I'll sort things out, get me out of here, get me to hospital, I'll pay you back, I'll get clean, just get me out of here."

Light flooded in through the front door as Gomez and Garcia were unceremoniously thrown through the entrance by one of Enrique's men. They knew they was in deep trouble and were trying to remain silent. As Gomez's eyes adjusted to the dim lights and he saw Paolo strapped naked to the chair lying on his back his resolve snapped. He jumped to his feet and rushed over to kick him in the ribs catching Max unaware. Rachel pulled him back and went to Paolo's side to protect him.

"Paolo you fuck shit...what have you done? What have you done, you'll get us all killed."

There was only the one guard. Enrique's other man was racing through the streets with Martin's men in the back of the car trying to catch up and join in the battle to save Bridget. He looked on impassively, he really didn't care if the prisoners took chunks out of each other; it wasn't his problem. He picked his mobile out of his pocket as he felt it vibrate and put it to his ear nodding as he listened to his orders. He slowly placed it back in his trousers and picked his glock out of his waistband turning towards five faces watching his every move. He smiled.

"Hey it's your lucky day, Bridget's been found alive."

He raised his gun and slowly squeezed the trigger releasing four rounds. The shots echoed round the building as blood and bits of brain splattered everywhere as the soft nosed bullets tore through two skulls. Rachel stood statue like before realising that she was covered in bits of brain stuck in her hair and hanging off the front of her blouse. She started screaming uncontrollably, hyper ventilating and pulling at her hair and clothes spreading the mess even further.

"Sorry about that." Enrique's man put his gun back in his waistband and turned to walk out of the door. Max suddenly came to his senses.

"Wait, wait...I've got to get my brother to hospital."

The man looked him up and down. "No Senor, you are supposed to kill him, the same as I have done with Gomez and Garcia, now I just have to dispose of the bodies."

"Look, I can't do it... I'll pay you, for the love of life get him to a hospital."

"Ha...words are cheap."

He stepped over to Rachel scrabbling at her rings on her fingers. "Rachel, give me your jewellery....now Rachel!"

She reluctantly removed her rings and diamond necklace placing them in Max's hands.

"Here, look. There's over fifty grands worth of diamonds. Just get him to a safe place where someone can treat him, it doesn't need to be a hospital a clinic will do, all you need to say is that he wasn't here when you arrived, or even better, you disposed of the body, nothing else." Max looked directly into his eyes desperately hoping that he would cooperate.

The man weighed the jewels in his hand, clearly thinking as he bounced them up and down.

"No guarantees senor; and I'll deny that this ever happened."

Chapter 61
No More Killing

BY THE TIME THE POLICE ARRIVED the battle outside the bar was over and they were left with bodies scattered throughout the neighbourhood and a group of witnesses that had no clue as to what went on. It was another day of senseless violence a typical result of the drug and poverty fuelled cocktail. The only man who knew the truth, the barman, was saying nothing; he had no intention of revealing that the girl had been central to the mayhem. His contact had told him to keep quiet and that he would be well rewarded and he preferred to place his trust in the underworld than risk dealing with a corrupt police officer.

Back at Enrique's compound the Doctor was treating the wounded. Bridget was sent to his clinic under heavily armed guard for an X-ray on her ankle, as expected it was just badly sprained although the Doc was at pains to point out that a bad sprain could take longer to heal than a break. She was heavily strapped up and forced to use crutches. Jack's injuries were fairly superficial; the bullet had torn through the skin and surface flesh on his bicep leaving nothing to stitch together. The medic used iodine and wound powder before dressing it. His body would recover, yes he'd have a scar as a reminder but it wasn't exactly life threatening.

Bridget was relaxing in a huge bath with her bad leg slung over the side to keep the dressing dry. Jack sat at the other end doing the same with his wounded arm. "Jack?"

"Yes, sweetheart."

"Did you send the message I told you to? You know the @EMERGENCY one."

"Yes, I did exactly as you said; wasn't I supposed to send it?"

"No, yes...no...you did exactly what you should do but we'd better get out of this bath and get to a computer. How long has it been since you sent it?"

"I don't rightly know, it's all been a blur, all I focussed on was finding you...where was I? I was in the back of the car off to visit Tony, it's gotta be three days, maybe more depending on the time zone."

Bridget pulled herself up with her arms and tried to put her bad foot to the floor. Jack rushed to support her stealing a kiss in the process. She hopped on one leg and grabbed a robe. "Come on Jack, relaxation can wait we need a computer now!"

Dressed in towelling robes and leaving a trail of wet footprints the pair of them made their way back to the lounge where the crew were sat out on the terrace relaxing and swapping stories. Enrique caught them out of the corner of his eye and headed them off in the salon.

"I thought you two were supposed to be relaxing, Doctor's orders."

"That can wait, I need access to a computer and the internet please Enrique, a fast link if possible."

"Use my study, through here, I'll put my password in and then you'll have full access."

Bridget sat in front of the screen and tapped away on the keyboard until a page that Jack recognised but without a blood tester he couldn't see how it was going to work. The screen flashed.

Stage 1: Please provide fingerprint, left index finger

"Put your left index finger on the scanner Jack and hold still."

The scanner whirred backwards and forwards. *Image not clean, please place right thumb on scanner.* The technology's not great Jack, just do as it says, I've a failsafe built in, don't worry. He placed his thumb on the scanner as instructed while the machine clicked and whirred repeating the operation.

Eighty five percent match: within acceptable limits but time constrained to five days.

Welcome Jack, stage one identity confirmed via fingerprint.

Stage two identification - DNA and blood stress testing delayed five days.

The machine beeped and a further message came up on screen.

Stage three bypassed. Please enter required digits as requested.

Letter or number 1

Letter or number 4

Letter or number 12

Jack leant over and tapped his password letters in. F,K,9.

Bridget kissed his cheek, who's a clever boy remembering his password then. He hugged her close and whispered in her ear. "It's a password I'll never forget say it for me."

"FuckmeJ4ck69"

"He laughed, later my darling."

"Jack, concentrate!"

"You started it..." She punched him playfully before holding his cheeks in her hands and kissing him passionately.

The computer was flashing patiently.

Accepted.

Eye scan delayed five days.

Enter location: Whose vault contains C4?

Jack knew the answer instantly and typed it into the box. Finley Fitzgerald's

Accepted.

Please read the following text in your normal voice. Jack read the third stanza from his favourite poem by kipling. The computer beeped and a final message scrolled across the page.

Thank you Jack, have a happy retirement....

Security questions Bridget Donovan.

Stage 1: Please provide fingerprint, right ring finger

Bridget worked her way through the same questions that Jack had just answered until the final words scrolled across the screen:

Thank you Bridget, have a happy retirement...

She let out a long breath before bringing up the C:\ prompt and typing in the command. *Cancel@EMERGENCY*

Enrique stuck his head round the office door. "All okay?"

"Yeah thanks Enrique, Bridget has cancelled the chaos on the IT systems so hopefully things will calm down a bit now. What about our other loose ends?"

"Still at the warehouse, the final decision is yours."

Bridget looked up pleadingly into Jack's eyes. "No more killing...please Jack."

Jack stretched his neck and contemplated the request. "I'll think on it sweetie, I'll think on it."

"No Jack, no more killing in my name, enough people have already died."

Chapter 62
Government Fallout

THE EMAIL FLASHED UP on Toby and Doug's screens simultaneously.

Tick tock, we've paused the clock

Bridget Donovan and Jack Fitzgerald have signed in to a computer and are no longer considered missing.

The Emergency command has been cancelled for five days when they will be required to confirm their full biometrics.

Unless requested to act all agencies should stand down. Information already posted is now in the public domain but no new postings will be made. You are advised to make sure that both Bridget Donovan and Jack Fitzgerald are cleared for travel at all borders.

Tick tock, stop watching the clock.

"Well, she's alive somewhere, I wonder who found her? Can you get any info out of the spooks Doug? It'd be nice to know."

"If I get told Toby, you'll get told, it's the least that you deserve. It's a bit late for some though eh? The Prime Minister has resigned over the water due to so called health problems, we've had people killed in bombings and our own Senate has had more than one or two ministers stand down."

Toby stretched out leaning back on his chair. "It just goes to prove that information, social media and IT systems are the new nuclear bomb. The damage done in the last week or two is huge, who'd have believed it? Ever read Animal Farm by George Orwell?" Doug nodded. "You know the thing about some being more equal than others...the old leaders with their snouts in the trough..."

"And?"

"Well...Who'd have believed that a girl from the back streets of Belfast could force people to accept the consequences of their actions?"

Doug leant back in his chair grinning and shaking his head. "It won't make any difference Toby, it never does. Some other over privileged upstart will step in to their shoes. Never had a proper job, worked as a researcher, pre- selected as a candidate and put into a safe seat...And they wonder why the country's fucked. It's very rare that a real person who's worked becomes an MP and rises through the ranks at speed these days, they need to change the rules...five years minimum in a proper job."

Toby sat bolt upright. "We could do that Doug."

"How?"

"Well for a start we could talk to Bridget Donovan."

A huge smile spread across Doug's face. "Yeah, we could, couldn't we?"

Chapter 63
Viva Brazil

MAX AND RACHEL WERE DESPERATE for a way out; they were sat in the back of the car with Paolo in the front seat and the bodies of Gomez and Garcia in the trunk. Both were ashen and gripping each other's hands. The past eighteen months had been a roller coaster of emotions and they had seen and heard things that they wished they could undo. Their bond was now as strong as it had ever been.

The car pulled up at a tatty shack of a building and the driver stepped out and into the slum. Less than a minute later he appeared with another man and they pulled Paolo out of the front seat causing him to scream with the pain.

"Hey be careful with him, what are you doing? I thought we were going to a medical facility."

"This is the medical facility senor...you have a problem?"

The stare from the man's eyes made Max back down. He'd seen him kill in cold blood, at least Paolo would have a chance...he might survive and be able to disappear.

They were dropped back at the apartment where they both stood under the shower trying to wash away the pain they had suffered today; with Paolo gone they only had each other. They turned to drink and sat through the night talking in whispers hoping not to be overheard.

Could they run? Would they succeed in hiding? Reality was stark; they both knew they had no hope of escaping the reach of Bashar. They were back to square one going over the same conversation they had in Los Milnos before they had departed for Brazil, there was no going back, all they could do was appeal to his better nature. It was almost midnight when both of their phones pinged.

We will all meet at the apartment tomorrow at midday to discuss things. Make sure you are there.

Bashar

Despite the alcohol neither of them slept well, both wondered what conditions Paolo was being kept in. They had left him in a dirty slum with people that they didn't know, it was Hobson's choice, that or death. The agreed story was that Max had killed him and Enrique's man had dumped the body along with Gomez. They had to stick to it no matter what, Bashar and Jack would both want confirmation.

Just after lunchtime the following day Max was huddled in a corner with Bashar.

"No Max, sorry, I really don't care whether we've killed your brother or not, you pulled the trigger as an act of mercy and maybe you should have done it years ago. Whether you like it or not you've signed up to our organisation, you've taken our money and yes I know that you've fenced some of our drugs, so what do you expect? Since fatherhood I've mellowed so here's the deal; you can marry your beautiful lady, build a nice villa in Vistamar and look after the development project. It won't be too hard and I can think of a lot worse places to be." The part left unsaid was the choice was probably death.

Max called Rachel over and Bashar repeated his offer. Rachel looked into Max's eyes and nodded, there was nowhere to hide and it was a fair deal.

"Okay Bish, you've got yourself a deal." Max held out his hand to shake with the devil.

"Good." He looked around the room to see that everyone had a drink before using a spoon to clink against the side of his champagne flute to get everyone's attention.

"Listen up people. Max and Rachel are going to get married and build a villa in Vistamar. Please raise your glasses to the happy couple."

"Viva Brazil!"

Epilogue

LYNETTE WAS SAT NURSING MILLIE out on the balcony trying to get some peace and quiet away from the hub bub of the crowd when Martin appeared with two glasses of fizz and sat down beside her.

"She's gorgeous isn't she...and eat...doesn't she ever stop feeding?"

"She certainly has an appetite but then look at how much growing is going on, I'm amazed every day at the changes." She looked down at Millie who had dozed off contentedly while suckling. "Have you finished sweetie?" Lynette pulled a pad out of the change bag and placed it inside her bra before hooking herself back together. "Right then poppet, go have a cuddle with Uncle Martin." Millie was placed unceremoniously on Martin's lap. Not being used to babies he virtually froze before Lynette moved Millie round to make them both comfortable. A smile broke out on his face as she snuggled down.

"So Lindy, why are you hiding out here with a big sad face and so deep in thought?"

"Oh, I don't know Martin...I'm just trying to process a lot of information about Baz and his business empire...Don't get me wrong I love him dearly but I'm just worried about some of the things he seems to be into and whether Millie is at risk in the same way as Bridget."

"Such as?"

"Well when I was given full powers over Baz's BVI companies he clearly hadn't thought things through before signing the documentation. I've gone through most of the files, well skimmed the files to be honest but I don't like some of what I've read, some of his trading activities are very dark to say the least." She turned her big brown eyes full bore onto Martin. "What do you know about the people trafficking and prostitution operations in Morocco?"

"It's really not for me to say ...I can't get between the two of you. You'll have to ask him directly."

"Come on Martin, if not for me, think of Millie, you said that you'd treat her as one of your own if anything ever happened to Baz so why not protect her now and tell me the truth. Look me in the eye...Now truth; has Baz got prostitution and people trafficking operation in Morocco?"

Martin wavered. How could he say no when he could swim in her deep brown firey eyes? He'd always had a thing for Lynette. "He'll kill me if he thinks I've told you...you do realise that." She nodded as Millie burped and shuffled on Martin's lap. As he cuddled her in he reached his decision.

"Okay...Yes he's got his fingers in both pots; I refuse to have anything to do with it....and I'll deny I ever confirmed it, it's up to the two of you to work it out."

A small tear fell formed in Lynette's eye and run down her cheek. *Why couldn't life be simple, why couldn't they just live on a beach in Brazil?*

One week on and Paolo was lying in a make shift cot in the corner of the dank slum hallucinating due to the fever from his various infections. The treatment was rudimentary, raw iodine on the burn wounds and shattered kneecap causing him to shriek in pain and basic stitching around the exit hole which was where most of the infection problems lay. His so called medic had given him the option of having his leg off above the knee, he said it would be better for him as they couldn't get the fragments of bullet and shattered bone out of the surrounding tissue. His knee would never function properly again and he would live with constant pain. His chest and his penis were healing but both with ugly scars where the blow lamp had burnt down deep into the flesh, his playboy body was destroyed, but his mind was still functioning. The mess on his face was something else. *Why had Max abandoned him? If I ever got out of here alive I'm going to get even.*

He was tossing his head side to side as he burnt up and relived the nightmare, a soothing hand placed a cold towel on his brow. "Be tranquil amigo, use your energy to fight the infection...you have a long road ahead."

Notes From The Author

Thank you

Viva Brazil is the last book in the three book series entitled "Dirty Money" which was inspired by events in England, Spain and Brazil.

I have another two or three books hidden away at the back of my head based in the City of London and of course Paolo could always make a reappearance but if I am honest I fell into writing book one after some life changing events happening to a good friend. Book two and book three were a lot more fun to write as I learnt the ropes but despite many of you leaving fantastic reviews the world of publishing is hugely competitive and it seems to make a book a success an author has to spend a lot of time on social media which is not a good use of my energy or something I enjoy.

If you enjoyed the series please spread the word by leaving a review on the site you purchased it from or by publicising the series on social media, it might just encourage me to continue my second career!

Thanks again for taking the time to read my books.

Facebook: www.facebook.com/roadblockpublications or Neil Andrews Author

Web: www.roadblockpublications.com

About Neil Andrews

Neil Andrews was diagnosed with M.E., Myalgic Encephalomyelitis, sometimes known as CFIDS or CFS, over ten years ago bringing an end to a successful career in business. He has struggled adapting to the restrictions placed on his life by this hugely frustrating illness, the support of family and friends has been invaluable to him. He fell into writing by chance during a conversation with friends and has enjoyed using it as an escape. Over the last few years he has learned not to take life too seriously and to live for today as one never knows what tomorrow might bring. He is lucky enough to live between the UK and Spain, is married with grown up children and needs another Weimaraner dog to keep him on his toes........unfortunately his wife has yet to agree!

For more information on the devastating effects of CFS or ME please go to

www.measussex.org.uk or www.actionforme.org.uk

Printed in Great Britain
by Amazon.co.uk, Ltd.,
Marston Gate.